THE
MEETING

THE
MEETING

HUGH L.

HAZELDEN

First published August 1990.

ISBN: 0-89486-693-1

Library of Congress Catalog Card Number: 90-81416

Printed in the United States of America.

Editor's note:
Hazelden Educational Materials offers a variety of information on chemical dependency and related areas. Our publications do not necessarily represent Hazelden or its programs, nor do they officially speak for any Twelve Step organization.

This book is fictional. Many characters are described. These characters are composites of a wide range of individuals. Resemblance to any one person is purely coincidental.

Permission to reprint the Twelve Steps and Twelve Traditions does not mean that Alcoholics Anonymous has reviewed or approved the contents of this publication, nor that AA agrees with the views expressed herein. AA is a program of recovery from alcoholism only. Use of the Twelve Steps and Twelve Traditions in connection with programs which are patterned after AA but which address other problems does not imply otherwise.

Contents

Introduction

Although the names and places in *The Meeting* are fictitious, the incidents are based on actual experiences in Alcoholics Anonymous meetings.

The central character in this collection of stories about alcoholism and recovery in the Step-by-Step group of AA is the group itself. The stories deal with some of the things newly sober persons in AA often must face, both in themselves and in their relationships with other AA members.

The people in the Step-by-Step group represent a cross section of AA membership. And the Step-by-Step group itself is probably as close to the "average" AA group as any one example could be in a country as diverse as the United States. No one example of any kind of group, though, is likely to be completely typical of all.

Groups tend to reflect the diverse personalities of their individual members. But the group itself may take on its own "personality," which is more than the sum of its individual parts.

Often, persons going from one group to another find they have some adjusting to do, both in the sense of simple custom and procedure, and also in dealing with new personalities. Persons with such problems of adjustment may find this book of help.

In describing some AA "characters," such as the "Thirteenth Stepper" and the "Old Guard," *The Meeting* does not mean to criticize, but simply to point out some fairly common kinds of behavior within AA groups. After all, as it says in the Fifth Chapter of the "Big Book," *Alcoholics Anonymous*, "We are not saints." The stories in *The Meeting* show that success in using AA as a recovery tool lies in learning to *accept* — people and life and one's own self.

First Meeting

Something was different in his car, but it was several miles from the time Nick became aware of a difference until he realized what it was.

There was no beer can or drink cup in the center console. It had been a long time since he'd taken a trip, even a short one like this, without having something alcoholic to drink.

Driving the twenty-odd miles from his hometown to his first meeting of Alcoholics Anonymous, Nick had time to experience both waves of relief and flashes of apprehension. Relief at having made, with some help, certain decisions; apprehension at having to carry them out.

It was six days since his most recent drink. The misery of the hangover and shakes was finally gone. He'd just learned this week that hangovers and shakes were symptoms of withdrawal from alcohol.

Withdrawal — he'd always thought of withdrawal as something that happened to narcotics addicts. The counselor at the mental health agency told him about alcohol being a drug, much like a narcotic in its action. The counselor, who specialized in chemical dependency, had cautioned him about the possibility of seizures in the third to fifth day after stopping drinking. The counselor wanted Nick to go into treatment, which Nick had refused. Nick hadn't experienced seizures, though the silent screaming of his nerves as they reacted to being off the bottle had almost changed his mind about accepting treatment. Stopping this time had been harder, physically, than any of the times before.

Stopping, not *quitting* — he now thought of it that way. *Quitting* was a word he'd used too many times in the past. He knew now that it was too final a word. He'd quit over and over, but it had never lasted. He knew now, deep inside, that he couldn't *not* drink without help.

It seemed ironic to Nick that he'd once told his wife Ellen, after a very bad night, that he'd never get drunk again, that he'd never *drink* again, that he'd do whatever it took; "I'll even go to AA," he'd said. As things had gotten worse over the years, he'd made many promises to his wife, the promises becoming more and more extreme. But the one about going to AA was the most extreme of all. He was now fulfilling that promise, one he'd never dreamed he'd actually have to make good on.

Going to AA had turned out to be a compromise, after the counselor had tried to get Nick to go into treatment. When Nick begged off, the counselor had set up an AA contact for Nick at a meeting in the next town. The counselor gave Nick the contact's full name; the man had given the counselor permission to break the man's anonymity.

It seemed a little like playing secret agents to Nick, this business of some people in AA not giving their full names. Not that he minded the practice; he was glad that the counselor hadn't sent him to an AA meeting in his own town.

Anonymity wasn't any stranger than some of the other things Nick had been learning. The counselor had used the phrase, "the disease of alcoholism." An odd word, *disease,* for something that for years Nick had told himself he did simply because he wanted to. But he now admitted to himself that many times, particularly in the last year, he'd gotten drunk when he hadn't meant to, had tried not to. At times he hadn't even wanted to drink and had gotten drunk.

He found the meeting site, a large Episcopal church at the edge of town, without too much trouble. The streets were quiet at this hour, seven-thirty on a clear August evening.

Already several vehicles were parked in the lot at the rear of the church — a new Lincoln, several late-model cars, a couple of old cars, a heavy-duty pickup.

Nick took a quick look at his face in the rearview mirror. The eyes weren't bloodshot now, and his skin was losing the greyish tinge. There were a couple of tiny ruptured blood vessels in his cheeks that some suntan would cover. His stomach was a little soft from the excess empty calories of alcohol, but he was in reasonably good physical shape; *amazingly good,* he admitted to himself, *for a thirty-eight-year-old man who'd been drinking heavily for over twenty years.*

Nick fought an impulse to look around nervously as he got out of his car. He would have welcomed the darkness of a winter's evening, rather than midsummer daylight saving time. Still, no one who knew him was likely to see him here, and there were no signs saying "Alcoholics Anonymous" to catch the attention of passersby.

A door on the annex at the rear of the church was propped open. Nick paused just inside. The sound of voices echoed from somewhere deeper in the building. The aroma of coffee floated down a hallway leading to his right. He followed the sound and smell around a corner and down the hall to an open door.

About a dozen people had already arrived. The room was big, and folding metal chairs were set out for four or five times that many. Several long tables had been arranged in a "U" shape with a wooden lectern placed at the open end of the "U."

A serving counter extended down one side of the room. Two big shiny coffeepots sat on the counter, steaming and staring at the room with red brewing lights. Stacks of disposable Styrofoam cups stood ready beside them.

Most of the people there were near the coffeepots, but a short, muscular man and a well-dressed woman were standing by a table near the door. Nick took a quick look at the literature laid out in neat stacks on the table. It all seemed to be about Alcoholics Anonymous, so he was in the right place.

The man broke off his conversation with the woman and moved over to greet Nick.

"How're you doing?" he said, sticking out his hand. "I'm Al O'Connor."

"I'm Nick." The counselor had told him it was up to him whether he gave his full name or not.

Al's hand was big and powerful, but he didn't try to impress Nick with his grip. He was in his late forties or early fifties, tanned, looking fit and healthy. He had short hair, what there was of it, and a tattoo on his right forearm. He gave Nick the impression of being a retired military man.

"First meeting?" Al asked.

"Yeah," Nick admitted. *Am I that conspicuous?* he thought. He'd later learn to recognize the first-meeting look on others.

"This is a good meeting," Al said. "This isn't my home group, but I like this group's meetings."

More people were arriving behind them. "Let's get some coffee," Al said, and they moved toward the serving counter.

"Are most AA meetings in churches?" Nick asked. He always felt uneasy in new situations, but since he'd been spotted as a newcomer, he might as well ask newcomer's questions.

"A pretty fair number," Al said. "There are groups that rent their own independent meeting rooms, and some meet in treatment centers and the like. But there are a lot of churches that give space for AA meetings, either rent free or very cheaply, and they can be Episcopal, or Catholic, or Presbyterian — practically any denomination." He grinned. "Though there are still some churches that aren't especially fond of Alcoholics Anonymous."

"Why's that?" Nick asked.

"Well, some churches look on alcoholics as sinners. They don't like the idea of a 'bunch of drunks' meeting in their buildings. And there are those churches that have the mistaken idea that AA is trying to horn in on what should be the church's job."

"How so?"

"Some churches see alcoholism as a question of good and evil. They think alcoholics need to become 'good' in order to recover."

"I just learned that alcoholism is a disease," Nick said.

"Not everybody agrees with that. There are people who see it as a moral issue. That's what I liked about AA from the start." Al looked squarely into Nick's eyes. "They said that alcoholics were sick people who needed to get well; they didn't tell me I was a bad person who needed to get good."

A couple of people were ahead of them at the coffeepots. Nick looked around the room again. At the front, on the wall behind the lectern, were two large posters with text on them. They looked as if they spent the time between meetings rolled up, as if they'd been unrolled many times.

Nick scanned each poster. One had the heading, "The Twelve Steps," and what followed seemed to be a list of behaviors or actions. At the top of the other one was written, "The Twelve Traditions." They seemed to deal with the way Alcoholics Anonymous was run.

Several of the Twelve Steps mentioned God, as did the Second Tradition. On plaques hung on each side of the two posters there were slogans; *Let Go and Let God* and *There But For the Grace of God* were two of them. *With all this mention of God, AA must be religious in some way,* Nick thought.

"I'm an agnostic," Al said, not making any effort to lower his voice. It was as though he'd read Nick's thoughts. "You'll hear people talking about God and a Higher Power, and so forth. I use the group as my Higher Power. It stands to reason that a group of people trying to do something, like stay sober, has more power than one person by himself."

Nick considered this as they moved up to the coffeepots. A skinny, middle-aged man was serving the coffee. At a distance, his skin had looked ruddy, like a person who worked outdoors. Up close, Nick could see that the color was from a vast network of broken veins underneath the man's pale skin, which had a rough texture like crumpled tissue paper. *He might not have slept under a bridge last night,* Nick thought, *but he had the look of a man who'd done so in the past.*

"Eddie," the skinny man introduced himself to Nick, reaching out to shake hands. His hand was bony and had the kind of tremor that Nick suspected was chronic.

Eddie poured coffee for Nick and Al. It was a small miracle that he didn't spill any. "Cream and sugar's down there," he said, pointing to the other end of the counter.

"Poor guy's in rough shape," Nick said to Al when they'd moved out of earshot.

"You should have seen him when he came in," Al replied. "Eddie's been sober almost a year now. He's what some AA's call a 'low-bottom' alcoholic. He'd lost almost everything before he hit bottom and became ready to try to stay sober in Alcoholics Anonymous. People who haven't lost jobs or families or a lot of other things because of drinking are called 'high-bottom' alcoholics." Al wasn't being demeaning toward Eddie, Nick realized, just stating a fact.

After a moment, Al asked, "How're *you* feeling?" It took Nick a second to realize what he meant.

"Pretty good," Nick replied. "I haven't had a drink in almost a week." It sounded pretty unimpressive, with a guy like Eddie having been sober for almost a year.

"That's good," Al praised. "At my first meeting, I was coming off a drunk. My hands were shaking so bad I sat on them to keep people from seeing." He sipped his coffee. "It's good that you're not drinking. It's hard to learn much about AA if you're under the influence at a meeting."

"Do people who've been drinking come in often?" Nick asked.

"Not too often." Al laughed. "An AA meeting is usually the last place a drinking alcoholic wants to be. We don't ask people to leave just because they're drinking, unless they're disruptive. But we do tell them to come back when they're not under the influence."

"Six days is the longest I've been able to manage without a drink in a long time," Nick said. "I know I need to stop for good."

"I don't say I've stopped for good any more," Al said. "I can't think about 'quitting forever' — that's just too damn long for me. I might get to thinking about 'forever' and end up drunk." He pointed to a plaque carrying the slogan, One Day at a Time. "I can just about manage one day," Al said. "I'll worry about the next one when it gets here. I may have been thinking about 'forever' when I had my last slip."

A slip meant drinking again, Nick guessed. Evidently you could come back into AA if you'd relapsed into drinking. He wondered if AA had some system for checking up on people, to catch them if they tried to drink on the sly.

Al led the way to a group of five men at the end of the counter and said, "Hey, the Step-by-Step group is represented in force tonight. What brings you over this way?"

After a chorus of replies, Al simply said, "This is Nick," by way of introduction to all of them at once, and each man introduced himself.

Richard was fiftyish with a well-trimmed, greying beard and a professorial air. Tom was a big, older man with a chew of tobacco tucked into his cheek and a hand like steel wrapped in leather. Joe was even bigger than Tom, a giant of a man in a leather cycle jacket and boots, with a black beard that looked fierce compared to Richard's. Henry was a compact, quick-talking man with a Brooklyn accent. John, a thin man, had, like Eddie, something of a low-bottom look about him, although John's hand was as steady as his gaze.

"These guys all belong to the same AA group, over in the next town," Al said to Nick. "It's not unusual to see AA members go 'visiting' like this — you get a meeting on the trip over and back, as well as at the meeting room, right, Tom?"

"Right," Tom said. "You live around here?" he asked Nick in a friendly way.

"Well, no," Nick admitted. "I guess I'm from the same town you guys just came from."

"No kidding?" Henry said. "You oughta visit the Step-by-Step group — it's a good group."

"I will," Nick said, not knowing if he really meant it. He'd driven twenty-odd miles to avoid going to his first AA meeting in his own hometown, and now it seemed that a part of that group had followed him here.

The people now rapidly filling the room seemed to be of every race, age, and social level. Nick saw a group made up of four middle-aged black men, three middle-aged white men, two older white women, and a dark-skinned young man with straight black hair whom he later learned was a Cherokee Indian, all chatting together. The members of minorities weren't all huddled together, as he'd often seen when people of different races got together in a group. Instead, they were mingling and talking with no apparent self-consciousness.

"Quite a variety, eh?" Al said, seeing Nick eyeing the crowd. "I had the idea when I first got here that AA was probably a bunch of guys with newspaper in their shoes who slept in flophouses and got their clothes from the Salvation Army. Now, Richard, who you just met, is a college professor. Old Tom has one of the biggest construction outfits in this part of the state. And young Lucy. . ." he gestured at a girl across the room who looked to be in her teens. "I was really amazed when I saw people young enough to be my kids."

"I guess Eddie's the only one here who's anything like the kind of guy I pictured in AA," Nick admitted.

"In the old days, the AA 'old-timers' used to say that if you came to your first meeting wearing a watch, you probably weren't ready, because you hadn't lost enough," Al said. "Today, Alcoholics Anonymous has people who've hit their own personal bottoms in every condition. AA says that you can get off the elevator on any floor — you don't have to sink all the way to the basement."

"I guess I'm real lucky," Nick said. "I haven't lost my driver's license, my job, or my wife, although I don't think she would have put up with my drinking for much longer."

Al looked at Nick very directly. "They told me, when I said I hadn't lost this or that, to always add the word 'yet.' I know that if I'd kept on drinking, I'd have lost all the things I hadn't lost 'yet.' That's if I didn't die first."

"I was having trouble on the job," Nick admitted. "I think my boss was about to tell me to get help for my drinking or get out."

"I heard a fellow say once, 'I didn't get into trouble every time I drank, but every time I got into trouble I'd been drinking,' " Al said.

Nick remembered the warning he'd gotten about absenteeism on Mondays; the parking lot wreck when he'd been half drunk but lucky enough to know the man whose car he'd backed into; the screaming-and-yelling quarrels with Ellen.

Nick suddenly realized that he'd forgotten to ask for the man whose name the alcoholism counselor had given him. He mentioned the name to Al, who said, casually, "He's not been around for a while." Al's tone made Nick think he didn't want to talk about it further.

Nick stayed close to Al. The crowd began to find seats as eight o'clock approached. Al and Nick took chairs closer to the front than Nick would have chosen on his own, but it was better than sitting by himself and feeling awkward.

Nick was breathing a bit easier now. It seemed that Alcoholics Anonymous wasn't a group of religious fanatics or skid-row bums.

He wondered what a person had to do to become an actual member. Maybe AA had a test, or required a person to promise to do certain things.

Nick wondered if you had to affirm a belief in God. He wasn't an agnostic like Al claimed to be, or at least he didn't think he was. He'd been brought up to believe in God and he supposed he still did, although he was hazy as to who, or what,

God was. But if Al was openly an agnostic, then maybe AA wasn't too strict on the God business.

At eight o'clock, a small, serious-looking man stepped up to the lectern and rapped on it for attention. The crowd quieted.

"I'd like to welcome everyone to this meeting of Alcoholics Anonymous," he said. "My name is George and I'm an alcoholic."

"Hi, George," said everyone in the room except Nick. He was taken by surprise. He'd seen some television drama in which an AA meeting was shown; the crowd had shouted out a greeting to a person who'd introduced himself as George had. This real-life crowd had said it in an ordinary tone, but the combined voices of forty or fifty people were loud enough.

"Those who'd care to, please join me in the Serenity Prayer," George said. George started it off, and the rest of the people followed with practiced ease:

God, grant me the serenity
To accept the things I cannot change,
The courage to change the things I can,
And the wisdom to know the difference.

Some of the group said a soft "amen" at the end. Nick noticed that Al hadn't joined in, although he'd bowed his head respectfully.

George read something explaining Alcoholics Anonymous; one phrase that stood out for Nick was, "The only requirement for membership is a desire to stop drinking."

Then George said, "I've asked Ted P. to tell how it works."

Ted was a man in his sixties. He stepped up to the lectern and said, "I'm Ted Parker and I'm an alcoholic." The group said, "Hi, Ted." Ted held the sheet of paper he read from at arm's length, catching it in the bottoms of his bifocals. "Rarely have we seen a person fail who has thoroughly followed our path... ," he began.

Nick had difficulty following what Ted was reading, though Ted's voice was clear and reasonably loud. Nick did recognize a part of what Ted read as the Twelve Steps from the poster hanging on the wall. The words seemed a little stiff and preachy to Nick. He wondered if people in AA actually did all the things in the Steps. In Nick's experience, there was almost always a large gap between what people *said* they were going to do, and what they actually did. Nick was glad he'd run into Al before the meeting started, for there really seemed to be a lot about God.

When Ted finished, George called on "Nadine M." to read the Twelve Traditions. Nadine was a neatly dressed, ordinary-looking young woman, the kind Nick would expect to see dropping off her kids at school or shopping in the supermarket.

She introduced herself as "Nadine, a grateful recovering alcoholic." Nick joined in this time when the crowd said, "Hi, Nadine." He realized that in the time directly before the meeting no one had asked him if *he* was an alcoholic, or had mentioned being an alcoholic. He saw what the counselor had meant now about how people gave their last names or not, as their own choice.

When Nadine finished reading the Traditions, George stepped back up and said, "Well, this is a speaker meeting, and the woman I've asked to tell her story has meant a lot to me in my own recovery. She was here in AA when I came into the program, and she's helped me a lot. I won't take up any more of her time; help me welcome Anna J."

There was applause from the crowd as the middle-aged woman whom Al had been talking to when Nick first arrived stepped behind the lectern.

"Hello, everyone, I'm Anna and I'm an alcoholic."

Nick joined in again with "Hi, Anna," but he was a little disappointed. The counselor had told him that alcoholics told their drinking stories at AA speaker meetings. He'd hoped to hear someone he could identify with. This graceful, slender woman in her summer dress and heels, with carefully done silver hair, could have been a model for a TV commercial concerning Mature Adults. He'd thought of female alcoholics as either blowsy, loud-mouthed women or frail, deathly looking wretches. *This woman must not have had a very exciting drinking history,* Nick thought.

"I come from a family of hard drinkers," Anna began in a soft Carolina Low Country accent. "My daddy was a bootlegger in Charleston, South Carolina, during Prohibition. I guess it was a good thing for us in a way, my daddy's liquor business. Our family wasn't as bad off in the Depression as a lot of folks." Nick glanced around and saw some amused looks. No one in the room needed to be told that drinkers were going to drink, whatever the law or the state of the economy.

"I was able to go to a private school for young ladies," Anna went on. "A 'finishing school,' I suppose you'd call it. They taught us how to be proper Southern ladies. I learned to say 'fantastic' instead of 'bullshit' when people shoveled it at me."

The crowd roared with laughter. Nick laughed as hard as anyone else. It felt good to laugh; he hadn't felt much like laughing for what seemed a long time. It had been a bit of a shock when this aristocratic-looking Southern woman had come out with the crude word, but she'd made it seem perfectly natural. *Evidently, the God stuff didn't make these AA people goody-goodies or stick-in-the-muds,* Nick thought.

"I always felt out of place at that school," Anna continued. "The other girls' fathers were doctors and lawyers and so on. Some of them had *ministers* for fathers, for goodness sake! Of course," she said with a sly smile, "my daddy knew some of those doctors and lawyers in *his* business." She paused while a chuckle began to build in the crowd. "He probably knew some of the ministers, too, if the truth were known." There was another round of laughter.

"It being the Depression, the school was as hard up for money as everyone else, I guess," she said. "I've often thought that that's the reason why they let me in."

Nick could identify with the feeling of not belonging at school; his father had been a career serviceman, and Nick was often the new kid in school because of his family's many moves.

"My daddy didn't have to change much when Prohibition was repealed," Anna said. "He just started operating out in the open." She paused to light a cigarette. There was a lot of smoke in the room. Nick's eyes were smarting a bit.

A man sitting close to the lectern handed Anna an ashtray. People got up for more coffee. *This is a pretty informal place,* Nick thought, *although the crowd is quiet for Anna's talk.*

"I didn't drink any hard liquor until I went away to college," Anna resumed. "My parents had old-fashioned ideas about women drinking, even though our family was supported by alcohol. We were good Southern Baptists, you see." Another soft round of chuckles. "I'd never had anything stronger than wine until I was a college sophomore.

"A girlfriend and I bought a bottle of mint gin." She shuddered. "I've never been able to drink mint gin since that time, though I learned to drink just about everything else. I guess I should have known there was something different about me from that first hard liquor. Although I didn't like the taste of the stuff, I drank it until I got drunk and threw up and passed out. But we don't learn that easily, do we?"

Anna went on to tell of marrying a young man whom her family disapproved of, a man who turned out to be alcoholic himself. She began to drink with him in an attempt to share his life, but quickly developed a dependence on alcohol herself.

The marriage failed, and she went to work to support the two children she'd had, too proud to accept help from the family who'd disapproved of her husband. Nick could understand her attitude; his family had been estranged from both his father's and mother's relatives, and he'd learned, without having to be told in so many words, that he shouldn't ever be beholden to other people.

Anna's drinking had progressed from weekends to weeknights and finally to working hours. She told of the struggle to keep her job despite having to drink during the workday. She'd used the words "having to drink"; she understood, as Nick was beginning to understand, that alcoholics had no choice when drinking had progressed this far. Nick knew he'd had to resort to deceit and lies and attempts to cover his tracks and make excuses for his behavior.

"Five years ago, I was seriously considering suicide," Anna said quietly. She'd spun out a few humorous drinking stories, the kind that were funny with hindsight, but now the room was quiet, the silence broken only by her voice.

"My suicide was something I didn't want to mess up, like I'd seemed to mess up everything else," she said. "I was afraid of dying, but I was even more afraid of trying to kill myself, and failing. I had a plan — I'm not going to go into all that — but I had a way of committing suicide that I thought would work, first time."

Nick had an eerie feeling. He had made such plans, all the while having decided that he must be insane and that he mustn't let anyone know it. He was afraid that either they wouldn't take his suicide thoughts seriously, forcing him to act to save his pride, or they *would* take him seriously and block his attempt by locking him away somewhere. He looked at Steps One (". . .our lives had become unmanageable") and Two (". . .could restore us to sanity"), on the wall behind Anna. His life had become unmanageable enough for him to consider ending it, and if only crazy people planned suicide, then maybe the part about needing sanity restored applied to him too.

Anna told of phoning an AA answering service in a blackout and of being surprised and embarrassed when two women showed up at her door the next day. She couldn't bring herself to admit she didn't remember calling AA, but the women guessed it.

She spoke of not drinking and coming to meetings, but of being miserable for a while, having a "lousy attitude." She spoke of self-pity and resentment, of working on these with the Twelve Steps until she became "sober" rather than "dry."

Anna finished by saying she had to continue to work on her "character defects" — Nick wondered if by character defects she meant the negative ways of thinking and reacting that had become a way of life for him. She thanked the group for help-ing her stay sober by letting her tell her story.

After the applause died, George passed out some baskets, saying, "These are for voluntary contributions. AA has no dues or fees. Please feel free to *not* contribute."

Nick noticed that most people put money in the baskets; a few didn't. A dollar bill seemed to be a common amount. He put one in a basket as it passed.

There were a couple of announcements, then George said, "In this part of the country, most AA groups have the chip system." He held one up, a white plastic disc the size of a poker chip. "They won't keep you sober, but they might make you think before you drink."

George looked around the room. Nick felt self-consciously new. "Accepting a white chip simply means that you want to try the AA way of life, of not taking a drink One Day at a Time. Accepting the white chip doesn't mean you're necessarily join-ing this particular AA group. If you do want to join this group, all you have to do is say, 'I want to join.' We don't have any initiation process here. We figure you've already done that, out there drinking and getting all the trouble you get if you're an alcoholic." There was another chuckle from the crowd. "We don't charge anything for chips, either," George said. "If you're the kind of drinker I was, you've already paid, many times over, in money and in problems." He held the white chip high. "Anyone want to start by picking up a white chip?"

Al leaned over to Nick and whispered, "If you'd like to give AA a try, go get your chip."

Nick found himself on his feet, the audience applauding — *applauding!* — as he went up to the lectern and got the white chip and a firm, friendly handshake from George. He was em-barrassed, but pleased at the same time. George's serious face was split by a wide grin. His eyes were smiling, too, as he gave Nick the chip.

A couple of different colored chips were given out, a green one for a young man who'd just accomplished nine months of sobriety, a blue one to Nadine, the woman who'd read the Traditions, who'd accomplished a year of sobriety. Nick's white chip had a stylized "AA" on one side, but an outsider wouldn't have recognized what it symbolized. An outsider — suddenly he was no longer one. For the first time in a long while, he didn't feel the loneliness that he had secretly felt for so long. It was true he hadn't understood a lot of what he'd heard tonight, but he resolved to try to learn.

The God Business

"Some days I get up and don't turn my stuff over," big Joe was saying.

Joe was six feet, four inches and weighed upwards of 240 pounds. He had a thick, bushy beard and shoulders wide enough for two average men. He wore a Harley-Davidson T-shirt, a belt made from a chromed motorcycle chain, and black boots.

"I try to run my life all by myself," Joe went on, "and it gets all screwed up. I finally have to just stop and turn it over to H.P." He grinned, his teeth white in the black forest of beard. "I just say, 'You better take over, 'cause my way ain't makin' it.'"

Phil was sitting across the aisle from Joe at this meeting of the Step-by-Step group of Alcoholics Anonymous. It took him a moment to realize that he'd just heard the big biker describing a personal version of the act of praying.

Buddy, sitting two rows behind Phil, was shocked at Joe's choice of term for God — "H.P.," for Higher Power.

Buddy had grown up in an atmosphere where God was spoken of in very reverent terms — "The Lord God Jehovah," "The Holy Spirit," "The Lord Jesus Christ." Buddy tried to picture his mother's reaction to Joe's "H.P." He could see her lips tighten and her eyes turn snappish with anger.

Phil, a slender man in his forties with thinning hair, wore a well-tailored suit that was a part of his workday. Buddy, in his mid-twenties, was also in his workday clothes — jeans, blue work shirt, and heavy boots. A construction worker, he looked the part with his lean frame and suntanned, calloused hands.

Sandy, a young woman in her mid-twenties, wearing skirt and sweater and glasses and looking like a graduate student rather than an alcoholic, was chairing this meeting. She had suggested AA's Third Step as a topic for discussion: "Made a decision to turn our will and our lives over to the care of God *as we understood Him.*"

The Third Step often came up at AA discussion meetings, in one way or another. Both Phil and Buddy were having problems with the Third Step.

The basement meeting room of the Step-by-Step group was fairly well filled tonight. The air was thick with the smells of coffee and cigarette smoke. The Step-by-Step group, unlike some other AA groups, didn't use a church or some other "ready-made" meeting place. Instead, they leased this room located in the basement of an office building on the town's main street.

After Joe finished speaking, Sandy called on Nick, a man who'd only recently begun attending meetings of the Step-by-Step group.

"I'm Nick and I'm an alcoholic," he said, and the group members responded in unison, "Hi, Nick."

"I'm pretty new in the program," Nick began. "I don't have much to contribute. I will say that I'm glad to finally be attending meetings in my own hometown. I had to go twenty miles away for my first few meetings." He grinned, looking sheepish. "I didn't want anyone to know I was going to AA, you see."

The group laughed. A lot of people in the room had had the same kinds of fears in the beginning.

"Al?" Sandy said to the man sitting beside Nick.

"I'm Al and I'm an alcoholic," he said. "Thanks, Sandy, I'll pass." Al frequently visited the Step-by-Step group; he belonged to another AA group in the area. Al, as many of the people in the room knew, considered himself an agnostic, which was doubtless the reason why he wasn't choosing to take part in a discussion in which the word *God* figured prominently.

Sandy next called on Richard, a handsome, professorial man in his fifties.

"I didn't realize how much I needed a Power greater than myself," Richard said after he'd introduced and identified himself. "When I was a child, my parents went to a fashionable, mainstream kind of church in our town. I think their church membership was like belonging to the country club, at least in a way. It was just something you do, worshipping in a proper, socially acceptable manner, for reasons that were at least partly social."

Phil reflected that his upbringing must have been much like Richard's, minus the churchgoing. His parents had never discouraged the idea of his going to church, but they'd never really encouraged it, either. Phil had occasionally gone to different churches with childhood friends, but he had not been particularly impressed. He had grown up looking on religion as a sort of casual superstition, nothing that an intelligent, educated person would consider especially important.

"I'm happy to say I now have a Higher Power," Richard went on, "one whom I choose to call 'God.' I feel very comfortable with that today."

Buddy was amazed and a little frightened at the idea of anyone *choosing* to call God anything. In his experience, a person had little leeway in such matters. Unless, of course, he wanted to risk eternal damnation.

"It seems to me," Richard continued, "that human beings everywhere, in every age, have needed to believe in some Power greater than themselves. Even those who say they don't believe in God have to believe there's some kind of order in the universe, even if it's just a scientifically defined order." Richard was, Phil suspected, a very good teacher. "Even people involved with Satanic cults seem to need to believe in a force greater than human energy," Richard said. "I'd known all that for a long time, of course, even during my drinking years. But

I had the alcoholic's arrogance — I thought that none of it applied to *me,* personally. I thought that education and knowledge — coupled, of course, with my great intellect — could take the place of a Higher Power in my life."

He laughed dryly. "I was wrong. When I first came into AA, I used the group as my Higher Power, figuring that a group of people trying to stay sober had more strength than just one person. And I was right, as far as it went. That worked for me for a while. But the longer I stayed sober, the more I began to find problems in my life that I couldn't address simply by not drinking and coming to meetings. I know now that I wasn't growing as a person. I was just not drinking, and I was beginning to feel miserable."

Richard's words were describing what Phil had been feeling for some time now. He'd found that he'd had what AA members sometimes called a "pink cloud." Almost immediately he'd had a sense of relief, of belonging in AA. An outgoing man by nature, Phil had found AA members to be fun loving and accepting of new members from the very start. Since returning to his job, however, he'd found himself gradually getting back into the pessimism and frustration of his drinking days.

"I tried talking to people in AA," Richard was saying. "I told them I was having trouble with the 'God business.' They told me to *act as if* I believed, whether I did or not. It didn't seem very logical to me. In fact, it seemed pretty stupid. But, after I'd hurt enough, I tried it. It took a while, but it worked."

It seems too simple, Phil thought. *How could pretending there was a God help anybody? It seemed like pretending there was water in the desert — you could die of thirst while you were trying to will yourself a waterhole. Well, at least Alcoholics Anonymous didn't require anyone to believe in God.*

Buddy listened to Richard and felt the old conflicts welling up within. Both Joe and Richard spoke of a Higher Power as a sort of friend, someone you could talk to like an ordinary person. Buddy had often wished he could just talk to God in everyday language.

The God Buddy had learned about in Sunday school and from the sermons he'd sweated through as a kid was not very friendly. Buddy had come to imagine God as a fierce, white-bearded old man who'd fling a sinner into the pit of hell — not just for big sins, but for simply not living a holy enough life. For Buddy, talking to God had meant using words that were strange to a child's ears, words like "thee" and "thou" and "thine." And there was the matter of God the Father, the Son, and the Holy Ghost. Buddy had never understood what his mother and the preachers meant by the Holy Trinity, and he didn't know how he was supposed to apply this concept to himself and his everyday concerns.

Sandy called on Annette, a petite, dark-haired woman in her early thirties, about the same age as Buddy's older sister.

"I'd been away from any church for a long time when I finally made it into AA," Annette said. "I've been able to get back into church since I've been sober. I know we don't talk about religion in AA, but worshipping God with other people is important to me. Alcoholics Anonymous has given my religion back to me, through sobriety."

Buddy glanced around the room. No one seemed offended at Annette's reference to church. AA seemed to make a big point of not being religious in itself. Buddy guessed that was why even agnostics like Al, who was sitting with the new guy, Nick, were comfortable in AA.

"I don't have any trouble combining AA with my church life," Annette said. "I know that I'm a lot better church member, sober, than I could have ever been when I was drinking!" There were nods and chuckles from other people in the room.

Phil knew that agnostics and even atheists were welcome in Alcoholics Anonymous. The often cited phrase, "The only requirement for AA membership is a desire to stop drinking," was from one of the AA Traditions. Phil knew that AA didn't pressure anyone to do anything — so where was this uneasiness he was feeling coming from?

Buddy felt uneasy too. Alcoholics Anonymous seemed too — well, *relaxed* — about God. It was as if AA said that anyone's personal idea of God, or even no idea at all, was all right. This went against everything Buddy had been taught as a child.

Several of Phil's co-workers at the advertising agency were confirmed heavy drinkers. Despite this, everyone seemed genuinely glad he'd gotten help at the treatment center for his drinking problem. When he came back to work after his twenty-eight days, they gave him a "glad-you're-back" surprise party.

The agency had done some public-service ads and commercials about alcohol and other drug abuse. This, and Phil's experiences in treatment and AA, caused the others to ask him a lot of questions concerning alcoholism and Alcoholics Anonymous.

"AA members sort of watch each other, don't they?" Harry asked Phil one afternoon in the office they shared. It was a couple of days after the Third Step discussion meeting. Harry had gone barhopping with Phil a few times in the days when Phil was still drinking.

"Not really," Phil answered. "They encourage you to call another member if you feel like you're ready to take a drink, but AA doesn't believe that anyone can keep another person sober by riding herd on him."

"Doesn't AA have some sort of redemption process?" Harry asked after he'd digested Phil's response. Harry was a big man with the ruddy complexion of a hearty drinker. Phil wondered if Harry might have more than a casual interest in alcoholism. "I mean, don't alcoholics get 'saved' or something in AA? I've heard they pray at meetings."

"AA meetings usually open with what we call the Serenity Prayer," Phil said. "And the meetings usually close with the Lord's Prayer — but, no, AA isn't religious at all."

"Umm," Harry said, sounding as if he wasn't convinced but also not anxious to pursue it further. Phil had felt awkward in trying to answer Harry's question about AA and God. He'd been unable to come up with the right words to explain AA's attitude toward a Supreme Being, and coming up with right words was an important part of Phil's job as an advertising account executive.

Buddy was back at his parents' home, his last drinking bout having cost him his driver's license and a good job. He was working again, though not on as good a job as the one he'd lost. With luck, he'd have his driver's license back before the year was out.

"The Reverend Allen asked about you Sunday," Buddy's mother said to him at the supper table. She liked having Buddy, her middle child, at home. It gave her an excuse to do more cooking than she usually did for just herself and her husband.

"He was glad to hear you're doing so well," his mother went on, her voice too casual as she passed the plate of chicken to Buddy. His mother's casualness was a warning sign to Buddy. "He asked when you might be coming back to church."

Buddy, his mouth full of biscuit, didn't answer. His defenses had begun to rise the moment his mother mentioned the pastor of the church she attended.

"We'd be glad to have you go with us," his stepfather said. John was a quiet, stocky man who, like Buddy's father before he'd died, worked for the railroad. John had met Buddy's mother at her church, two years after Buddy's father was killed in a railroad accident. John was as involved in religion as Buddy's mother and was the opposite of Buddy's father in that way.

The railroad company had been kind enough to not mention that Buddy's father had been drunk when he missed his footing and fell under the moving boxcar he'd been trying to board. No one had talked about it, openly, although Buddy's father's drinking habits were all too well known to everyone who knew him.

Buddy knew he was going to have to say something about going back to church. He swallowed his mouthful of food, took a sip of milk, and said, "I just don't feel...," he paused, looking for a word, "...right, somehow, about going back to church. Just yet, anyway."

"What do they say at those AA meetings about going to church?" his mother asked. Her voice, usually pleasant, sounded grim. Her plump features had the look of someone who suspected a possible crime in progress.

"They don't talk about it one way or the other, Mom," Buddy said. "Some AA's go to church, some don't. AA leaves it up to each person."

"Hmmph," his mother said. "It seems to me that an organization that doesn't take a stand for salvation can't be a very good influence."

"Mom," Buddy replied, trying to keep his voice calm, "I'm twenty-six years old. I don't need to be 'influenced,' like some little kid."

"Some of the guys from the railroad have joined AA," John spoke up. Buddy stared at his stepfather in surprise. "They seem to have really been helped. A couple of them have been 'born again' since they joined AA." Because John was as devoted a churchgoer as Buddy's mother, he was the last person Buddy would have expected to defend AA.

"That's well and good," Buddy's mother said. "But it seems to me that if they'd repented and given their hearts to God in the first place, they wouldn't have needed this Alcoholics Anonymous business." She looked at Buddy's plate. "Don't you like the chicken, son?"

"It's fine, Mom," Buddy said. "I guess I just don't feel like eating very much this evening." He put down his knife and fork, excused himself, and left the table.

Buddy was staying in the room that he had shared with his younger brother. He lay on his bed and stared at the ceiling. He hadn't wanted to have hard words at the table. His mother and stepfather had, after all, been very good about taking him back in after his troubles with drinking.

His mother had worked hard to provide the best family life possible for her children. Buddy's father had made good money on the railroad, but the family had always seemed to be short on cash. Buddy now realized that his father had been an alcoholic, as Buddy himself had become.

It seemed to Buddy that for years he and his mother had spoken different languages, perhaps lived in different worlds. His mother's world seemed to be a black-and-white place, where something was either right or wrong. Buddy now sometimes wondered if his mother was always as sure of things as she claimed to be. She'd considered his father's drinking sinful and had often told the children so. She'd always added that they must never talk about it, to anyone. Buddy supposed that if his father had not been killed, his mother would still be married to him. Divorce was one of the many other things besides drinking that she considered to be morally wrong.

As Buddy grew older, his world had become less black and white and his ideas of right and wrong less certain. He still believed some of what he'd been taught about sin and evil as a child — or supposed he did — but there seemed to be so many unanswered questions. . . .

Phil found himself drifting toward Richard before and after meetings, and he listened to Richard closely during discussions. Richard seemed to have what AA's called "good sobriety," meaning more than just not drinking. He also felt a kinship to Richard in the way they thought.

"I had a lot of trouble with the 'God business,'" Richard said to Phil the night Phil confided the problem he was having with the idea of a Higher Power. It was after a meeting and they were having a last cup of coffee, most of the people having already left.

"I'd read about Bill W.'s 'spiritual experience,' of course," Richard said. "I didn't think *I'd* be likely to have one of those!" He was referring to the writings of Bill Wilson, one of AA's co-founders, concerning a supernatural experience Bill W. had while lying in a hospital bed after his last binge. "It would've probably scared me to death," Richard added. "I'd have thought I was going into D.T.'s!"

Phil joined in a laugh at this inside joke, the kind he'd begun to enjoy sharing with other sober alcoholics.

"I don't know. . . . Maybe I need to come to some understanding of a Higher Power, but. . . ."

"I know," Richard said. "It seemed like a lot of superstitious nonsense to me in the beginning. I mean, the whole idea of a God — it was something nobody could *prove*. Oh, I thought Alcoholics Anonymous itself was a great idea. 'Peer group therapy,' the psychologists call it. I was willing to accept that, because psychology was something an intelligent, educated person could understand. And I thought there were people in AA — other people, of course, not *me* — who probably needed the idea of a God."

"I'm not saying I'm *better* than other people," Phil objected.

"Of course you are," Richard said, looking at him very directly. "Just like me. You don't necessarily *want* to feel that way; neither did I. But the fact was, I *did* feel superior to the people who seemed to need a God."

"Well. . . . ," Phil said.

"I don't mean better or superior in the sense of wanting to lord it over people," Richard said. "But I had a kind of false pride, an intellectual arrogance that kept me from admitting that I was no different from people everywhere when it came to a basic human emotional need. I didn't want to admit that I needed a belief in some Power greater than me." He shook his head. "That 'I'm different' attitude almost killed me. I've heard people in AA say that they almost died of 'terminal uniqueness.'"

"Well, what the hell do you *do?*" Phil asked in frustration. "I mean, if you do feel a certain way, how can you just stop feeling that way?"

"It's not easy," Richard replied. "I didn't, for a while. I went to meetings, I tried to work the Steps — the ones without God in them, I mean — but I was feeling more and more miserable. I complained to other AA members about how miserable I was. I wallowed in self-pity; here I was, not drinking, and I still wasn't very happy or serene. I was seriously thinking of checking myself into a mental hospital. Or maybe drinking again — I figured if I was going to be miserable, I might as well be drinking!"

"So what happened?" Phil asked when Richard paused.

"I got some 'tough love,' " Richard said. "I was in a discussion meeting, complaining about how bad I was feeling, about how AA didn't seem to be helping me very much anymore. Some of the other members talked about how their Higher Power had helped them with the kinds of problems I was having. I said that I couldn't, just couldn't, get hold of something as vague as the idea of God.

"There was an AA old-timer there, an ex-Marine named Dan. He sat and listened to me for a while.

"Finally I guess he got enough and spoke up. He said, 'Kid' — Kid, and me forty at the time — 'Kid, I've been hearing you bitch and moan and wallow around. You seem to think that spirituality in AA is some kind of superstitious religious belief. You ain't going to get this program until you figure out that spirituality in AA ain't got a goddamn thing to do with religion!' "

Phil whistled. "What did you say?"

"What could I say?" Richard spread his hands. "He had me. Oh, I was angry for a while, of course. But after I cooled off, I had enough honesty to admit to myself that Dan was right.

I knew that he was anything but some wild-eyed religious freak. If a guy like that needed a Higher Power, then who was I to think I didn't?"

"And that did it for you?" Phil asked.

Richard shook his head. "It got me started in the right direction. But it wasn't easy. I couldn't just will myself to believe all at once. People told me, 'Fake It 'Til You Make It,' meaning to *act as if* I believed. I felt like a fool at first, trying to pray. I wondered if there was anyone or anything out there listening. But I kept trying. And it began to work. I began to feel less anxious and less depressed. I began to have some hope that I might really learn to believe in God. And damned if it didn't happen!"

"That sounds really good," Phil said, making an effort to seem enthusiastic.

"And you think it's a lot of crap, right?" Richard asked with a grin, not seeming offended.

"No, no," Phil said quickly, "Not 'crap. . . .'"

"It's all right. I don't take it personally. I know how hard it is. Just give it a fair chance. What have you got to lose, besides some misery?"

"Do you really, you know, pray?" Buddy blurted out the question.

"How's that?" Big Joe, the biker, was pulling on his leather jacket. Buddy had followed him outside after the meeting. Joe's big Harley was parked close to the door.

"Do you really pray to, uh, 'H.P.,' like you said the other night in the meeting about the Third Step?" Buddy felt uneasy just quoting Joe's offhand term for God.

Joe's thick black beard made it hard to read his face. His nose had been broken at some time. In a wreck, Buddy guessed, or maybe in a fight. Joe leaned on the Harley's saddle. Even half-sitting, his eyes were on a level with Buddy's. Buddy would've hated to meet Joe when he was drunk and feeling mean. Buddy wasn't so sure he'd been wise to accost Joe now.

"Havin' trouble with the God business, are you?" Joe asked.

"I don't know, exactly, but...yeah, I guess I am."

"What's the biggest problem you got with it?" Joe asked.

"Well..." Buddy found it hard to explain. "I mean, I believe in God, and all. My mom had me in church every time the doors opened until I was old enough to say no and make it stick, but...." His voice trailed off.

Joe grinned. "Sounds like me. My old man was a lay preacher. He dragged my brothers and sisters and me across half the state, going to revivals and camp meetings and such." He leaned forward a little so he could see Buddy's face under the light mounted over the door. "You got a bad case of it, ain't you?"

"Case of what?" Buddy said.

"The fear of God," Joe said. "My old man taught us kids to be God-fearing, but he mostly left out the God-loving part. I wasn't afraid of the Devil — that showed well enough when I got out on my own and started raising hell — but I was scared to death of God."

Buddy considered this for a moment; he'd never thought of it that way before. "My folks believe in a real, live Satan," he said finally.

"Oh, yeah," Joe said, "My daddy did too. A Devil complete with horns and a long, forked tail." He fished a cigarette out of his jacket pocket, struck a wooden match with his thumbnail, and lit up.

"The way I understood it," Joe said, squinting through the smoke, "God was the one who had the final say on who Satan got to grab. That meant to me that God was the Man, the one I had to be afraid of."

He flicked the ash off the unfiltered cigarette. "I used to have a '48 Harley with a hundred-and-two-cubic-inch engine. It had a throttle without a return spring. That ol' scooter'd just run at whatever speed it was doin' when I let go of the twist grip.

I stood up in the saddle one night, running sixty miles an hour, and beat my chest and screamed into the wind, daring the Devil to take me."

"Were you drunk?" Buddy asked.

Big Joe laughed. " 'Course I was drunk! I ain't *that* big a damn fool to do something like that sober."

Buddy kicked at a broken place in the concrete in front of the door. "What if our folks were right?" he asked. "I mean, what if we really are supposed to go to a certain church and talk to God in a certain way and all?"

"I got no answer for that one, except here," Joe said, jabbing himself in the stomach with his thumb. "I know what I feel here in my gut, and that's all I have to go on today. I can't prove I'm right and everybody else is wrong, the way my old man used to with his Bible. And the thing is, I don't *have* to prove anything."

"But, what about heaven and hell and all...the hereafter?" Buddy asked.

Joe rubbed his black beard thoughtfully. "For myself, I have to say that the things I've been through — the D.T.'s and hallucinations and withdrawal — were my own private hell. And I don't have to go back there. The Higher Power I believe in now gave me Alcoholics Anonymous. AA keeps me from having to go through that hell again, and that's enough for me."

"How'd you get to know this Higher Power?" Buddy asked. "The one you have now?"

"I had to lighten up," Joe said. "I had to put all I'd learned as a kid out of my mind and start from scratch. The people in AA helped me do that. They didn't try to 'save' me, or 'convert' me, or tell me who God was and what He was like and how I was supposed to deal with Him.

"I met a man in AA who'd done time for murder. He told me that he'd learned that God loved him. I hadn't ever really believed that God could love me. But there was old Ray, who'd killed somebody, and yet he really meant it when he said that he believed God loved him. Ray told me that he didn't believe God had ever punished him for anything that he'd done, that God had just let him punish himself."

Buddy thought about this. "Looking at it that way, I guess I've punished myself some," he said.

"We all have; all us alcoholics," Joe said. "I thought about the times I'd been in jail; about the time I wrecked and broke both my legs, running from the law and me drunk out of my mind. I realized that Ray was right. As a practicing alcoholic, I'd been punishing myself for a long time."

Joe took a final drag on his cigarette, then ground it out under his boot. "Get to know the Power yourself," he said. "That's what I had to do. There probably ain't too many churches who'd want me as a member, even now, but that's all right too."

Buddy pictured the looks on the faces of his mother and her fellow church members if Joe were to walk into a service with his beard and Harley T-shirt. He grinned.

Joe straddled his bike, its suspension sagging under his weight. "Churches and doctrines and rituals: they're all just too complicated for this ol' drunk," he said. "I have to Keep It Simple." He started the Harley. "Just do like they say: don't drink and go to meetings, and try talkin' to the Man," he said over the rumble of motorcycle pipes. He pointed upward, gave Buddy a thumb-up, then rolled away. Buddy stood there until the Harley's exhaust faded in the night.

It wasn't until the new Barringer account came up that Phil saw the other side of his agency's attitude toward his alcoholism.

Kevin, the head of the agency, called a staff meeting on a Friday afternoon to make the announcement.

"As you all know," Kevin began, "Barringer, Incorporated is the largest account this agency has ever handled. Barringer, like other American textile firms, has been hit hard by foreign textile imports." Kevin, a lean, handsome man in his fifties, looked ten years younger. He was a type most alcoholics can never fully understand — the true social drinker.

"Barringer is going to go national in a new campaign," Kevin went on. Phil's excitement began to mount. He had handled the Barringer account when Barringer was doing local and regional advertising. "Barringer wants to use a 'Buy American' theme. They want network television and national magazine and newspaper coverage." Phil knew the sales and public relations people at Barringer; as the account executive for an ad campaign like this one, he'd have a chance to really make a name for himself.

"We're going to begin gearing up immediately, starting Monday," Kevin said. "I'm putting Harry in charge of the campaign." He avoided looking at Phil as he said this.

Phil couldn't believe his ears for a moment. He looked quickly around; the others were avoiding looking at him too. He was the one who'd handled the Barringer account from the first. Not two months ago he'd wrapped up a series of local TV commercials for them, right before he'd gone into treatment.

So that was it. He'd opened his mouth to protest, but he closed it and kept his silence. For the rest of the meeting, he was aware, if not of what was said, of the rest of the staff's careful avoidance of looking directly at him. They were obviously embarrassed at this rejection of Phil as Kevin's choice to handle the most significant job the agency had thus far been offered.

After the meeting broke up, Phil made a pretense of needing something from the storeroom to be alone for a few minutes. He played in his head the things he could have said to Kevin in protest at being passed over. He also played the things Kevin could have said to him: *You missed an entire month of work while you were in treatment; your work had fallen off before you left; Harry had to take over the stuff you were working on while you were gone; we'll need to see how well you're going to do now that you're back, won't we?*

Phil knew, or at least a part of him knew, that Kevin would be justified in saying any of these things. *They don't trust me and why should they?* Yet, it still hurt bitterly to be passed over.

Phil put a smile on his face when he came back into his and Harry's office.

"Congratulations!" he said, shaking Harry's hand.

Harry looked very uncomfortable. "I swear, Phil, I didn't mean to shoot you out of the saddle. I didn't know. . . ."

"I know, I know," Phil said, slapping him on the shoulder. "I guess Kevin's just not wanting to put too much pressure on me right now. He's afraid the company alky might get drunk if he's put under the gun." His good humor was false, even to his own ears.

Phil left early that afternoon, making up a phony errand to run. He went down alone in the elevator and out to the parking lot at the rear of the building. He unlocked his car, climbed in, put the key in the ignition, but paused before starting up.

A small, sour voice was beginning to speak inside his head. *If I hadn't spent time at a drunk farm, they'd have trusted me with an important account,* it said.

It had been a mistake to be so honest about where he'd been for the twenty-eight days of treatment. Kevin would have had to know, of course, but. . . .*I could have made up something to tell the others — then Kevin wouldn't have found it so easy to pass me over for Harry. Look at where my new honesty has gotten me; maybe in a year or two they'll let me handle something bigger than used-car dealers and furniture stores. Or maybe they'll just find a way to ease me out completely.*

Phil started his car and pulled out of the lot, heading in the general direction of home. He'd be an hour early; his wife would wonder why. *She'll think I'm playing hooky from work, the way I did when I was drinking.* Phyllis was not a naturally suspicious person, but she'd learned not to trust him when he was drinking. It seemed to Phil that the whole world was a giant bandwagon of people who didn't trust him.

Life seemed to stretch ahead of him — his career roadblocked, people always lacking trust in him — and all because of something that, if the people in AA and the treatment center were right, wasn't even his fault! An involuntary illness; a disease, many people called it, and he was a victim.

It was Friday afternoon, the time of the week when he'd most appreciated having a few drinks — back when he could really have a *few* drinks. Fridays were for either celebrating or getting over the past week, depending on how things had gone. This would be a Friday to get over something. And he couldn't drink. *It's not fair,* the voice screamed inside his head.

A liquor store where he'd done a lot of business was in the next block. He was in the right lane. He would be caught by the light at the corner past the liquor store anyway. It seemed like fate.

He pulled the car into a parking space in front of the liquor store and shut off the engine. He thought about the first drink, how it would smell and taste and feel.

He felt the outline of the white plastic AA chip that he'd picked up at his first meeting, smooth and round in his right front pants pocket. He thought of having to drive somewhere since he couldn't take his liquor home, with Phyllis there. He thought about her finding out he was drinking again; he knew he couldn't fool her for long. He thought about having to pick up another white chip — if he could bear to face AA again. He thought about how the first drinks would wear off, leaving the dull, dead feeling. He thought about having to drink more, but never regaining that first glow, just postponing the sick, depressed, hopeless feeling that would finally come, no matter what. . . .

He reached for the ignition switch to restart the engine, but his hand fell away. He was a fool; he had been a fool all along, to think he could survive in life — real life, not some treatment center or AA meeting — without alcohol. But he had no illusions about ever being able to drink successfully again.

"What am I supposed to do?" he heard himself saying out loud. He was gripping the steering wheel with both hands, his knuckles white. "Just what the hell am I supposed to do?"

Buddy had been nervous about speaking to Annette. The fact that she reminded him of his older sister helped, but he still had to crank up his courage to go over to her after the meeting.

"You said you went back to church after you got sober," Buddy said to her. "What if your church had said you didn't need AA?"

Annette's eyes had widened in surprise at Buddy's question, but now she looked thoughtful.

"Well...," she began, "it didn't come up, and I'm glad." She was a little taller than his sister, but she was about Janet's age and had the same trace of country in her voice. "But I think...." She paused. (Buddy had noticed that most of the people he'd encountered in AA seemed to really *think* about a question before giving an answer.) "I have to say, speaking for myself, that if my church had told me I shouldn't need Alcoholics Anonymous, I'd have had to find another church."

"But..." Buddy struggled with his question. "What if a church, your folks' church, the church you were brought up in, told you that *its* way was the only right way?"

Annette smiled dryly. "There are some people in *my* church now who seem to think that way," she said. "Fortunately, my pastor isn't one of them. He took the trouble to learn about AA and he thinks it's great for alcoholics. But there are those ministers, and churches, who're narrow-minded and judgmental."

"My mother doesn't understand why I don't want to go back to church — her church — right now," Buddy said. "To tell the truth, I'm not sure I ever want to go back to that church. Maybe not to *any* church."

"I know what you mean," Annette said. "I wasn't brought up in the church I'm in now. The church my folks went to taught that there was just one way — *its* way, of course — to worship God. When I got sober, even though I was already in a church that wasn't as rigid as my folks', I realized that I couldn't just accept what other people told me about God. I had to find Him, or 'Her,'" she smiled, then added, "by myself, for myself."

"My mother's church says it's sinful to doubt or question," Buddy said. "It says that to even think that other people's understanding of God might be right for *them* is wrong, if their understanding is different from the church's."

Annette shrugged. "I have to use the Serenity Prayer on folks like that," she said. "I know I can't change them. I have to accept that they're that way. But I can have my own beliefs; Alcoholics Anonymous has taught me that."

"I don't think I could be a member of a church and not agree with its beliefs," Buddy said.

Annette nodded. "I think that's personal honesty, the kind AA tells us we need if we're going to stay sober. I think that personal honesty is more important for an alcoholic than some religious doctrine."

Buddy thought about this. It made sense, but there was still the fear. . . .

"I can't help thinking about the stuff they taught me about heaven and hell and all," he said. "About what would happen to me if I died and wasn't ready to go."

Annette made an irritated, snorting sound. "That's where the churches that put AA down really get my goat," she said, then smiled. "I have to use the Serenity Prayer a lot when I think about that." She turned serious again. "AA is about staying sober. AA doesn't try to prepare anyone for a life after death. It doesn't say that the hereafter isn't important; it just says that it isn't AA's business. There's a saying I've heard: 'Religion can help save your soul; Alcoholics Anonymous will help save your butt.'"

Buddy stared at Annette for a moment, then burst into laughter. This soft-spoken woman, a church member and so much like his sister, could talk as tough as anybody when she needed to.

"I guess that means I need to stay sober, whatever else I may plan to do," Buddy said.

"Absolutely," Annette replied. "I would be a lousy addition to a congregation — Protestant, Catholic, Jewish, or anything else — if I didn't stay sober. I believe personally that God gave Alcoholics Anonymous to people like me. I'd be not only ungrateful, but a fool if I didn't use AA!"

She laughed. "I sound a little like I'm in a pulpit, don't I?" She gave Buddy's arm a sisterly pat. "Just Keep It Simple, like the slogan says. Don't let your confusion over religion keep you from using a Higher Power in staying sober. If you don't drink and come to meetings and listen, you'll find that all the other stuff will work itself out in time."

"It's called 'planning the drunk, not just the drink,'" Richard said to Phil. Phil had arrived early for this evening's meeting and was grateful that Richard, too, had arrived early. They'd gotten coffee and found a private corner of the meeting room.

"'Planning the drunk'?" Phil asked.

"It means thinking through what will be likely to happen after you take that first drink," Richard said. "Most of us, in the old days, never thought beyond the first drink."

"That saying's a new one to me," Phil admitted. It had been several hours now since his near-relapse, but his hand still shook as it held his coffee cup.

"You hadn't heard of it, yet you practiced it," Richard said. "Interesting, isn't it?"

"I drove away from that liquor store feeling as if I'd just missed being run over by a truck," Phil said. Even now, several hours after his near-relapse, his stomach felt fluttery.

"I wonder, do you suppose your Higher Power saw fit to give you a tool, in the form of that slogan that you'd never heard of before?" Richard asked, his eyebrows raised.

"I don't know. . . ." Phil shook his head. "The God business is still a little hard to swallow."

"I'm told by people in AA that spiritual experiences come in all shapes and sizes."

"Maybe. . . ." Phil was remembering that he'd seemed to be asking *someone*, something, about what he was supposed to do when he was about to go into the liquor store.

"I know you're still having trouble," Richard said. "You know, you can look on it as having had the people you know in AA supporting you in spirit when you were about to take that drink."

Phil nodded, remembering the feel of the white plastic chip in his pocket as he fought the urge to drink.

"I ran across an interesting definition of *faith*," Richard said, sipping from a steaming cup of coffee. " 'A belief in something that can't be proved in concrete terms.' I can't show you God, the way I could show you the White House or the Grand Canyon. But does that fact mean you were any less anxious to get some kind of help this afternoon at the liquor store?"

Phil struggled with himself for a moment. Honesty won out; he shook his head. "No," he admitted.

"Try having faith in something — the group, or Alcoholics Anonymous itself, or whatever," Richard suggested. "Just take it easy; don't force it."

"Maybe I *have* been letting my intellect get too mixed up with my gut-level needs," Phil said.

"It's possible to resolve that conflict between your intellect and your emotions," Richard said. "Just relax, and don't worry about having to 'prove' or 'disprove' God's existence. It's not your intellect that needs to believe, it's your gut emotions. I have to say that my Higher Power is more comfort to me than any 'proof' — including the kind of proof that comes in whiskey bottles."

The Slipper

Bonnie finished writing the new listing and looked at her watch, surprised to see that it was a quarter to seven in the evening. She'd lost track of time after the other brokers and the clerical staff had left at five.

She hurriedly gathered her purse and coat and went out, locking the front door behind her. Ordinarily, she'd not be in a hurry at this hour, having only a skimpy meal and her moonlighting work to look forward to for the remainder of the evening, but tonight was different.

The battery in her five-year-old Chevrolet was starting to die; it complained but turned the engine over until it started. *Have to do something about that,* she told herself. *It wouldn't do to be showing a house and have my prospects stranded because my car wouldn't start.*

She disliked the Chevrolet on general principles. It represented a part of her failure, the failure that had climaxed with twenty-eight days in an alcoholism treatment center. She had had to sell her new Buick, along with the condominium she'd bought after separating from Paul and dividing the proceeds with him from the sale of their house.

Now, six months after completing treatment, she was stuck with the Chevrolet and the dumpy little furnished apartment to which she was now returning. She didn't mind the apartment as much as the car, since she used the apartment only as a place to sleep, bathe, keep her clothes, and do her moonlighting as an accountant. But she missed her new Buick. She used her car every day in her real estate work, and the Chevrolet had been a used car when she got it. A good one, admittedly; she supposed she should be grateful to find a decent vehicle she could afford, considering the state of her finances. But it was a *used* car — with that struggling, just-making-ends-meet kind of sound.

Tonight was special. It was to be her first real date since her divorce and since completing treatment. She arrived at the apartment a few minutes after seven; her date was due to pick her up at eight. She frantically tore off her workday clothes, put on sweat suit and sneakers, and jogged for twenty minutes through the quiet neighborhood.

With a little over half an hour to get ready when she returned from running, she showered quickly and blow-dried her short, reddish-blonde hair — "strawberry blonde" her mother had called it. Bonnie had often wished that it was a more dramatic color, pale-gold blonde perhaps, or striking brunette.

Still, she was reasonably well-satisfied with her looks at this time in her life. In her early thirties, she was as slender as her rather sturdy bone structure would allow; *sturdy peasant* was a term she often thought of when considering her figure. She would've liked to be either taller and more statuesque, or smaller and more petite. But at least she'd lost the puffiness she'd had when she was still drinking, and her eyes and skin were clear and healthy-looking.

She took out her dark-red dress and the accessories that went with it. Her wardrobe was still reasonably nice, which was fortunate since she'd been able to add precious little to it in the time she'd been sober. Her old job as sales manager at a large real estate brokerage had carried a considerably larger income than she was presently making. Being just one of several brokers in a smaller agency had definitely put a crimp in her style, one she was working hard to correct.

Jerry was prompt, arriving a couple of minutes before eight. Bonnie called to him to come in while she finished putting on her makeup.

Jerry's eyes showed his approval of her appearance when she came out ready to go. He was a nice enough looking guy and reminded Bonnie vaguely of her ex-husband, which was one reason she hadn't rushed to accept his invitations to go out. Jerry had the same tall, big-shouldered build as Paul, with the same widow's peak of hairline that was starting to recede.

Jerry seemed to be doing well in his job as a broker for another real estate agency, judging from his BMW sedan and stylish clothes. He held the door open as she climbed into the car and then drove her to the country club for dinner. It was the first time Bonnie had been to the club since completing treatment, though she and Paul had been regular patrons B. D. — Before Divorce.

The club's dining room with its solid mahogany paneling, giant stone fireplace, and leather-upholstered chairs and banquettes was at once remotely familiar and strange to her. Familiar in that she'd been here in vastly different circumstances; strange for its luxury, a luxury she'd once taken more or less for granted, but which now seemed much more impressive.

The AA rooms that had recently been the focus of most of her off-work socializing — such as it had been — were for the most part rather shabby. They ran to mismatched and battered furniture, cramped rest rooms, and the smell of cigarettes and coffee. The people here tonight at the country club were all well-dressed, down to the waiters, who were smartly turned-out in evening clothes. They seemed a far cry from the kinds of people one rubbed shoulders with in Alcoholics Anonymous.

There was a short wait to be seated, and they passed the time in the club's bar. Bonnie ordered a Perrier, Jerry a scotch and soda. Bonnie had to make a conscious effort to order the imported mineral water rather than a martini. She blessed the health and fitness trend among the upwardly mobile population that made ordering a nonalcoholic beverage rather fashionable.

When they were seated, however, and Jerry was ordering their meal, she couldn't very well stop him as he ordered a bottle of "good" wine. *To make a point of it,* she thought, *would've been — uncivilized.*

The meal was delicious, though she picked at it carefully, not wanting to break the self-imposed diet that had allowed her to drop two sizes in six months. She made a conscious effort to sip the wine very slowly and was surprised and relieved — though with a vague sense of disappointment — to feel no effect from the alcohol.

Jerry was not a witty conversationalist, but he was flatteringly attentive. He was also good-looking enough that being seen with him in public made Bonnie's ego feel better than it had in months.

At the end of dinner, when Bonnie had refused dessert and cognac, Jerry suggested going to a nightclub. Bonnie declined, pleading work to do at home and an early day at the office tomorrow. He took her back to her apartment, didn't appear to be irritated when she turned aside his hint about coming in for a nightcap, and gave her a pleasant if not soul-stirring kiss.

Bonnie managed to work for an hour on the books for one of the small businesses for which she was doing accounting on the side. Getting ready for bed after she'd finally decided to call it a day, she felt quite virtuous and more upbeat than she had for some time. Underneath, though, was a feeling of physical letdown, more than simple fatigue. It was the sort of feeling, in mild form, she remembered when the effects of alcohol were wearing off. She'd felt no intoxication, no euphoria, from the modest amount of wine she'd drunk with dinner. But, for the first time since she'd left treatment, there was a small but definite craving for a drink.

The next day was another busy one. Bonnie again worked until nearly seven in the evening, showing a house to a couple who both worked during the day. They weren't a completely sure sale yet, but they signed an offer, and the prospects of selling them the split-level seemed excellent.

She went home, ran and did exercises, ate a small cup of yogurt and a salad — the first food she'd had since breakfast — and busied herself with another set of books until nearly eleven. She was exhausted by the time she went to bed, but this night she slept fitfully.

The following afternoon she finished at the agency a little after five. She had more time this evening, but the idea of going back to the apartment to work on more monthly statements suddenly seemed repulsive.

There was an AA meeting tonight. But after the atmosphere of the country club, she wasn't anxious to go to the tacky, smoky little meeting room and listen to people talking about the benefits of sobriety and taking one's inventory and resentments and acceptance: all the standard AA things. Besides, AA members, while they didn't come right out and ask you where you'd been after you'd missed some meetings, showed an interest in your welfare that was — embarrassing — to say the least.

The thought had occurred to Bonnie in the last couple of days that perhaps she wasn't a *true* alcoholic after all, the kind that needed to keep going to AA meetings all her life. She hadn't felt any real effect from the wine she'd had at the country club, and yet, technically, it was what Alcoholics Anonymous called a "slip." She hadn't really wanted to drink since, not seriously; to hear some of those AA's talk, one drink of *anything* alcoholic would send you off on a roaring drunk!

There was one of the better class of motels not far from the agency, with a well-managed lounge, a place where riffraff didn't hang out. It was a nice place where a lot of business and professional people stopped after office hours to share a drink and informal socializing. Bonnie remembered it well from the old days.

On a sudden impulse this late afternoon, she pulled into the motel lot and around to the side where patrons of the lounge parked. Several expensive cars were already parked there. Bonnie paused a moment before getting out, then squared her shoulders, locked her car, and went inside.

Sure enough, there were Alice and Pat, two of the gals she used to see here in the old days. Alice was office manager for a large insurance agency, Pat a loan officer at a local bank.

As a rule, Bonnie was not fond of the company of other women, but Alice and Pat were neither young-matron types, preoccupied with homes and children, nor young singles, on the make for men. Alice was a tailored, no-nonsense woman in her early forties; Pat was about Bonnie's age, a redhead whose dizziness seemed odd considering that she worked in banking.

They, of course, immediately began catching up on old times. Bonnie told, in a falsely humorous way, of her breakup with Paul and her divorce. She did not mention her treatment for alcoholism. There was still enough caution in her to cause her to order Perrier again, even though she'd felt a loosening in her attitude toward drinking since the wine at the country club.

Alice, a very casual drinker, sipped her gin and tonic infrequently as they talked. Pat was more the style of drinker Bonnie had been; Bonnie smiled inwardly, remembering how she herself had been famous among Paul's male friends as a woman who could drink most men under the table.

The waitress came to renew their drinks just as Alice was in the midst of a bit of office gossip she was passing along to Bonnie. Pat ordered. When the drinks came, Bonnie's was a martini, like in the old days when she used to meet Pat here.

She fingered the stem of the glass as she half-listened to the end of Alice's story. She considered sending the martini back. Pat was well into her current scotch. Even Alice had finished her first drink by this time.

Bonnie tasted the martini. It was cold, with the glass properly chilled the way she remembered the bartender mixing martinis here. It was dry, with just a suggestion of vermouth. It was like suddenly running into an old, half-forgotten friend by accident, not expecting the joy of reunion that welled up inside. . . .

A tremendous sense of well-being came with the alcohol's first effect. The five-year-old car, the stodgy little apartment, the lower income all seemed to be truly temporary conditions. They now seemed not only bearable, but even gave Bonnie a sense of pride at the idea of pulling herself up by her own boot-straps. She was now slender, had all but just closed a sale, had attracted the attention of a successful male — she was amazed that she'd been feeling so discontented with her present life.

Bonnie had the impression that it was nearly ten when she left the lounge, though it was too dark on the way out to her car to see her watch clearly. She called out a laughing good night to Pat; Alice had left much earlier. It wasn't until Bonnie had coaxed the battery to once more stir the engine into life, that a sudden, sheer terror overtook her: The police. Arrested for drunken driving. Her name in the paper. It seemed that half the patients with whom she'd gone through treatment had been cited for driving while impaired. That's all she needed, a DWI and loss of her driver's license, which was an absolute necessity for a real estate broker.

She sat huddled over the wheel at the edge of the parking lot until she mustered enough courage to edge her way cau-tiously out into the street. She did so only from the sheer desperation of having to get home somehow. She remembered hearing from one of the DWI patients that the police looked for drivers going abnormally slow as well as for speeders and weavers, so she forced herself to nudge the accelerator up to a normal speed. She had to half-close one eye to watch the mirror. The drive home was an agony of suspense, but she made it without seeing a police car.

The next morning Bonnie had a mild hangover and a terrible sense of guilt. It had been so *stupid*, putting herself at such risk. It would have been the ultimate cruel irony to lose her driver's license *after* having gone through alcoholism treatment.

She managed to get to the office on time and worked extra hard as a sort of penance for the previous night's mistake. She would never, *never* drink again when driving was called for afterward.

Jerry called her at the office that afternoon. She accepted his offer of dinner quicker than she might have otherwise.

On the way home, she realized that if Jerry again wanted to come in after their date, and she decided to let him, she'd need to offer him a drink. She stopped at the liquor store and bought a fifth of gin, a bottle of vermouth, and a bottle of scotch.

Bonnie ran, did her exercises, and cleaned the already spotless apartment. She then showered, did her hair, and began choosing an outfit.

She tried on an off-white, frilly blouse and a navy skirt. She didn't like them. The green silk dress went well with her hair, but it was a bit large for her new weight. A dark-brown skirt and yellow blouse fit, but they were not really suitable for an evening date. In the last few months, she'd bought mostly things to wear at work. She didn't have an evening outfit she really liked now, apart from the dark red dress she'd worn on her first date with Jerry.

Jerry was due to arrive very soon. She still hadn't decided what to wear. She was feeling jittery and tense.

She mixed a quick-and-dirty martini, glass unchilled and no olive but *dry,* strong enough to almost gag her with the first swallow. But the drink did what she knew it would — the rough edges of her nerves smoothed out, and choosing an outfit suddenly became much easier.

She managed to finish a second drink before Jerry arrived. She used mouthwash and became aware of pronouncing words very carefully.

This time they went to a restaurant called the Coachlamp a few miles out of town. It had a sort of Medieval English decor and a menu without prices listed.

There was another short wait in the bar for their table. Bonnie had one more martini. She knew her face was flushed from the alcohol, but that didn't hurt her looks — Jerry's eyes were admiring as he looked into hers.

There was wine again with the meal, and brandy afterward. With the brandy, things began to not go so well. Bonnie couldn't make the waitress understand that she wanted a proper, large snifter glass for the brandy. Jerry was looking at Bonnie a bit oddly. She tripped on a piece of gravel on the way out to his car.

Jerry dropped her at her door and said nothing about coming in for a nightcap. She'd more or less planned on letting him come in, but it was just as well, she supposed, that he didn't; she was feeling a bit fuzzy-headed. She had her nightcap alone, and another, and that was the last she remembered.

Bonnie came to at four in the morning with a raging thirst and the shakes so bad that she could hardly hold a glass. She knew from experience that short of the detox medication they'd used on her at the treatment center, alcohol was the only thing that would calm her screaming nerves and let her go back to sleep. She mixed gin half-and-half with orange juice, managed to get two glasses down, and crawled miserably back into bed.

There was no question of going to the office in the morning. She called in sick, pleading a virus — she remembered hearing hangovers called "Irish influenza" while she was in treatment. Although she did have some Irish ancestors, she didn't find the joke at all funny. She was glad it wasn't a Monday morning; calling in sick on Mondays was always more suspicious.

Somehow, she made it through the day, venturing out once to the liquor store despite her resolve to never drive after drinking again. She wore her largest pair of sunglasses and a scarf around her head and drove carefully. The day was to become fuzzy in her memory by four in the afternoon, and after six the blackout became complete.

At seven the following evening, Bonnie took a deep breath, squared her shoulders, and began putting on eye makeup. Looking at herself this closely in the mirror was something she'd been putting off as long as possible.

The drinking had left her with dark, puffy circles under reddened eyes. She had realized, had admitted this morning that she was on a flat-out binge. She had somehow managed to avoid drinking more today. The Valium she'd found in a seldom-used purse helped. The staff at the treatment center had warned her about Valium and other prescription drugs. But she'd felt as though she was going to explode as she went through the withdrawal from alcohol and that she had the choice of either taking the tranquilizer or drinking more.

Bonnie gritted her teeth as she put on shadow and liner and mascara with hands that were still none too steady, despite the passage of time and the Valium. *The thing about the progression of alcoholism continuing even when you're not drinking must be true,* she thought. She'd been skeptical when they told her that at the treatment center, but now she'd only been drinking — what? — two or three days this time, and she was in almost as bad a shape as she'd been when she'd entered treatment.

"AA can't make you stay sober, but it can sure mess up your drinking." It was a saying she'd heard in Alcoholics Anonymous and which she'd more or less dismissed at the time as not applying to her. But now the self-disgust and guilt she was feeling seemed to prove the truth of the saying.

She knew she needed to get back to AA, although the prospect wasn't very appealing just now. If she'd been pressed to say exactly *why* she needed to go to a meeting tonight, she would have had a hard time putting it into words. But it was a compulsion, almost as strong as the compulsion to drink had been.

She'd not been to many meetings in the past month; she paused and realized with a start she hadn't been to *any* meetings in the last thirty days.

She'd gotten thoroughly tired of AA meetings, of the way people seemed to talk at agonizing length about the same few basic things, the cautions and admonitions they were always giving. They'd even warned of involvement with the opposite sex for the first year — *year!* — of sobriety.

But despite this, Bonnie felt the pull of an AA meeting tonight. AA was the one place where people would understand, without having to be told, exactly how she was feeling right now.

Jerry wouldn't understand, no matter how hard she tried to explain. She'd made a scene at the Coachlamp Restaurant arguing with the waitress, she now realized. And she'd stumbled — no, be honest — *staggered* on the way out to Jerry's car. He had undoubtedly marked her down by now simply as an obnoxious drunk, the way Paul had done when he left her. She felt the old sense of injustice and self-pity and anger well up inside her. . . .

Bonnie decided on the dark red dress to wear to the meeting. It looked good on her, and her ego needed all the help it could get. She gave her hair a final brush and pat and studied herself in the full-length mirror on the closet door. Thank God she had not been drinking again long enough to start putting on weight. She'd been bloated by the time Paul left; she still wasn't convinced he hadn't found another, more attractive woman.

Bonnie arrived at the meeting room of the Step-by-Step group of Alcoholics Anonymous a little before eight o'clock. Going down the alley, passing the Dumpster, entering the door that was marked only by a stylized AA symbol that an outsider wouldn't recognize as such, she was struck by the contrast between this and the country club and the Coachlamp. It was ironic that while most of her destructive drinking had taken place either in her own tastefully and expensively decorated home or in stylish and grand public surroundings, her sobriety — what there had been of it — had been in seedy places like this.

There was the usual blue haze of cigarette smoke and smell of coffee as she walked into the meeting room. She was greeted by several members in a way that was enthusiastically friendly but without any questioning looks at her long absence from meetings.

She moved into the room past small knots of people, avoiding the one in which Annette was talking to a couple of other members. Annette had been a sort of unofficial sponsor to Bonnie, making a point to talk to her when she'd first started coming to meetings of this group. Bonnie had never formally asked anyone to be her sponsor. You didn't need a sponsor to join AA; sponsors were simply people to whom you could talk on a one-to-one basis.

"Bonnie!" said Tom, a big old bear of a man with a bear's lovableness. He gave her a hug, and she smelled the sawdust on his clothes. He was a successful building contractor; Bonnie had sold a couple of houses he'd built and had been surprised when she'd first run into him at AA.

There was Phil, a well-dressed man in his forties with thinning hair and glasses who was in advertising; Richard, a handsome, bearded man in his fifties who was a professor at the local college; Buddy, a good-looking young man in his twenties who showed his male appreciation of Bonnie by his shyness around her. There was Chuck, a fashionably dressed man in expensive casual clothes; *attractive enough but rather vain,* Bonnie thought. Chuck was talking to a tall, pretty, dark-haired young woman, a newcomer who was with Janey. Janey was a petite blonde whose looks belied her age; she was in her forties, with teenaged children.

Nick, a husky, dark-haired man in his late thirties, was chairing the meeting tonight. He called it to order at eight o'clock, pausing long enough to let latecomers get coffee and find a seat. He opened the meeting by leading the group in the Serenity Prayer. Nick was an attractive man who was (unfortunately from Bonnie's point of view) married.

Bonnie never ceased to be amazed by the diversity in Alcoholics Anonymous. There was Joe, a huge, black-bearded man who wore a motorcycle jacket and boots; John, a man who often described himself as a "low-bottom drunk," meaning he'd been on skid row in his drinking days; Anna, a beautiful and aristocratic-looking middle-aged woman; Sandy, a pert teenager given to denims and fantastic hairdos; Martha, a former nun who was now a horse trainer and wore jeans and boots most of the time.

This was a "speaker meeting" of the Step-by-Step group, and after Nick had finished the routine of opening the meeting, he introduced the person who was to tell his story tonight.

This turned out to be young Buddy, who was speaking before an AA group for the first time. She half-listened to Buddy and wondered if Jerry would call her again. Had he perhaps called while she was in a blackout? She could have literally said *anything;* her mind reeled under the possibility of the embarrassment of such a situation. She had learned in treatment that blackouts were a form of alcohol-induced amnesia; she'd thought for years that it was normal for people who drank to not remember some things they did and said.

She wondered if she should mention her relapse to anyone here tonight. She decided not. Perhaps she should go back to the psychologist she had been seeing before she went into alcoholism treatment. Perhaps having been an overweight teenager was her real problem, that and her parents having divorced when she was eleven. On second thought, the psychologist wasn't such a good idea, at least not *that* psychologist; he'd pressured her into going into treatment for her drinking.

She applauded along with the others when Buddy finished telling his story. *He didn't make a very good talk,* Bonnie thought, remembering some of the really good speakers she had heard in AA, *but he had tried at least.* She hadn't paid a great deal of attention to what he had had to say.

Nick passed the baskets after making the usual explanation that AA has no dues or fees and that everyone is free to contribute or not. There were a couple of announcements. Then Nick picked up the chip box.

The chips were for various lengths of sobriety, except for the first, the white chip.

"The white chip is for newcomers who'd like to try the AA way of life," Nick said, holding one up. It was the size of a poker chip, with a stylized AA logo like the one on the door on one side. "Or, the white chip's for anyone who's been out in the weeds and wants to start over."

Bonnie winced inwardly at Nick's casual AA term for a drinking relapse. "Out in the weeds" sounded so — *disreputable.*

Nick held the chip higher. "Anyone need a white chip?" he asked.

Bonnie felt a sudden panic. She'd decided to say nothing to anyone about her slip. Now, she suddenly felt that everyone in the room knew; that they were sitting there, waiting to see how honest she was.

It would be easy enough to just get up and get the stupid chip, she thought with a quick flash of anger. *But what business was it of theirs, all these self-righteous sober alcoholics?* She busied herself pretending to look for something in her purse while Nick went on to the colored chips that denoted various lengths of sobriety.

After Nick read the closing statement about taking what you liked and leaving the rest, everyone rose and formed a circle with joined hands to say the Lord's Prayer. Bonnie's left hand was in Tom's and her right in Richard's, and she felt the nervous perspiration on her palms and was sure they knew.

"So, how've you been?" Annette asked, suddenly materializing in front of Bonnie as the crowd milled around after the meeting's close.

"Oh, uh, fine," Bonnie stammered. "I've missed some meetings, thought I ought to get back, you know. . . ."

"Umm," Annette said. "I've been concerned about you. Especially since I hadn't seen you in awhile." Annette was a pixieish brunette about Bonnie's age. She had a slightly countrified accent that seemed to belie her quick, disturbingly perceptive mind.

"Well, you know," Bonnie said, "work and all. . . ."

"Yes, I know," Annette said. Bonnie didn't much like her tone, which suggested Annette really *did* know. "That's a pretty dress," Annette added.

"Thanks," Bonnie said uncomfortably. Ordinarily, she thrived on compliments, but now she felt overdressed and overly made up, beside Annette. In her jeans and sweater, Annette looked as if she'd simply stopped doing whatever she'd been doing at home to come to the meeting. Compared to Annette, Bonnie suddenly felt rather vulgar in appearance.

It's all very well for her, Bonnie thought as Annette turned to respond to someone calling her name. *She's a mother and housewife; she doesn't have to worry about looking good all of the time. . . .*

"Looking good, Bonnie," Chuck said. She started a little at his use of the words she'd just been thinking. "That dress really becomes you," he added.

Bonnie was glad now for a compliment that she could feel all right about, even though she didn't especially like Chuck. He was, she sensed, a womanizer, what some AA's called a "Thirteenth Stepper," meaning he was constantly on the prowl for new, attractive females in the group. Still, talking with him now, flirting a little, helped push away some of the uncomfortable things speaking with Annette had brought to mind.

She noted with some amusement that Janey had swept the pretty newcomer away from Chuck right after the meeting. *The newcomer would do well to avoid Chuck,* Bonnie thought as she played the familiar game with him, keeping him at a conversational arm's length while doing a discreet amount of flirting.

She finally disengaged herself from Chuck and turned to leave. As she was walking out, however, Annette stopped her once more and said, "Some of us gals have started a women's meeting. The first one's Thursday, tomorrow night. Why don't you come to it?"

"All right," Bonnie heard herself agreeing, insincerely. It seemed the quickest way to get free. On the way home she shuddered a little at the thought of an all-female AA meeting. The coed meetings could be dull enough at times!

Jerry didn't call again. Bonnie found herself depressed because he didn't, even though she'd been only casually interested in him.

She had two tiring days at the office and in her moonlighting business. The sale fell through with the people who had signed the offer; the seller was agreeable but the would-be buyers couldn't get acceptable financing. She'd been late in finishing the books for one of her accounting clients because of the drinking episode, and they had taken their business elsewhere. The battery in the Chevrolet finally died, and she had to pay for road service in addition to a new battery.

Bonnie had felt that she'd learned her lesson from the three-day slip, but by Friday afternoon she was strung tight and desperately wanted a drink. She thought of going to an AA meeting that evening, but there was the issue of the white chip and whether to acknowledge that she had had a relapse. She didn't think she could bear another session of being around AA members with her guilty secret.

Bonnie didn't allow herself to think long about stopping at the motel lounge after work. But when she got home and began cleaning the kitchen, she found, under the counter, the bottle of scotch she had bought when she had thought Jerry might come in after their last date. Somehow she'd overlooked the scotch on her drinking spree.

She set it on the counter for a while, unopened. Then she broke the seal, but quickly set the bottle down again when she remembered she hadn't eaten since that morning. She fixed soup and a small salad and ate the frugal little meal. Then, with a slump of resignation, she poured a generous slug of scotch over two ice cubes and added a little soda water.

Bonnie didn't like scotch, but she drank it until she was what she had once thought of as comfortably high. But this time, though the physical relaxation was there, the mental release wasn't. She knew now, with a saddening certainty, that she would have to drink more. She couldn't get through the weekend without it.

She finished the scotch, then managed to get to the liquor store and back without incident. Large portions of that weekend were lost to Bonnie. She actually managed to do some running on Saturday, though her heart pounded frighteningly and her perspiration came with a slick, greasy, unhealthy feel. She remembered being grateful that she and Paul hadn't had children; it came to her in a brief moment of partial clarity what a disaster she would be as a mother. She'd always thought she wanted children, someday, but "someday" was being pushed further and further into the future while her biological clock kept ticking away, louder than ever, it seemed.

Sunday went by in such a haze that she had no real memory of it. Monday morning she awoke with a raging hangover and the shakes so bad that she had to use both hands, one guiding the other, to punch the office telephone number. She pled a reoccurrence of the flu; the broker-in-charge sounded skeptical.

She found the number of Ridgeview, the treatment center where she'd been introduced to sobriety and AA. They'd told her to call if she ever needed help. At the time, she'd believed it highly unlikely that she would ever have to make such a call. Now, she asked for Sally, the woman who had been assigned as her counselor at Ridgeview.

Sally came on the line after a couple of minutes. Bonnie could picture Sally in her mind when she heard Sally's voice. Sally was a sturdily built woman in her fifties with warm, deep blue eyes, a contrast to the sternness of her face. Sally's voice had become husky from years of smoking cigarettes and drinking.

"Not doing too well, are we?" Sally said as soon as Bonnie identified herself. Sally was not one for beating around the bush.

"I'm doing lousy," Bonnie admitted.

"I imagine. Well, was it any better this time?"

"It was worse." Bonnie was surprised and disgusted to find herself crying.

"Have you been back to AA?" Sally asked.

"I drank last week and went to a meeting after that," Bonnie sniffled. "But I haven't been back, and I started drinking again this past Friday." She knuckled at her eyes like a little child. "Oh, Sally, I feel so damn *rotten!*"

"Of course you do," Sally said. Bonnie felt she could have sounded a little more concerned. "That's the practicing alcoholic's natural state, feeling rotten." Sally had her virtues, but unbridled sympathy wasn't one of them.

"What am I going to do?" Bonnie almost wailed.

"You know what to do, kid," Sally said. "You spent twenty-eight days here learning what to do. Do you need to come back and repeat the course?"

"I. . . ." Bonnie paused, seriously considering going back to treatment. "I don't see how I can. My insurance won't pay for more than one treatment per year, and my new boss isn't thrilled by my being out of work even for a couple of days."

"Well, a lot of people make it in AA without going through treatment," Sally said. "You've actually got a head start, you know, over somebody coming into AA off the street."

Bonnie didn't particularly want to think about her supposed advantage right now. She didn't reply. After a moment, she heard Sally sigh.

"So what's the problem you're having with AA?" Sally asked.

"Oh, I don't know," Bonnie said, impatience fighting with her tears of self-pity.

"You *are* having a problem, though?"

"AA doesn't seem to help me with my. . . . specific problems," Bonnie said. "All they talk about are the Steps and the slogans and not taking a drink."

"Don't you think talking about not taking a drink is appropriate, considering your last couple of days?" Sally didn't bother to disguise the sarcasm in her voice.

"But I have special problems," Bonnie said.

"Such as?"

"Well —" She thought quickly. "Like trying to catch up on my finances and keeping my weight down and having some kind of a social life. . . ." These things had seemed urgently important to Bonnie until she had to say them out loud to Sally; now they seemed somehow trivial.

"It sounds as if you may have what I've heard called a case of 'terminal uniqueness,' " Sally said.

"What do you mean?"

"Considering yourself a special case. Don't you think that among the members of any Alcoholics Anonymous group there are people who've had the same kinds of problems as yours?"

"I suppose so," Bonnie said grudgingly. "But I still don't seem to be getting much help out of AA anymore."

"Do you have a sponsor?"

"Not yet." Bonnie admitted to herself that the "yet" could give the impression that she was actively in the process of getting a sponsor, something she'd never seriously planned to do.

Sally sighed again. "Are you doing any of the other things that AA suggests? Working the Steps? Practicing HALT?"

"HALT?"

"I thought we covered HALT while you were in treatment. HALT — not getting too Hungry, Angry, Lonely, or Tired."

"Well. . . ." Bonnie now vaguely remembered it. She thought of skipping meals and dieting, getting angry at her ex-husband, missing meetings, working long days and moonlighting in the evenings. . . .

"I see," Sally said when Bonnie didn't go on. "Bonnie, you have some choices. You could come back to treatment, but you say that's not possible. You can go to meetings and work the AA program, but you say that AA doesn't help you. That leaves you with the alcoholic's other alternative — you can drink."

"Well, this is really great," Bonnie said angrily. "You tell me to call if I'm in trouble and now you tell me this! I'm sorry I bothered you!" And she slammed down the phone.

Bonnie was miserable, angry, and despairing. She had tried, hadn't she? People in AA just talked about the same old things, and now her former counselor had done the AA thing with her.

Bonnie spent most of the rest of Monday in bed, recuperating from the weekend's drinking bout. She thought several times of going to get more liquor, but instead of it being a way to cope, the idea simply brought home the fact that she was, indeed, an alcoholic, a real alcoholic. Besides, Sally's brusque third alternative still rankled Bonnie. She would at least not let Sally be right about that. Bonnie took a couple more Valium and made it through the day in a sort of dull blue funk.

Tuesday, she returned to work. She got the Valium prescription refilled, and the drug's effect made it easy enough to display symptoms that could be those of getting over a bout with a virus. She didn't like Valium's effect — it made her dull and listless. But at least she had no desire to drink and didn't feel as if she was going to jump out of her skin.

Bonnie dragged herself through the day and came home exhausted, falling into bed and a heavy sleep. Wednesday, she felt calmer; she took only one Valium, and her day was less exhausting. For some reason, she decided to go to the speaker meeting that the Step-by-Step group held on Wednesday nights. Perhaps Sally had been at least partly right — maybe she hadn't given AA enough of a chance.

Annette was the speaker; it was the first time Bonnie had heard her story. She was surprised to hear that Annette, whom Bonnie had thought of as the ultra-typical young wife and mother, had been unattached for a number of years as an adult alcoholic. Annette told of relationships with a number of men in which she'd compromised her personal standards as a result of trying to find fulfillment through love affairs.

Bonnie thought of the way she'd let Jerry, a man to whom she'd felt no more than a mild attraction, cause her to feel down on herself simply because he hadn't called her again. She thought of the way Paul's leaving had caused her to hate him and feel unattractive, washed-up. She still resented Paul, but seeing Annette, attractive, self-assured, and obviously happy in sobriety, gave Bonnie an inkling of hope.

To her surprise, Bonnie went to the women's meeting on Thursday night. She wasn't sure what made her change her mind about going. She had a profound distaste in general for women-only activities. *But,* she told herself, *the women's meeting is new; by going, I'd be lending some support for it and for women who might need such a meeting.*

Janey, the blonde woman who'd taken the new member, Laura, under her wing, chaired the meeting. The turnout was larger than Bonnie had imagined it would be. Besides herself, Janey, Annette, and Laura, there were over a dozen other women. Bonnie hadn't thought of the Step-by-Step group as having that many women in it. She held the popular misconception of Alcoholics Anonymous as a male-dominated fellowship, at least in numbers.

Janey called the meeting to order, and when the opening formalities were taken care of, she said, "I've gotten some kidding from some of the male members about this meeting. They seem to think that we sit in here and talk about *men*." There were some laughs from the group at this.

"Actually, though," Janey continued, "the topic I have in mind does have to do with men. It's a topic that probably wouldn't fly at a general meeting, but then that's one reason we gals decided to start this one. If no one has an immediate problem they need to talk about —" She looked around the group, and when no one spoke up, she said, "My topic has to do with some of the messages we all received from the time we were little girls, from the older females around us.

"As a little girl, I got the idea, from my mother and my aunts and my older sisters, that maybe the most important thing in a woman's life is her relationship with men. Not just men in general, but with one man, that Special Man." She paused and sipped her coffee.

"Now, my mom and aunts and sisters didn't give me these messages in so many words. I doubt they were even consciously aware, most of the time, that they were giving me messages at all. But by the time I was an adolescent, I had the idea firmly in my mind that a woman defined herself in terms of what kind of guy she was, or was going to be, attached to. A couple of my aunts weren't married; they were known to the rest of the family as the 'old maids,' meaning they didn't have men. Of course, no one said that to their faces, but there was a kind of ridicule in the term."

Bonnie looked around. There were heads nodding in agreement to Janey's words. She remembered her own mother assuming the label of the Divorced Woman after her parents broke up.

"As I grew older," Janey said, "the thing about having a guy became more and more important to me too. And as my alcoholism progressed, so did my need for the security of 'having a man.' My alcoholism distorted everything in my life and my need for the security of a relationship was no exception.

"I got into some pretty sick relationships because of this fear of being alone. I'd be in a bad relationship with a guy, finally get free of it, and then I'd jump right into another one in a sort of panic at the fear of 'being an old maid' like my two unmarried aunts.

"My point in bringing this up as an AA topic is that when I got sober, I was an unattached female and that bothered me a lot. I was two years sober before I met the guy I'm married to today. I was lucky enough to find a woman as sponsor when I was new to AA who set me straight on this business of 'needing a man.' " She smiled.

"My first sponsor," she continued, "was married to a practicing alcoholic when she got sober. She stayed in that marriage quite awhile, even though his drinking got steadily worse and he refused to admit to a drinking problem. Even though she'd become the primary breadwinner after getting sober and did all the head-of-the-family stuff with the children, she was still hung up on the notion of 'needing a man' to be a complete person.

"She said that it suddenly just came to her one day — more or less hit her in the face — that for all practical purposes she didn't have a husband anyway. By this time he was so far gone in his alcoholism that he wasn't able to be anything to her or the rest of the family. She said it was a great relief to discover that she didn't have to depend on someone else for how she felt about herself."

She stopped and smiled again. "I've gone on long enough. I'd like to hear from some of you. Has anyone here ever experienced the kind of thing I'm talking about?"

Doris, a woman about Bonnie's age, raised her hand. Doris wore no makeup, and her clothes were plain to the point of being frumpy.

"They say that alcoholics don't have relationships — they take hostages," Doris said. There were some laughs at this. Bonnie was surprised — she hadn't heard Doris say more than a half dozen words, it seemed, in the time she had been coming to AA meetings.

"I set myself up as a hostage for a long time with alcoholic men," Doris went on. "Alcoholic women seem to have a greater risk in relationships than alcoholic men do. We're chemically dependent ourselves, but we are often also codependents. I think it has to do with the thing you mentioned, Janey, the fact that we've been taught to think of ourselves in terms of a relationship with a man.

"I think I had more than just an addiction to alcohol — I was an excitement junkie. I lived with a drug dealer for a while during my drinking years. I was hooked on not only booze but my own adrenaline from the constant fear and anxiety of living that kind of life."

Bonnie was amazed — Doris was one of the last women in the group she would have picked to have been involved with a drug dealer.

"After I got sober," Doris said, "I had to learn to be a person in my own right, not just somebody's wife or girlfriend. And I had to learn that life doesn't have to be a series of crises in order to be interesting."

Janey looked around the room when Doris had finished. "Fran?" she said to a slender, fortyish woman with short dark hair, a slightly older version of Annette.

"I was a kind of codependent," Fran said, "the way Doris mentioned. My husband wasn't an alcoholic, but he was addicted to work. Hank was the kind of man who spent fourteen hours a day in his business. It paid off well in material terms; we had a lovely house and a lot of nice things. But there were a lot of times when I wished for less money and more of his time.

"I used to yell at him when I was drinking, accusing him of neglecting me. Of course, my yelling just made him want to stay away from me even more." Fran was another quiet one; Bonnie tried to imagine her yelling. Alcohol certainly caused personality changes!

Fran said, "After I got into AA, I began to realize that I couldn't depend on other people, their attention to me or lack of it, to feel good about myself. Hank and I are still married, and since I've been sober for a while and become more of a partner and easier to get along with, he doesn't work quite as hard as he used to. But I still have to keep in mind that I can't let other people, including my husband, determine how I feel about *me*."

Bonnie felt some identity with Fran: Paul had been very conscientious about his work. Although his obvious drive to be successful was one of the things that had attracted her to him in the first place, it got to the point of causing her to feel left out at times. She suddenly realized that she'd shown a certain amount of perversity in becoming angry at Paul for the same thing she'd admired in him in the beginning.

"Annette?" Janey said.

"I can identify with your sponsor," Annette said to Janey. "I'm lucky that the guy I'm married to now isn't alcoholic, but I had some boyfriends that were doozies!"

Annette looked around at the rest of the group. "Some of you heard me tell my story last night," she said. "Since it was an open meeting I toned it down a bit. But when I was drinking, I was what some people would probably call a not-very-nice girl. I used to pick the best-looking guys with the prettiest girlfriends and bet myself that I could take them away from their women. And a lot of times I did; I'm not bragging and not proud of the way I was, but to me being able to turn men's heads meant power, with a capital P.

"I ended up doing a lot of things that didn't make me feel very good about myself. That's one of the problems alcoholics seem to have — we're cursed with high moral standards and the inclination to break those standards because of our disease, our drinking."

She shook her head with a wry smile. "You should have seen me when I first came into AA. I wore clothes that were up to here and down to there, and loads of makeup. I did that until my first sponsor took me aside and gave me a little picture of myself from her perspective. She was nice enough not to say that I looked trashy, but she made her point. I had to stop trying to get one over on the guys and start changing myself. In the process, I found that the little gal who'd acted so self-confident, actually had very little real self-esteem; my act was all a big cover-up for some pretty strong inferiority feelings."

The discussion was passed along. Bonnie listened to the others and was further amazed by how different people were before and after getting into Alcoholics Anonymous.

Close to the end of the meeting, when she was one of the few who still hadn't spoken, Bonnie was called on.

"I'm Bonnie and I'm an alcoholic," she said, echoing the standard AA introduction. The group's, "Hi, Bonnie," felt better than she'd imagined it would.

"I. . . ." She paused and took a breath. "I've been drinking again. I don't have anything to add, but I'm glad I'm here." The words came out in a rush. She hadn't planned on admitting to her relapse, but she felt a ton lighter for having done so.

"We're glad you're here too, Bonnie," Janey said, and Bonnie felt her eyes moistening a little.

When Janey offered chips, Bonnie picked up her second white one, to the applause of the other women. After the closing, Annette came up and gave Bonnie a hug.

"Annette," Bonnie said, not being able to stop herself from looking around to see if anyone was listening, "would you consider being my sponsor?" It was the second surprise, after owning up to her relapse, that she had given herself in the space of a quarter of an hour.

"Sure," Annette said without hesitation. She got a pen and a small pad from her purse and wrote her phone number. "I'd like you to call me every day for a while," Annette said, tearing the sheet off the pad and handing it to Bonnie. Her tone suggested she expected Bonnie to do it. Bonnie surprised herself a third time by nodding meekly.

Bonnie was having second thoughts about asking Annette to be her sponsor by the next evening. But the urge to drink, or at least thoughts about drinking, had come to her when she had left the office a short while earlier. She knew she had to at least make an effort this time.

"Sure, hold on a second," said the male voice that answered when she had rung Annette's number. She could hear the squeals and laughter of young children in the background.

"Did I catch you at a bad time?" she asked when Annette came on the line.

"No, no," Annette laughed, "It's just the usual craziness around here."

"I could call later. . . ."

"No, this is fine — " Annette paused and said something in an admonishing tone to one of the children. "I'll tell you what, though, why don't we meet for coffee somewhere, where it's quieter and I won't be distracted by my *very* immediate family?"

"Well. . . .fine, if you're sure it's no bother. . . ."

"No bother. Papa has agreed to babysit and give Mama a little break this evening. Taking it with another AA member is ideal." They agreed to meet at a small restaurant that was reasonably near to both of them.

Annette drove up to the restaurant parking lot just after Bonnie. They went inside. Finding a private table was no problem since it was late for dinner and early for people coming in after a show.

"So, how's it going?" Annette asked after the waitress brought their coffee.

"I've been better," Bonnie confessed. "I had a strong inclination toward drinking after work."

Annette looked at her watch. "You must have worked late."

"I seem to do that a lot these days."

"I know what you mean about the after-work craving," Annette said. "I was working on a regular job when I got sober, and those days got awfully long without the promise of a drink after hours. Now, staying home and taking care of the kids, I seem to work even harder, but the emotional strain is a lot less." She grinned. "But who am I kidding? If I was still drinking, keeping two preschoolers would be an excellent excuse to have a few!"

"I used to think I was good at handling stress," Bonnie said. "I guess maybe I'm not. I just used alcohol to keep the stress in check."

"I know," Annette said. "I did the same thing. And it seemed to work for a while. But eventually the drinking began to create its own extra stress in my life."

Bonnie nodded, absently swirling the coffee in her cup. "I just don't seem to be getting anywhere in my life."

"Sometimes we reach plateaus," Annette said.

"I'm afraid I've been falling back," Bonnie replied.

"Well, we do what we have to do," Annette said. "Maybe you *needed* to drink some more."

Bonnie didn't much like the almost casual way Annette said it. It was a great deal like what Sally had said, but it wasn't what Bonnie had expected from an AA sponsor.

"You mean I needed to have a slip?" she asked.

"Some AA members think that 'slip' isn't a very good term," Annette said. " 'Slip' sounds like an accident. Very few alcoholics drink by accident."

Bonnie thought about this. She had to admit that her fall back into drinking hadn't exactly been an accident, but then it hadn't been something she'd premeditated, either.

"I didn't plan to drink," she said to Annette. "You make it sound as if my drinking again was almost — inevitable."

"Bonnie, alcoholics — this alcoholic, anyway — can only stand to hurt for so long. When we can't stand the pain anymore, we do something about it. My drinking finally caused me so much pain that I had to get help to stop.

"Alcoholics who aren't drinking aren't so different, you know. If we hurt long enough, we'll do something about the pain. That something may be growing in the AA program, or it may be drinking again. You've heard people say in AA, 'We're either going away from a drink or heading toward one.' That's what that saying means to me."

"I just can't seem to find what I need in life since I've been trying to stay sober," Bonnie said stubbornly.

"You mean getting back all the nice things, and the social life, and finding Mr. Right?"

"So what's wrong with that?" Bonnie asked. "I'm not desperate for a man, but I would like to have a better car and a nicer place to live; there's nothing wrong with those things, is there?"

"There's nothing wrong with wanting the nicer car and place to live, and even Mr. Right, for that matter, Bonnie. The trouble comes when we get our priorities screwed up."

"Well, we do have to set priorities, don't we? I mean, who else is going to do that for us?" Bonnie asked.

Annette leaned forward over the table. "You asked me to be your sponsor, right?"

"Well...yes."

"Okay. Being a sponsor sometimes involves telling people things they don't want to hear. Are you willing to accept that?"

"Yes," Bonnie said, but her stomach felt uneasy.

"Let me tell you some things I'm seeing you do," Annette said. "One — I see you working a lot; you worked late this evening, right? Two — I see you've lost a good deal of weight since you've been coming to meetings. Three — it doesn't take a degree in psychology to see that you've got a lot of anger inside; it shows on your face. Four — I expect you've isolated yourself a lot; you'd practically stopped coming to meetings before you started drinking again. Have you heard of HALT?"

"Yes, I just had a lecture about HALT from my former counselor at the treatment center."

"Well," Annette said, spreading her hands, "there you are. Playing the catch-up game, trying to get back everything our drinking has cost us in a short time, is a sure way to get too tired. And not eating: women, especially, who are alcoholic are also prone to eating disorders, and we all want to lose that empty-calorie flab we've gotten from alcohol. We can overdo dieting, especially if we're working too hard to eat regular meals. Low blood sugar is a good way to set ourselves up for physically craving alcohol. And anger: I carried a lot of anger into Alcoholics Anonymous — anger at former husbands and boyfriends, my family, society — you name it."

"Do I really come across as an angry person?" Bonnie asked.

"Anger is the common cold of alcoholism," Annette said. "I only need to know a person's alcoholic to know there's a lot of anger inside."

The waitress came by and refilled their cups. When the waitress had gone, Bonnie said, "I guess that makes some sense. I've been working pretty hard lately. And I've skipped meals and been alone in the evenings. And I've been pretty bitter about my ex-husband — not that I don't think he deserves some blame."

"Justified resentments," Annette said. "The most dangerous kind. Silly resentments aren't hard to let go of. We're not stupid people; we know the difference. Resentments over the *real* injustices people have done us are hard to get rid of, but they'll get us drunk if we don't."

"Well, how *do* you get rid of resentment at things people really have done to you?" Bonnie asked. "I mean, you just can't smile and say, 'That's all right,' can you?"

"No. Pretending that things are different from what they really were won't get us anywhere. But we have to accept, in our hearts, that what's done is done; no one, no matter who they are, can simply go back and undo things. That's what acceptance means. We have to accept things, get on with our lives, and not let the past keep the power to ruin our present lives."

"Easier said than done."

"Ain't it?" Annette grinned. "What did you think about the meeting last night? How did you like the topic?"

"It was a good topic," Bonnie said automatically.

"Now tell me what you *really* thought of it," Annette said.

"Well. . . . I guess I did get some messages about men from my mother when I was a child," Bonnie said. "But I like to think I'm pretty independent today when it comes to men."

Annette studied her thoughtfully before responding.

"In some ways, I agree," she said. "I don't see you as the kind of woman who needs a man to get the car fixed, or make financial decisions, or support you. But in other ways —" She shook her head slightly.

"What does that mean?" Bonnie demanded. "I mean, I'm unattached, I don't have a husband like a lot of the other women in AA — like you — but that doesn't mean —"

"I know, I know," Annette interrupted her. "That's not what I'm talking about, just the fact that you're unattached."

"What, then?"

"Can I tell you what I see when I look at Bonnie?" Annette asked. She set her cup down carefully.

Bonnie nodded, but she didn't like this line of discussion very well.

"I see," Annette said, "a very attractive, intelligent woman who has a great need for approval. I understand that, God knows; most alcoholics are approval junkies, and I'm no exception.

"But I see you coming to AA meetings, which are about the most informal gatherings in the world, all gussied up like a page out of a fashion magazine. I see you spending a lot more time talking to men than to women. I know, the guys are more than willing to pay attention to a good-looking woman, but I don't see you making much of an effort to make friends with other women in the group. I see some seductive behavior —" She held up her hand at the expression on Bonnie's face at the word *seductive*. "And I know it's innocent flirting, but it's still flirting, which I know *you* know, if you look at it honestly."

"Just a minute," Bonnie said. "Are you making me out to be some kind of...cheap hussy?" She hadn't heard the word hussy in years, let alone used it.

"Take it easy," Annette said. "I'm not calling you anything. I'm not talking about cheap, obvious behavior; that used to be more *my* style, but you're a pretty sophisticated woman. And I'm certainly not making any moral judgment about anybody's behavior. I'd like you to take a look at *why* you might come across the way I've just described. To dress up sometimes just for the feeling of looking good, or even sexy, is fine; even old married women with kids, like me, do that sometimes. And I don't mind a little flirting, however terrible that may sound coming from a wife and mother. But I learned, the hard way, that feeling good about myself has to come from within, not from the way other people react to me — especially when I've manipulated their reactions."

"Well, that was quite a speech," Bonnie said sarcastically. "Maybe I should get my clothes from the Salvation Army thrift shop, and not wear makeup or shave my legs, or ever talk to men at AA meetings."

Annette leaned back and sighed. "Okay, you're mad at me. That's all right; it won't be the first time I've made somebody mad. But after you're over being angry, think about what I've said."

Bonnie set her cup down in the saucer harder than was necessary. "I need to get home," she said. She got money out of her purse for the coffee, slapped it down on the table, rose and left without saying good-bye.

Driving away, she was furious. How did Annette dare to talk to her that way? Her anger was all the stronger for being mixed with some embarrassment. If Annette saw her that way, maybe some of the other AA members did also. Well, to hell with Annette; to hell with all those self-righteous sober drunks!

She had worked her anger into full-fledged righteous indignation by the time she was nearing the liquor store. *To hell with sobriety, too,* she thought as she wheeled into the parking lot.

She came to at three in the morning on the sofa. She hadn't made it to bed, hadn't even taken off her clothes. Her head ached hellishly and her mouth had the taste of a shoe sole. The small lamp still burning on the end table seemed bright enough to furnish an interrogation room.

She dimly remembered having tried to talk to someone on the phone. *Oh God, had she tried to call Jerry in a drunken stupor?* She remembered being sorry for herself because he hadn't called her.

She made it into the kitchen. There was an empty gin bottle beside a half-bottle of vermouth. She drank some water and felt her stomach begin turning over. She barely made it to the bathroom on time.

Her throat and nose burned after she'd finally stopped throwing up and what had seemed an eternity of dry heaves. She sat on the floor and leaned against the toilet, too weak to stand. *Praying to the porcelain God,* she thought, remembering the AA joke about alcoholics and toilets. It wasn't funny now. Nothing would ever be funny again. AA *had* ruined her drinking, just the way they had said it would.

She managed to get up after a bit and washed her face. She felt less faint if not less depressed. She went into the bedroom and picked up the phone.

It rang several times. Bonnie chewed her lip as she waited. Finally, a sleepy voice said, irritably, "I thought I told you to call me when you weren't drunk!"

"Annette," Bonnie said, and then began crying. So Annette had been the person she half-remembered trying to talk to. She was embarrassed, but it was a tremendous relief to at least not have called Jerry.

Despite the irritation in her voice, Annette didn't hang up. Finally, Bonnie managed to get herself under some control.

"Oh, *damn,* I did it again!" she said.

"I figured that out," Annette said, with more sarcasm than humor.

"But — you were so *mean* to me!" Bonnie said.

"I didn't hold you and force booze down your throat afterward, did I?"

"No, but —"

"Look, Bonnie, I don't know what kind of shape you're in or if you can grasp this. But when I was drinking, there were people who almost killed me with kindness. It wasn't until I'd run out of people being nice to me and I'd begun to get some honesty that I had a chance to get better. And even then I had to go a little further in my drinking. Now, hear this: I am *not* responsible for your drinking. I won't go on that guilt trip, understand?"

"Yes," Bonnie said, leaning her head on the pillow as she held the phone to her ear. "I feel so rotten."

"Of course you do. If drinking didn't make alcoholics feel rotten, there'd be no reason to quit, would there?"

"But my life — it's just going down the toilet!"

"Only if you choose to let it."

"What can I do?"

"Let's Keep It Simple," Annette said. "Let's do it by the numbers. One — don't drink anymore. Two — go to bed. Three — don't drink. Four — come to the meeting tomorrow. Make that tonight; it's already tomorrow. Five — don't drink. And six — don't wait until *after* you've had the drink to call me next time."

"You mean, you'll still be my sponsor?"

"You aren't going to get rid of me that easily," Annette said, and hung up the phone.

The meeting had already started when Bonnie slipped in and took a seat toward the rear. She was wearing the old jeans she'd been wearing around the apartment all afternoon, an old blouse, and a sweatshirt. She'd put on no makeup. She guessed that she looked as bad as she felt.

The real estate brokerage office closed at noon on Saturdays, and she'd managed to make it in for the half-day. Afterward, she'd read some AA literature, washed a few clothes, watched part of an old movie on TV. It had been a strange kind of day, a feeling of half-floating through time. She had started to take more Valium to quiet her withdrawal nerves, but the realization that she would be using a drug to fight the effects of another drug had come to her, and she had flushed the remaining Valium down the toilet. She sensed some kind of change in herself, its nature unknown and therefore disturbing. But there was also a glimmer of hope.

She didn't pay close attention to the discussion that night, but just sat there in the atmosphere of brewing coffee and cigarette smoke. There was now more than tobacco and coffee in the air for Bonnie; it seemed thick with comfort and hope, things that she realized had been in short supply for her for quite some time.

When the chips were offered, she went up and picked up her third white one. She felt no embarrassment or elation at the applause, just a sense of relief.

After the closing, she went directly to Annette, greeting, but not stopping to talk to, several male members.

"I did the first five things," she said to Annette.

"Good," Annette said. To Bonnie's surprise, Annette gave her a hug. "I see you came as you were," Annette said with a grin, looking at Bonnie's clothes.

"I look and feel like a slob, but I didn't get 'all gussied up,'" Bonnie said, returning Annette's smile with a small one of her own.

"There are things that it's all right to do," Annette said, "as long as we're sure we're doing them for the right reasons."

"I'm beginning to believe you're right. Annette...thanks, for still being my sponsor."

Annette gave her another hug. "Maybe you won't have to apply Number Six," she said. "You don't ever *have* to drink again, you know."

Bonnie nodded. "Having" to drink had taken on new meaning. She hoped Annette was right, that the program's promise applied to her too. She knew that she had a lot of work to do to make it come true, but it was a promise she hadn't allowed herself before.

Finding A Sponsor

"...And I found a really tough sponsor, who gave me just the kind of help I needed...."

It was a speaker meeting of the Step-by-Step group of Alcoholics Anonymous. Brad, a small, white-haired man in his sixties, was telling his story.

Brad had already told of his drinking years, what AA members call the "drunkalogue." He was now telling of his life since joining AA.

Buddy, sitting close to the front beside big Joe the biker, shifted uncomfortably on the hard folding chair. It wasn't the chair that caused his discomfort; he had become well-accustomed to the chairs and the smoky atmosphere and smell of coffee in the few months he had been a member of this AA group.

His discomfort came from a growing sense of uneasiness and guilt, for Buddy had not yet found a sponsor.

He'd learned early that having a sponsor wasn't a prerequisite for joining AA. The Third Tradition of the Twelve Traditions of Alcoholics Anonymous stated that the only requirement for membership was a desire to stop drinking.

A *sponsor* is someone to whom you could talk about things that you felt were too confidential or specific to bring up in a general discussion meeting. While having a sponsor wasn't a strict requirement, it was strongly recommended.

Buddy, with the tanned skin and tough hands of the construction carpenter, was one of the youngest members in the Step-by-Step group. Most members were in their thirties and older.

It seemed to Buddy that his sobriety was turning into a series of hurdles to be overcome. First, of course, there had been admitting and accepting that he was truly powerless over alcohol, and that his life had become unmanageable — AA's First Step.

Then there had been the God business and his difficulty in overcoming the effects of a rigidly religious upbringing to find his own personal understanding of a Higher Power.

Now there was the sponsorship thing. Buddy knew, on a gut level, that he needed to give his best effort to staying sober. But the process of choosing and acquiring an AA sponsor seemed more and more difficult the longer he put it off.

Another man, sitting near the rear in the same meeting, was also concerned with the sponsorship issue. But just now he had a more immediate concern. Ken, a tall, thin man with red hair that was turning grey, had the permanently blackened fingernails of the professional mechanic. He was back tonight to begin again and was now dreading the point at the end of the meeting when the chairperson asked if anyone wanted to start the AA way of life — or needed to start over.

Relapses were referred to variously as "slips," "research," and "trips out into the weeds," among other things and were treated as an unfortunate fact of life. But that didn't make Ken's plight seem any less embarrassing or depressing.

Ken wondered if having a sponsor might have prevented his relapse. He could have called a sponsor before going to see the drunk at the motel. He'd often heard in AA meetings that *Twelfth Step calls* — going to talk to practicing alcoholics about the AA program usually at their or a family member's or friend's request — should never be done alone. A sponsor would have been the natural person to ask to accompany him.

Unfortunately, Ken had forgotten this piece of advice when the wife of an alcoholic acquaintance had called him to say that her husband was holed up in a cheap motel on the edge of town, on a drunk. The man, who to Ken's knowledge had never passed through an AA meeting door, had indicated he'd be willing to talk to Ken, who was six months sober at the time. Ken had gone to the motel to talk to him, alone.

Sick and remorseful, the man had gone home to his wife after Ken talked with him. Ken, however, faced with an abandoned half-case of liquor and a motel room paid up until the end of the week, had not left. He took over the booze and the room to begin what turned into a two-week binge.

"...my sponsor told me that I'd gotten into trouble trying to think for myself," Brad was saying from the speaker's lectern. "He said, 'Brad, whenever you catch yourself starting to think seriously about *anything,* you'd better call me!'"

Buddy joined in the laughter with everybody else, but Brad's description of his first sponsor made the man seem a rather overbearing sort. A lot of speakers described their sponsors that way. Buddy was a quiet young man, but he didn't take to being browbeaten. Was that what sponsors were supposed to do?

Ken, too, didn't much like the sound of Brad's sponsor. Ken had left his job in the service department of a large car dealership to open his own shop. One of the big reasons for making the move had been his not liking to take orders.

The group gave Brad a nice round of applause when he finished. John, the chairperson tonight, thanked Brad and passed around the baskets for voluntary contributions. John was even thinner than Ken, with sunken cheeks and an unhealthy pallor suggesting that he had not been as fortunate as the many alcoholics who regain their physical health in recovery.

After a couple of announcements, the moment came that Ken had been dreading — when John picked up the chip box.

"The Step-by-Step group has the chip system," John explained. He held up a round piece of plastic the size of a poker chip with the stylized AA emblem. "We have a white chip for any newcomers who'd like to try the AA way of life, or for anyone who's been out doing some research and wants to come back." He looked around the room, which was well-filled for this speaker meeting. "Anyone for a white chip?"

Ken felt mashed down in his chair as if by a huge weight. He simply could not make himself get up.

John laid down the white chip, picked up a red one, similar to the white except for color. "Anyone have three months continuous sobriety?" No takers. He held up a yellow chip. "Six months?" He offered the green for nine months, the blue chip for a year or any multiple of years. This seemed to be a chipless night. He was about to put away the chips, but he held up the white once more. "Any second thoughts on the white chip?"

Ken found himself on his feet, moving numbly toward the front. The applause began. John rose, shook Ken's hand as he gave him the white chip. "Don't let it bother you," he said, softly enough so that only Ken could hear. "I collected enough white chips in the beginning to tile the bathroom!"

Ken grinned weakly at John's joke and made his way back to his seat amid the sustained applause.

As the crowd began to break up after the closing, Buddy shook Ken's hand, as did most of the other members. Having a relapsing member come back was a genuinely joyous event in AA. Buddy felt a humble gratitude that it hadn't been him having to pick up another white chip. But as he left, he was still uneasy about the idea of having to ask someone to be his sponsor and of what having a sponsor might mean.

Ken went back to the two-room apartment he now called home, after his slip and two-week binge. His wife had firmly asked him to leave *their* home when he had come off the drunk that had ensued from his ill-advised solo Twelfth Step call.

He couldn't truly blame Mary. Or rather his rational, practical mind couldn't. Nevertheless, he was still angry and hurt at her rejection.

She had been quietly firm about it — no screaming or shouting or name calling, just her mouth set in a tight line, her grey eyes tired and dull as she told him she wanted a separation.

It was hard to think of Mary, his wife of over fifteen years
— the grey in her auburn hair matching his own — as his estranged wife. He'd made many promises typical of an alcoholic
during his drinking years, promises that his alcoholism hadn't
allowed him to keep. Mary had had trouble believing in Ken's
new self when he finally got into Alcoholics Anonymous.

Yet she'd seemed to relax a little in the past six months, with
him not drinking and going to AA meetings conscientiously.
The slip had cruelly jerked her back to the old days and fulfilled
her worst fears. *It was ironic*, Ken thought now, *that living with a
sober alcoholic for those few months had given her the strength to
do what fifteen years of his drinking hadn't — ask for a separation.*

His new bachelor lodgings were in a big, old, two-story house
that had once been a rather grand single-family home. Now,
like many other such houses in the slowly decaying neighborhood, it had been cut up into apartments.

To reach his two rented rooms, he had to enter at the rear
of the house and climb a creaky stairway. The old-fashioned,
paneled interior doors acted as soundboards for the slightest
noise in the house. His bathroom was an added-on cubicle in
the corner of the little kitchen. The kitchen appliances looked
to have been secondhand when the landlord bought them. He
had no telephone. The old black-and-white portable TV with
a rabbit-ears antenna pulled in only two stations, neither of
them very well.

Ken had never thought of himself as depressed, but what he
was feeling now would do until a real depression came along.

He still had his work; being self-employed meant he at least
hadn't been fired. But his business had suffered in the two
weeks of his relapse. He felt obligated to continue to help Mary
with the support of the house, even though they had no written
separation agreement as yet. There was the overhead on the
shop, including the wages for Bill, the mechanic he'd hired to
help out when the first two months of his sobriety had seen
an encouraging increase in business. He had the rent on this
dumpy little place in which he was now living. He'd probably

be able to keep his financial head above water for the next few months, but that was about all.

He stared around at the walls of the apartment — to be forty-eight years old and reduced to these slim prospects was enough to sour a man's outlook on life.

Buddy, too, was not pleased with his current situation. He was still staying at his mother and stepfather's house, still having to catch rides to work and to meetings as best he could. He wouldn't have his driver's license returned for another three months, and then there would be the matter of how to afford a car. His credit had gone down the tubes when he had let his car be repossessed after losing his license to a DWI.

The wages of sin, Buddy thought with sour humor. He was twenty-six, single, reasonably good-looking, but for all the good these things were doing him he might as well have been living in the wilderness or a monastery.

Buddy had been working on the same project for several months, the construction of a large condominium complex. On a job of this length, the crews of the primary builder and the various subcontractors got to know each other. Many struck up friendships, especially the younger, single men. Drinking tended to play a big part in the social life of most young construction workers, at least in Buddy's experience. In his drinking days, Buddy had done more than his share of partying with the guys from the job. Now he knew he had to avoid drinking situations, especially the lusty, two-fisted kind of drinking sessions his co-workers indulged in.

And then there was the matter of dating. Like a lot of alcoholics, Buddy's experiences with the opposite sex had mostly included drinking. And now, in addition to not being able to drink, Buddy had been warned by many AA members about serious involvement with the opposite sex during his first year of sobriety. A *year!* Between the dangers of drinking situations and cautions about involvement with females, Buddy was feeling like the all-time has-been.

Ken at least had little idle time during the day. The shop, having almost gone under in his days before Alcoholics Anonymous, couldn't stand another long-term slack period. His binge had cost a few customers, whose vehicles Bill hadn't been able to get out on time working single-handed. There was plenty of backed-up work now to keep Ken busy well into his evenings.

He was careful to make time for AA meetings after having to pick up his second white chip. He knew well enough that missing meetings would be courting trouble. But there was still the sponsorship question. Ken knew that the frustration and resentment and general dissatisfaction he was feeling were things that, in theory at least, he could talk over with a sponsor.

Yet, every time he thought of confiding his personal problems to someone, even another AA member, Ken couldn't help remembering that his father used to say, "Kill your own snakes, Son." It had been one of his father's favorite sayings, and his father would turn over in his grave if he knew Ken was telling deeply personal things to anyone who wasn't family. For that matter, there hadn't been much of that kind of talk even between Ken's father and himself.

And there was his independence to consider, something that Ken felt very jealous of. He'd left the dealership because he wanted to be independent of a boss telling him what to do, which was the way some AA's seemed to think a sponsor was supposed to act. A small part of Ken's mind admitted, reluctantly, that another factor in his opening his own shop had been the fact that doing so let him drink when he wanted, with no boss to call him on the carpet for it.

The following evening there was a discussion meeting. It was chaired by Nick, a husky, dark-haired man in his late thirties who hadn't been in AA a great deal longer than either Buddy or Ken.

Nick opened the meeting at eight, led the group in the Serenity Prayer, called on a couple of people to read the Traditions and "How It Works" from Chapter Five of the Big Book. Then he opened the floor for suggestions on a topic of discussion.

This was what AA members often laughingly called the "moment of silence"; it wasn't unusual for no one to speak up at this point.

"Well," Nick said, "I've been told that my duties as chairperson involve opening the meeting, closing the meeting, and cleaning the coffeepots." Another standard AA joke. "I was also told that it was my responsibility to suggest a topic, if nobody else had one. Since no one did, I do have a topic in mind — sponsorship."

To Buddy and Ken, this was one of those coincidences that seem to happen surprisingly often in AA. The discussion topic was particularly relevant to each of them.

"When I first joined AA," Nick was saying, "I went to meetings in another town. I didn't want anyone here in *my* town to get the wrong idea about me, going to AA meetings." There was laughter from the group. "I had a sort-of sponsor at the first meetings I went to, a guy who more or less took me under his wing. But when I got over being afraid of someone seeing me going to AA and started attending meetings here in the Step-by-Step group, I knew I needed to get a regular, permanent sponsor.

"My sponsor's been a lot of help to me. If it's all right with everyone, let's talk about sponsors and sponsorship. I'll call on someone to start, and when that person's through, he or she can call on someone else, and so on. Tom — can you tell us something about your experience with sponsors?"

Tom, a tall, big-boned man in his sixties, was dressed as usual in khaki work clothes. He had the big knobby hands of a man who has done a lot of manual labor in his life. Although he was now a successful building contractor, he still worked alongside his men a good deal of the time.

"I was lucky," Tom said, after identifying himself and getting a "Hi, Tom" from the group. "I had Buck, one of the founders of this group, as my first sponsor.

"I was a pretty sick man by the time I got to Alcoholics Anonymous. That was going on thirty years ago. I guess today, somebody as sick as I was would be sent to treatment, but there weren't many places to send a drunk in those days, nor any insurance to pay for it.

"Buck kind of nursed me along, helped me get through the shakes and the alcoholic fog of my first few days. I didn't realize it at the time, but I was using him as a sponsor from the beginning. I did my first Fifth Step with Buck and got rid of the garbage I'd collected in my Fourth Step."

Tom paused, grinning in recollection. "Buck kept me from trying to sober up the whole world. I wanted to do that at first, get all the drunks I knew into AA, whether they wanted to be there or not. Buck used to say, 'Tommy' — he always called me that — 'Tommy, AA is for people who want it, not for people who just happen to need it.' He told me that Twelfth Stepping can be mighty thirsty work. He used to take me on Twelfth Step calls with him. He told me never to go on one by myself, and to always talk to a sponsor if I was thinking about talking to a drinking alcoholic."

Ken could certainly vouch for that last bit of advice, after the fiasco at the motel.

Tom called on Richard, a handsome, well-dressed man in his fifties with a neat, short beard and glasses. Richard looked like what he was, a professor at the local college.

"I made the mistake in the beginning of getting a sponsor too much like myself," Richard said. "My first sponsor was another teacher, a man who'd been in the AA program only about a year at the time. Now there are good sponsors who have only a year or so, but most advice I've heard in AA recommends at least a couple of years of quality sobriety in a sponsor.

"Anyway, this man and myself would sit and solve most of the problems of the world, and have opinions on all of them.

I have a tendency to over-intellectualize at times, and I'm afraid he did also. We'd analyze the AA program and find all the ways in which we were different from the 'average' AA member.

"I'm sorry to say that my first sponsor didn't stay sober. I almost came unglued when he started drinking again. Fortunately, I didn't imitate him! People in AA told me, 'Don't ever put anyone on a pedestal, even a sponsor.'

"I needed a sponsor, and I'd begun to realize that maybe I needed someone not so much like me, someone who'd cut through my intellectualization when I needed it.

"As it turned out, the second guy I asked to be my sponsor hadn't finished the eighth grade. Dan was a retired Marine sergeant. He didn't have the formal education I had, but he had a great AA program and a Ph.D. from the School of Hard Knocks.

"I'd be going on to Dan about some high-sounding notion or another, and he'd get this sly little grin on his face. He'd let me wind down, and then he'd just say, 'That's real nice, Richard,' and I'd know I was doing another snow job on myself. Dan and I were as different as night and day in a lot of ways, but I gained a tremendous amount of knowledge about living sober from that man."

Richard passed it along to big Joe the biker.

"I was afraid of somebody saying no if I asked them to be my sponsor," Joe said. To hear Joe admit to being afraid of anything seemed rather odd, especially something as mundane as simple rejection. Joe was well over six feet tall and seemed half that wide. He wore a leather cycle jacket and boots and his jeans were held up by a belt made from chromed motorcycle chain. He had a heavy black beard as thick as his hair, which was caught in a short ponytail at the back of his neck.

"I always operated on the principle that if I kept people away from me, they'd never have a chance to reject me," Joe said. "Being big helped. So did being mean, which I'm afraid to say I learned pretty early. I went around being bad and not needing anybody — or so I wanted you to believe — and it ended up almost killing me.

"When I got into AA, I didn't know how to go about asking anybody for anything. I'd always figured that what I couldn't just grab, I didn't need.

"And now, I was supposed to go to somebody in AA and ask them to be my sponsor?" He snorted. "No way! Ask them to be in a position to tell me what to do, to point out my mistakes and shortcomings? I figured it would be a cold day in hell before I'd do *that*.

"It took this rough ol' boy a long while to get up enough courage to ask a guy to be my sponsor. And you know what happened? He said no!

"I thought, all this humiliation, and the guy turns me down! I copped a bad attitude for a while; I almost went out and got drunk at the guy. That would've fixed him, by God!" Everyone laughed.

"Anyway," Joe said, "I didn't get drunk and I asked another guy, and he agreed to be my sponsor.

"Ray had done time for murder. He wasn't some kind of monster, he was just an alcoholic who'd gotten mixed up in a bad situation and ended up killing somebody. The same thing could've happened to me in my drinking days.

"I hear a lot of people talk about having these real rough sponsors. Ray wasn't like that. He was actually a gentle kind of man in a lot of ways. He was soft-spoken and quiet. But he could look me in the eye and tell me what I needed to hear if the occasion demanded it. I don't think a sponsor who tried to throw his weight around would've worked very well with me; I had operated that way myself for a long time and I'd have probably just played the macho game with a sponsor who tried to be super-tough."

Joe called on Bonnie, a woman in her early thirties who sold real estate. Bonnie seemed a bit surprised to find the discussion passed to her.

"I've had several slips back into drinking," Bonnie said. "I didn't have a sponsor then, and I think that's one reason why I didn't stay sober. I have a sponsor now, I'm glad to say."

She paused, collecting her thoughts. "I didn't relate very well to other women," she said. "AA tells us that men should have male sponsors, women should have other women to sponsor them. I didn't like that very well.

"I'd always gotten along better with men than with other women — or so I told myself, despite the fact that I'd had a failed marriage and some pretty disastrous relationships. I realize now that I preferred the company of men to women because I thought I could manipulate men better."

She smiled ruefully. It was easy to see how Bonnie, with her reddish-blonde hair, creamy complexion, and trim figure, would be able to captivate men.

"Only a woman could talk to another woman about that kind of thing and back it up," Bonnie said. "I think that's why, subconsciously at least, I didn't want an AA sponsor. I wanted to go on operating in the same way I had for years, even though that way hadn't worked out for me very well.

"I now have a sponsor who isn't afraid to look me in the eye and tell me when I'm up to my old ways. I don't always like that, but it seems to be something I need. And she does it in a kind and loving but firm way. I agree with Joe that a sponsor doesn't have to be like Attila the Hun."

Bonnie passed to Henry, a short, energetic man in his late forties.

"I think my first sponsor might've had a major ego problem," Henry said. "I know we aren't supposed to take other people's inventories, but this guy —" Henry had a quick, almost explosive way of speaking and an accent that was pure Brooklynese.

"I was living in New York when I first got sober," Henry said. "This guy comes up to me after a meeting — I'd been in AA a couple months maybe — and says, 'I'll sponsor you if you want.'

"Well, I figured, great, I won't have to ask nobody. I found out since that people who just volunteer to sponsor may have some over-inflation of the ego. Anyways, this guy gives me a lot of advice I don't ask for, and not just about staying sober and AA stuff, but all kinds of things, you know? I began to realize he was practically trying to run my whole life. He'd even get bent out of shape if he saw me talking very long to another group member after a meeting.

"Now I know good sponsors may tell you things you don't especially want to hear, but there's a big difference in that and in taking the responsibility for running somebody's whole life. I'm glad I didn't let that guy sour me on sponsors. I found another guy who seemed to be down-to-earth and solid AA and *I* asked *him* to be my sponsor. The first guy quit speaking to me, but that's all right; I learned that you can 'fire' a sponsor in AA if you want to."

Henry called on Chuck. Chuck was a man in his thirties who dressed in expensive casual clothes and wore Italian loafers and a Rolex watch. Buddy had heard that Chuck was the dee-jay on a local radio station from six in the morning until noon, although he used a different broadcast name. It was typical of Chuck that he was sitting tonight beside an attractive female newcomer named Laura, a tall woman with black hair and striking blue eyes.

"Well, I think sponsors are very important," Chuck said. He had a beautifully modulated voice. "Sponsors are people we can talk to when we're having problems...." Buddy had the feeling, though he couldn't have explained exactly why, that Chuck was carefully paraphrasing standard AA talk in his own well-chosen words. Still, Chuck was an example of one kind of successful sobriety; he drove a silver Corvette and dressed well and often brought good-looking female 'earth people' — an AA slang term for nonalcoholics — to open meetings.

Chuck called on Annette when he finished. Annette was a brunette in her thirties. She was married, the mother of two small children, but in her jeans and sweater she could have passed for a teenager at a fairly close distance.

"I did get a sponsor pretty soon after I got into AA," Annette said. She had a soft, slightly countrified voice, but Buddy knew Annette was anything but a hick. "Like Tom, I was lucky — my first sponsor was not only a person whom I liked and admired a lot, she turned out to be a terrific sponsor."

Annette laughed, white teeth flashing in her small, olive-skinned face. "I was awfully pitiful at first. I would try to just dump all my problems on my sponsor. I think I wanted her to fix me and all my troubles. I didn't understand at first just what an AA sponsor could and couldn't do.

"My sponsor would always be kind and share her own experiences with me, but she'd very firmly hand my problems right back to me. She helped me learn that I had to take responsibility for myself.

"She was tactful about showing me the way I came across to people. I was a sort of low-rent *femme fatale* when I came into AA. I acted real bold and wore these godawful clothes and makeup an inch thick. She helped me tone it down by talking about the beautiful person she said I was trying to hide under all the supposedly sexy clothes and makeup. She let me see myself, but in a way that I could accept — although it still wasn't easy.

"My sponsor helped me learn that I had to look life squarely in the eye. I had to see things as they really were, not as I'd like for them to be or the way my fear told me they were. I'd tried to use alcohol for years to make everything all right, even though it wasn't. My sponsor was able to see my problems from an unbiased point of view. I think that's one of the most important things sponsors can do for us. They're not caught up in the middle of our personal problems, the way family or close friends are."

Annette passed to John, the man who'd given Ken his second white chip. John had more of the look of the stereotype of the alcoholic than anyone else in the room. John often described himself as a "low-bottom" alcoholic; he'd spent his share of days on the streets and nights under bridges. He'd been sober for more than three years, but his health had been permanently affected; it showed in his emaciated body and the pallor of his skin.

"Some of you know how I'd been living the last few years before I came to AA," John said. "I didn't have a pot to — well, you know the old saying.

"I came to AA at first looking for handouts, at least that was part of the reason. I really did want to stop drinking by that time, but I wanted to *want* to stop drinking, if you know what I mean — I wanted it to be easy and painless.

"I tried to borrow money off AA members; nobody'd loan me any. They told me money would take care of itself if I stayed sober. I asked for help then in trying to find some kind of job. They told me that if I stayed sober, I could find my own job.

"In my days on the streets I had some drinking buddies I used to hang around with. There was a mission over on the seedy side of town. We used to go to the mission to get a hot meal, or a place to sleep when it was cold or rainy. My buddies and I conned some of the newer mission volunteers out of money from time to time with hard-luck stories, until they'd wise up. We bought wine with the money, of course. The mission folk meant well, and I guess they helped some of the street people who weren't alcoholics or other addicts, but my buddies and I just used them as a way to survive and keep on drinking.

"When I got to Alcoholics Anonymous, I learned that it isn't a welfare agency, doesn't loan money, isn't an employment bureau or a housing authority. When I was ready to find a sponsor, I'd learned that what AA offers the alcoholic is sobriety — period.

"My first sponsor was a man not much like me, at least on the outside. He was a successful businessman who'd never bummed money for wine or slept in back of Laundromats next to the hot-air vents. But he knew — *knew* — how I felt inside. He was never condescending to me, never made me think he looked down on me for having been on skid row. And after I'd been sober six months, he helped me find a job, and I didn't even ask him."

In spite of himself, Ken felt a shiver of gratitude that he hadn't gone as far down the scale as John. He wasn't at all sure he could have gotten sober if he had. But, given the things he had been hearing a sponsor couldn't do, he was beginning to wonder more than ever what one could do for him.

John called on Phil, one of the newer members of the group. Phil was a slender man in his forties, dressed in suit and tie, with thinning hair and glasses.

"I had a lot of false pride when I first came into AA," Phil said. "I guess I was a 'high-bottom' drunk, John." He grinned at the man who had called on him. John grinned back. "I hadn't lost a lot of the things that some alcoholics do — I've learned to add the word 'yet' when I say I haven't lost this or that, since if I drank again I could lose it all. Anyway, I figured that a smart guy like me didn't need a sponsor to steer him along in sobriety. Oh, I could see how some people might need a sponsor, but I've always been quick on the uptake and I know a lot of arm-chair psychology. I thought that while a person without my advantages might need an AA sponsor, *I* surely didn't.

"As some of you know, I had a lot of trouble with the God business. That was another reason I didn't want a sponsor: I was afraid I'd get some wild-eyed religious freak with a 'message,' trying to save my soul.

"Well, I almost got drunk. It scared me so badly that I decided I'd better do something about this Higher Power that people talk about in AA, since it seems to be an integral part of the program. And that led me into deciding I'd better start doing something about the other things recommended by AA, and getting a sponsor was one of those things."

Phil paused. "You know, a thing that I think has been very important for me is learning to practice *all* the elements of the AA program, even if I don't see a good reason at the time.

"That false pride I mentioned had always told me I could figure the best angles on my own. My alcoholism fed off that attitude and made it even worse. I had to get rid of the atti-tude that I knew everything — that I, and only I, knew what was best for me. I had to start doing things even if I couldn't see a reason why. It's a kind of humility that's been very im-portant for me to develop. Sometimes I think that simply letting go of *my* way has been as important in itself as the new ways I've been learning."

Other people spoke, Chet and Wylie, and Arnie and Grady. The meeting wound down. Nick called for announcements, passed the baskets, offered chips, and closed.

Ken went back to the cramped little apartment and sat in front of the snowy black-and-white picture on the battered TV. He thought of Mary, of the house that had once been his, too, of the big color TV and his comfortable recliner. Mary would probably let him have the recliner, but there was no room for it in this two-by-four place.

He thought of calling Mary. It was all well and good to say that things worked out for the best, the way a lot of the AA members talked. But he missed his home and his wife. He had told himself he was as well rid of a woman who let one relapse — all right, a two-week binge, but still technically one slip — sour her on him. But here, alone, staring at the bad TV picture, he felt tremendous self-pity. Alcoholism was supposed to be a disease, at least that's what a lot of AA members said, and he surely hadn't asked to become an alcoholic....

He went out the back and down to the corner to the little convenience store there, a "beer store" in the parlance of alcoholics. There was a pay phone outside the store. It was nearly ten, but he hesitated only a moment before dropping the coin in the slot and punching out the familiar phone number.

After several rings Mary answered.

"Hi," Ken said. Now that he had her on the line, he suddenly couldn't think of anything to say.

"Hello, Ken." Her voice was civil but not friendly.

"I, uh, just wondered if you were doing okay?"

"Fine, thank you."

"Good, good. I'm all right too."

"I'm glad to hear it." Her voice was flat.

There was an excruciating silence. Finally Ken said, "Do you miss me?" He cursed himself silently; he had planned to be a lot more cool than this.

Mary didn't reply immediately. "Yes," she said at last. "But I'll get over it."

"I miss you too." His throat, not to mention his pride, hurt as he said it. "I wish things were — different."

"So do I," she said wearily. "But they're not, are they?"

"Oh, hell," he said suddenly. "Why don't we stop this, Mary?"

"Ken, this is hard for me too. Although I'm sure you're not thinking of me."

"That was kind of a lousy thing to say."

"It's true enough, though, isn't it?"

"You think I don't care about you?"

"I think you care about me when you get lonely," she said. "I guess your AA friends aren't always enough."

"That's a nasty thing to say."

"So I say a lot of lousy and nasty things. Maybe I feel lousy and nasty."

"You don't have to blame Alcoholics Anonymous. AA didn't make me drink again."

"Didn't it? I thought you'd gone to 'carry the AA message' to a drunk when you fell off the wagon."

"I can't believe you're saying this."

"Why not? You seemed to want to stay sober more for your AA friends than for me."

Ken felt his back up against the wall. He'd never realized Mary's resentment of AA.

"So what do you want from me?" he asked in frustration. "Do you want me to quit AA?"

"I want you to let me go to sleep," she said. And with that the connection was broken.

Ken stared at the now-dead phone for a moment before slamming it back into the cradle with a curse.

He went directly into the store, heading for the beer coolers at the rear. *Go ahead, get drunk at her,* a voice said to him from somewhere inside. He stopped. *There's nothing wrong with an alcoholic that a drink won't make worse,* came another voice from the same spot inside his head. He muttered a curse and bypassed the beer cooler, opened one of the glass doors, and took out a sixteen-ounce bottle of cola.

After the bored clerk took his money, he headed back to the apartment. The AA sayings he had heard at some time or other had saved him this time, but he was thinking, *Now would be a good time to talk to a sponsor, if I had one.*

"That girl Pam called," Buddy's mother said when he came in after the meeting. The use of the term *that girl* indicated that his mother didn't particularly approve of Pam. "She left her number," his mother added.

Pamela was a woman Buddy had dated on a more or less casual basis in his days before Alcoholics Anonymous. She was fun, a real partier, but a nice woman. His first instinct now was to grab the phone. Then he stopped.

Pam was not, apparently, an alcoholic; she liked to drink a little and dance a lot. In Buddy's experience, alcoholics didn't let things like dancing get in the way of their drinking.

Still, Pam was a part of his old life. He wondered if talking to her was the wisest thing to do. But Pam knew he wasn't drinking now — and why — and if she had called him in spite of it . . . .

"Hi, Buddy," Pam said. "I was just wondering how you were getting along."

"Oh great, fine," he said. He had almost said, "Not drinking and going to meetings," before he remembered she wouldn't be familiar with the AA saying. "How've you been?"

"Oh, all right, I guess. Jody and I broke up."

"No kidding?" he said. "Sorry to hear that," he added insincerely.

"It was just as well. We weren't that serious anyway."

Buddy wondered how serious "that serious" was, and if Pam still looked as good as she used to, in the days before his drinking had gotten a little too wild for her and she had started dating Jody.

"So, what are you doing for yourself these days?" Pam asked.

"Building condominiums and going to meetings. Ol' straight arrow Buddy."

"I'm glad," she said. Her silence afterward was more effective than anything else she could have said about being glad he had done something about his drinking.

The pause stretched on longer; he knew now that he was supposed to act. Pam was a fairly hip, modern young woman. She'd call a guy, but Buddy doubted that she would come right out and ask him for a date.

"We ought to get together," he said.

"That sounds good," she replied, with enough enthusiasm to let him know he had been right. "Oh, have you heard from Charlie, or Barbara and Eddie?. . ."

She'd changed the subject quickly enough to not make her reason for calling him too obvious. Buddy found himself enjoying talking to Pam immensely. He'd missed the little games with a member of the opposite sex in the last few months.

He almost asked Pam out for the following weekend, but his lack of a driver's license and the necessity of using her car stopped him. There was also the uncertainty as to whether going out with a girlfriend from his drinking past was a good idea, or if dating at all might be advisable.

This was the sort of thing he needed to talk over with a sponsor, Buddy realized. He couldn't put off calling Pam back for too long; she wasn't the kind of young woman who went begging for dates. He needed some advice on the best course of action, and soon.

He began considering potential sponsors in the Step-by-Step group. It depended, he supposed, on what qualities in a sponsor you ranked highest.

Guys like Tom and Brad had been in AA for a long time and had a ton of sobriety. But both Tom and Brad were in their sixties. Could a guy that old understand an issue such as whether or not to go out with Pam?

There was Richard, not so old, but a college professor. Buddy had never been to college, and the idea of talking much one-on-one with Richard made him uneasy. Nick and Phil were closer to his own age, but they didn't have much more sober time than himself. And big Joe the biker had helped Buddy with the God business, but Joe was intimidating, to say the least.

Old John was a low-bottom alcoholic; he wouldn't have much in common with a guy who'd never been on skid row. And Henry struck him as a big-city, fast-talking kind of guy; Buddy was admittedly a small-town boy, and he didn't think he would be comfortable with Henry.

There was Chuck. He was older than Buddy, but not so much older. He was active socially, which to Buddy meant he dated a lot. Chuck seemed pretty smooth and knowledgeable; he'd understand Buddy's natural inclination to want to date and socialize with people his own age. Chuck did seem a little superficial at times, but that was probably just his personality.

"Sure, why not?" Chuck said. Buddy had mustered up all his courage and asked Chuck the following night after the meeting.

It hadn't been easy to catch Chuck alone long enough to ask if he would be Buddy's sponsor. Chuck hadn't brought a date to this closed meeting, but he had gone over and begun talking to Laura, the young newcomer, as soon as the meeting was over.

Waiting, Buddy had had some second thoughts about Chuck. Laura had only been to a few meetings, and Chuck was unmistakably trying to hit on her. Buddy had heard this kind of behavior referred to as "Thirteenth Stepping," and it was frowned on by most AA members.

But Buddy had had too hard a time making up his mind to ask Chuck to be his sponsor to back away now. He put his misgivings out of his mind.

"Let's go grab a bite to eat when we leave here, what do you say?" Chuck asked after he'd casually agreed to sponsor Buddy.

"I, uh, don't have any wheels," Buddy admitted. He'd made arrangements with his stepfather to pick him up if he didn't catch a ride with someone after the meeting.

"No problem," Chuck said. "Ride with me and I'll drop you off at your house afterward."

So Buddy climbed into the passenger's seat of the silver 'vette and Chuck whisked them over to the pancake house where some of the group's members often went for informal "meetings after the meeting."

Chuck might not have brought a date with him to the closed meeting, but there was a blonde in a new Pontiac waiting for him in the parking lot of the pancake house. She was dressed and made up to turn a rather average face and figure into something that was eye-catching if not subtle.

"This is Buddy," Chuck said to her when they had gotten out of the cars. "Buddy, this is Angela."

"Hi," Buddy said, feeling awkward.

"Hi," Angela said, smiling up at him from under lashes that had had their share of cosmetic help. She flashed Buddy a smile and linked her arm in Chuck's as they went into the restaurant.

Chuck chose a booth a little apart from the other AA's who had driven over after the meeting. Chuck and Angela ordered food, but Buddy had only coffee.

"So how's it going?" Chuck asked him after the waitress had left.

"Fine," Buddy said automatically. He had planned on bringing up the issue of dating, but with Angela there it didn't seem appropriate.

The rest of their time at the pancake house was filled mostly with small talk, with Buddy doing the least of it. Angela was pleasant enough, but she made it obvious that Chuck was her main interest, and Chuck seemed to enjoy it hugely. As the three of them were leaving, Chuck and Angela moved apart for a moment, obviously making plans for later.

The ride to Buddy's parents' home took only a few minutes, not time enough to bring up the matter of Pam. After Chuck had driven away, Buddy had the feeling he might have made a mistake in acquiring his first sponsor.

Ken went early to his shop the morning after Mary hung up on him. Instead of going immediately to work, as was his habit, he walked around the shop, inside and out, looking it over thoughtfully.

A cinder block building, it was solid and neat if not especially handsome. Three roll-up doors opened onto service bays. Along one inside wall were sturdy shelves where he kept a stock of commonly used parts. In the opposite corner was a small boxed-off room that he used as an office. The lot on which the building set was enclosed by a six-foot-high chain link fence. The three bays each held a customer's vehicle, and there were four more vehicles waiting outside.

Ken always felt more optimistic when he took time to look over his little operation and dream for the future. There was room enough on his lot to expand, and he was buying, not leasing. He was thinking of going into servicing diesel trucks, in addition to regular automotive work. The drinking had set those plans back, of course, but he could get a second mortgage to finance expansion, and he already had enough work to justify a helper.

Ken thought again about the sponsor question. Last night he had almost decided to get a sponsor, but the light of a new day caused him to look at things differently, as did his shop, with its well-stocked tool cabinets and growing business.

The drinking had held him back in the past, true, and the relapse had been a setback, but there was no need to panic. He hadn't bought any beer last night, after all. There was no need to rush into anything.

Buddy made up his mind; he went to old Tom after the next meeting and said, simply, "I'd like you to be my sponsor, if that's all right with you."

Asking the second time was easier, so Buddy's experience with Chuck hadn't been entirely a wasted effort.

"Well," Tom said, eyeing him thoughtfully, "you think you want to listen to an old codger like me?"

Buddy felt a little embarrassed; it was as though Tom had read his earlier thoughts.

"I want to stay sober," Buddy said. "I figure you've got a lot of experience at that. Maybe some of it will rub off on me."

Tom nodded. "You know it works both ways. Being a sponsor is a help to me in my own program. It helps keep my memory of my early sobriety alive. And being a sponsor forces me to take the same advice I pass along."

"Well," Buddy said, "there's this woman I used to date, and I'm thinking about going out with her again, but..."

When Buddy got home from work one day about three months later, there was an envelope in the mail for him from the Department of Motor Vehicles. In it was his driver's license.

He stared at the small plastic-coated card with his picture on it and thought that now he could seriously start looking for a car he could afford. Oddly, he didn't feel any great urgency now.

He and Pam had been dating casually but fairly steadily. He'd gotten over the discomfort he'd felt at first at having her drive her own car when they went out. Still, it would be nice to be able to drive legally again. *The benefits of good clean sober living,* Buddy thought with a grin.

On the day Buddy got his driver's license back, Ken was packing, preparing to be discharged from the treatment center. He finished and closed his two suitcases, leaving them on the bed in the room where he'd lived for the last twenty-eight days.

Ken had gotten the second mortgage on his shop, but the money had gone for this course of alcoholism treatment, rather than for the expansion of his business.

The formal separation agreement Mary's lawyer had sent Ken had been the final straw. He'd gone out and bought a bottle within an hour of having signed the separation papers. By this time, he had been missing more AA meetings. He'd thought briefly of calling someone in AA before he bought the bottle, but there was no one he felt close enough to. He hadn't, of course, gotten a sponsor, and he now knew that waiting until he was at immediate risk of drinking was cutting things a little too fine.

It had turned into the worst drinking bout he'd ever had. He'd almost gone into D.T.'s, or so they told him at the treatment center. He had no memory of arriving at the center, although they had told him he'd called and gotten a cab to bring him there.

Now Ken was faced with the need to again rebuild his business. Bill, his mechanic, had quit in disgust at having to be responsible for the shop and do the work of two men. All the shop's customers had picked up their vehicles, repaired or not.

Waiting to be discharged, Ken picked up the folder that he'd been given at the beginning of treatment, after he'd come out of his alcoholic fog and could begin the center's program. In the folder were the notes he'd taken in the various classes, the handouts that the counseling staff had given him, and his copies of his treatment plan and aftercare plan.

The aftercare plan, which he and his counselor had discussed as part of his predischarge interview, covered the things Ken needed to do to stay sober when he went back out into the "real world." Featured prominently in his aftercare plan was a recommendation, underlined in red ink by Ken himself: *GET A SPONSOR!*

Thirteenth Stepper

"Are you going to the meeting tonight?" Laura's mother called from the hallway.

"Yes," Laura called back, managing not to add *Mother* in the petulant tone of a teenager.

She felt like a teenager, and not in the pleasant sense of regained youthfulness. A return to adolescence wouldn't be that welcome, anyway. It had been a time of emotional pain, and things seemed to have gone downhill from there for Laura, except for the times when she had been able to kid herself that her life was terrific. That had been during the drinking times, and those had, in the end, let her down too.

"Would you like for me to drop you off?" her mother called.

Laura made a face in the mirror, but kept her voice pleasant as she answered, "No thanks, Mom, Janey's coming by." The fact that at thirty-two years of age she was back living with her mother wasn't her mother's fault, but that knowledge made her feel, if anything, worse.

She heard her mother's footsteps move away and she relaxed a little.

Her mother had been very supportive while Laura was in treatment, and Laura was grateful. Treatment had been a time when she had been able to view her life as if from a distance. Her marriage breaking up, David returning to his childhood sweetheart, losing her job after the last drinking bout, losing

103

her license for driving while impaired — all these things seemed to have happened to someone else.

In treatment, she'd felt herself a part of a family — made up of the other patients sharing misfortunes and pain and fears for the future — in a way that kept her from feeling alone.

Now it was her first full day back in the "outside world." The feeling of an exciting new sober life ahead of her had been replaced by the grinding awareness that she was at present unemployed, without a driver's license, with no friends from her former life with whom she could safely or comfortably socialize, and living with her mother like a little child.

She studied herself in the mirror over the dresser. Being off alcohol and other drugs for a month, eating balanced meals, sleeping regularly, and getting outdoor exercise had brightened her eyes and given her complexion a healthy tone. Even her hair, which she had never considered her strong point, was lively and shining.

I was a real mess, she thought ruefully. She remembered seeing herself in a mirror three days after her mother had gotten her to the treatment center. Her eyes stared out of darkened, puffy sockets. She had bruises from falls she didn't remember taking and the pasty skin of a terminally ill patient.

She'd learned that she indeed suffered from an illness that was terminal if not arrested. *Alcoholic and addict,* she had thought wryly, *something to take to my next high school reunion.*

She and David had been voted boy and girl most likely to succeed. *I succeeded, all right — in taking myself back to square one.*

She'd taken David away from Sheila as a high school junior; now Sheila had him back again. *It had a certain poetic justice to it,* Laura thought. It was probably better that things had worked out this way. Taking David away from Sheila had been a challenge, but in their marriage, once the first thrill of living together had worn off, their insecurities had clashed rather than complemented each other. The marriage had become a cycle of fighting and making up, with the fights growing more bitter and the making up less sincere.

Laura thought carefully about what to wear for her first evening out of treatment, even though AA meetings tended to be very informal. Classes and patient groups had involved a good deal of sitting around, and the treatment center's food had been plentiful. She'd put on several pounds in her twenty-eight days. Although she had the height to carry it, her clothes seemed more snug than she liked.

She finally decided on a grey skirt and white blouse that set off her vivid complexion and straight black hair to advantage. "Black Irish," her father used to call this combination of vivid dark complexion, black hair, and blue eyes that characterized his side of the family.

She still missed her father terribly at times. He'd left her mother when Laura was nine, and he'd died when she was twelve. She hadn't been allowed to go to his funeral. In treatment, she had had to work on her resentment of that, and on her grief, which had been thwarted for years. She now realized that her father had, in all probability, been an alcoholic himself.

"Don't you look nice!" said her mother when Laura came downstairs.

"Thanks, Mom," Laura said, pushing down the annoyance she always felt at direct compliments from anyone close to her. She had learned in treatment that this reaction to compliments from loved ones probably stemmed from the fact that she, at least unconsciously, discounted anyone's positive opinion of her. "If they think you're special or competent," her counselor had told her, "then they must be stupid, right? Because *you* know you're really inferior." Her counselor had been a tough older woman named Sally, with the tact of a Marine drill instructor and a warm heart under her tough exterior. "Older" was relative; Sally was actually no older than Laura's mother.

Absently, Laura watched her mother now as she dusted the living room furniture — Laura was sure it couldn't have been more than a couple of days since it had last been dusted. Still attractive in her late fifties, with hair almost completely white, her mother had a face softened rather than hardened by the lines around eyes and mouth. Laura had gotten her tallness from her mother's side of the family; her mother's bustling attack in whatever she did kept her figure trim. Her mother had lived a stressful life as first the wife of an alcoholic and then the mother of one. Laura now guessed that her maternal grandfather had also been alcoholic, though her mother never spoke of his bouts of drinking.

The things she'd learned in treatment about alcoholism in families had helped Laura better understand her mother's constant striving for a "perfect" home, despite having to raise her only child alone. Laura was thankful that she and David had never had children, although there was a sense of void in her life at times because of it.

"You say Janey's coming by?" her mother asked, busying herself with her dust cloth the way one does who wishes to appear very casual in her questioning.

"Mom," Laura said, taking the dust cloth from her mother's hands and putting her arm around her mother's shoulders. "I'm going to an AA meeting my first evening home, just like the counselors told us to do."

"Well, I didn't mean —"

"I know, Mom," Laura said, shaking her head. "I thought I'd say that just in case you *might* be worried." She gave back the dust cloth, and her mother began absently flicking it at imaginary dust.

"I'm proud of you, for going through treatment. . . ." Her mother's voice faltered a little, and just then Laura heard Janey's horn outside.

"I love you, Mom," Laura said, giving her a peck on the cheek. "I'll see you later." With that, Laura headed out the door.

"Hi," Janey said. "I'm glad you're going." Her tone suggested that not all the alumni of the treatment center where Janey had been a patient were so diligent in following the advice of the treatment staff.

"Me too," Laura said. "I'm not craving a drink," she added as Janey glanced at her before pulling away from the curb.

Laura had met Janey, a petite blonde woman in her forties, while Laura was in treatment. Janey, as a former patient now recovering, had come to speak to her women's group. Janey and Laura discovered that they lived close to each other, and Janey had agreed to be Laura's AA contact upon Laura's discharge.

"I think craving a drink might be simpler," Laura said now as they rolled along the quiet streets of their small town.

"Having trouble adjusting?"

"I guess that's it. I just feel so — juvenile — or something. When I was drinking, I thought I was the sophisticated woman of the world. Now I feel like an overweight, lumpy teenager, wondering if anyone will ever ask me for a date."

Janey's deep, rich laugh was a contrast to her slight build and delicate features. Janey had teenaged children, but at a distance she could easily have passed for a teenager herself.

"I know what you mean," Janey said. "My husband, in my last few weeks of boozing, had hired a maid. I was of absolutely no help in taking care of the house and children, of course, and my poor hubby was having to be father and mother both.

"When I was coming out of detox and the fog was beginning to lift, I began wondering exactly what that maid looked like. I vaguely remembered that she was young, but was she pretty? I felt completely washed up — as a woman, a wife, a human being. I could imagine my husband having an affair with the maid, or one of our female friends, or somebody at the office. God knows I hadn't been able to be much of a wife to him for a long time."

"Well," Laura said, "my ex-husband is having his fling, and I'm afraid I know exactly who he's having it with." Laura's bitter tone surprised her. "It's not that I mind the marriage breaking up so much — it was on rocky ground for a long time before I went into treatment — but I just feel so washed up, or something."

"It'll get better," Janey said with conviction.

"I suppose." Laura's answer lacked enthusiasm.

Laura had become accustomed to the lack of pretension in Alcoholics Anonymous. Exposed heating ducts and a concrete ceiling didn't put her off the Step-by-Step group's meeting place.

Janey began introducing her to what seemed like dozens of people as they made their way toward the inevitable coffeepot. John and Tom and Annette and Doris and Buddy and Nick and Chet and Wylie and Phil. . . .

It was the usual varied group she'd come to expect in Alcoholics Anonymous. Like most of the meetings she'd attended while in treatment, there were more men present than women. Some of the women patients had complained about this, but Laura liked men — she found them easier to get along with than most women.

It had not been, she could truly say, just the company that had attracted Laura to Alcoholics Anonymous. She had given herself quite a surprise by taking so readily to AA; there was, for her, an immediate feeling of belonging that she'd never experienced before in the company of other people.

She and Janey stopped just short of the coffeepot for another round of introductions. She'd shaken hands with a couple of people when a hand tapped her on the shoulder and a voice asked, "Can I get you a cup of coffee?"

He was a man of medium height, about David's size, and a little older, between thirty-five and forty, she guessed. He was well-dressed, if a little youthfully so, but he had the lean physique to carry it off. He had a firm chin and an interesting nose (Laura liked noses), brown eyes, and a touch of grey in his temples.

"My name's Chuck," he said, holding out his hand. He didn't try any phony-romantic stuff, just gave her a firm, friendly handshake.

"I'm Laura," she said. "And thanks, but I can get my own coffee."

It sounded a little irascible on her part, but he just smiled and didn't make a point of insisting. She wasn't truly irritated;

offering to get coffee was not necessarily a chauvinistic gesture.

"I haven't seen you here before," he said when she'd poured herself a cup of coffee. "Are you visiting?"

"Not exactly," she said. "I'm staying here in town; this is my first meeting here. I just got out of treatment." She could have, had she been painfully honest, added, *And I'm living with my Mummy.*

"This is a good group," Chuck said. "I go to a lot of meetings around the area, but this is my home group."

"Have you been in the program long?" Laura had learned that this question gave a person an opening to tell their length of sobriety if they chose to.

"A few years," Chuck said casually. He had a dimple on one side of his mouth that was a little deeper than its counterpart on the other, giving his smile an engaging lopsidedness.

"I've got thirty whole days, as of tomorrow," Laura said, fall-ing into AA small talk.

"That's great," Chuck said. He made it sound as if it really was great, instead of just a beginner's length of sobriety.

He sipped his coffee and looked around casually as he said, "Did you come with someone?"

Laura felt a little lurch in her stomach, unsettling but not unpleasant. Chuck's question had sounded like a prelude to a pass, done in a tasteful, low-key way.

Her defenses began to go up, as she remembered what the counselors had said about the risk of new romantic relation-ships the first year of sobriety. In treatment, there had been patients, male and female, who had tried to start treatment-center romances, which the staff, of course, firmly discouraged. It made sense to Laura that being just out of detoxification was no time to be forming an intimate relationship. But a *year!* She was just out of the treatment center's sheltered environment, already feeling adrift and alone, and tomorrow would only be her thirtieth day of sobriety.

"I came with Janey," Laura answered, a bit more firmly than was probably necessary, but he just nodded, smiling pleasantly.

People were starting to find seats as the starting time for the meeting approached. She and Janey sat together, and Chuck made no attempt to pursue or sit close to them. He sat with another man and a woman about Laura's age, a striking-looking strawberry-blonde whose name Laura remembered was Bonnie. Chuck was wearing no wedding band. *AA was a place to meet unattached males,* Laura thought, feeling a little less resentful toward David and Sheila.

It was a discussion meeting, and after the preliminaries, the woman who was chairing asked if anyone had a problem or topic they would like discussed or help with. Then she mentioned the AA Moment of Silence and got a chuckle from the group.

The topic that the chairperson suggested when none was forthcoming from the group was practicing the AA principles in one's everyday life. Laura was glad the time to close the meeting came before she was called on; she'd hardly had a chance to begin to live an everyday life, sober.

Chuck had been called on, and he had a good, concise, and articulate comment on the topic. Laura was feeling a little silly — suppose she'd been wrong, suppose he hadn't been intending to make a pass at her at all? With his length of time in Alcoholics Anonymous, Chuck would be aware that one's first year was an uncertain time and not advisable for beginning intimate commitments. She decided he was probably simply being friendly. He might find her attractive — she certainly hoped he did — but that didn't mean there was necessarily any sort of romance in the offing for them.

Laura had half-hoped to talk to Chuck at the end of the meeting, and she was a little disappointed when the opportunity didn't arise. She was tempted to ask Janey about Chuck on the way home, but to do so would seem obvious and rather premature, since Laura didn't count on any relationship in the near future. She decided to avoid the subject for now.

The following week, Laura began looking for a job. She knew in advance that it was going to be no picnic. She was a reliable worker, when she was in good shape. She'd had a variety of jobs as an adult because, like many alcoholics, she'd never taken the time out of her life to prepare for a profession or plan a career.

She'd decided to be frank about her alcoholism and her treatment when she applied for jobs. It was perhaps making a virtue out of necessity, since she would have to find a way to explain the reason for leaving her last job. Most of the people she talked to were kind, expressing admiration for Laura's honesty in admitting her alcoholism and her efforts at recovery. But that first week the admiration didn't seem to extend to offering her a job.

She'd gone almost every night with Janey to one AA meeting or another in the area. On the evening of an especially bad day, however, Janey called and said she'd be unable to attend the meeting that night.

"Bad news?" her mother asked when Laura put down the phone after Janey's call.

"Just Janey saying she can't go tonight." Laura realized that this was exactly when she needed AA the most. There was no bus service in the little town where they lived, and if Laura called a cab she'd have to borrow money from her mother to pay the fare since she'd used a lot of her cash on cabs in her job-hunting.

"I'd be glad to take you," her mother said. Laura's first reaction was to decline, but she *really* needed a meeting. . . .

"Thanks, Mom," she said. They talked a lot in AA about not being too proud to ask for help. Pride was one of her worst problems, Laura knew. If she was going to be able to go to meetings, though, it looked as though she'd have to make some adjustments.

Tonight's meeting was at the Step-by-Step group's basement meeting room. Laura was secretly relieved when her mother seemed to assume that she was to drop Laura off rather than coming into the meeting with her. It was an open meeting, but somehow having her mother come with her because Laura was not legally allowed to drive was more than Laura could bear the thought of.

"Shall I pick you up at nine?" her mother asked as Laura was getting out of the car.

"I'll get a ride with someone," Laura said impulsively. It would be as good a time as any to start putting into practice accepting help, from someone besides Janey.

"Are you sure? It'll be fairly late, and —"

"Don't worry, Mom," she said quickly. "If worse comes to worst, I can always call you from the phone booth on the corner."

It felt a little odd, walking in without Janey, but by now Laura knew a lot of faces and names. She was greeted by Fran, Grady, Richard, and others as she made her way to the coffeepot.

She had gotten a cup of coffee and was just turning back to resume her pre-meeting socializing when she almost bumped into Chuck.

"We're going to have to stop meeting like this," he said, peering around in mock-furtiveness. She laughed. "I haven't seen you around," he said.

"I've been going to other meetings around this area. I guess we've just missed running into each other."

"And now we almost did that, literally," he said. "How've you been?"

"All right," she said automatically. Then she said, "No, that's not true. I've had a lousy week."

She told him about her so-far unsuccessful job search, the applications filled out and the polite but noncommittal personnel officers she'd talked with. While she talked, Chuck subtly steered her away from the crowd to a quiet spot near a corner of the room. She was aware of what he was doing, but she welcomed having another alcoholic to share some of her frustration with and she welcomed the privacy.

"Do you have a ride home?" he asked when she had run down a little.

She was trapped with the truth — either tell him she could call her mother, or else shake her head.

"I'll be glad to drop you off," he said when she'd given the negative reply. "Drop you off" was reassuring; he didn't seem to consider it as anything more than a friendly gesture of one AA to another.

When they sat together during the meeting, it seemed perfectly natural. Chuck had a nice smell, a subtle cologne. When everyone joined hands to close the meeting with the Lord's Prayer, Chuck's hand was big and warm and comforting.

"You have a sparkle in your eye," her mother said when she came in. "You were looking down before."

"It was a good meeting," Laura said.

"Did you have any trouble getting a ride home?"

"No, one of the gals lives not far from here."

The lie had seemed to pop out of its own volition, although she'd felt a quick flash of irritation at her mother's question.

Her mother had always worried about Laura and men — not without reason, judging from some of the things that had happened, Laura had to admit to herself.

Still, Laura needed to feel like an adult, and independent. Chuck had chatted in a nonsuggestive way as they rode over in his Corvette; he'd let her off in front of her mother's house without any attempts to detain her or set up a future meeting — she'd felt a trace of disappointment at this. But as a counter-balance, there was the feeling that he was a trustworthy AA member, someone she could feel relaxed with.

The counselors at the treatment center had emphasized the need for a sponsor, someone with whom the recovering person could talk one-on-one. They'd also emphasized a sponsor of the same gender. Janey was so far the only woman Laura had gotten to know in AA. She'd thought of asking Janey to be her sponsor, but she'd heard the AA stories about "tough" sponsors. Although Janey didn't seem to be the overbearing type, Laura still had reservations. Something happened the following week, however, that pushed Laura into action.

She and Janey went together to the midweek meeting of the Step-by-Step group. Laura had secretly hoped that Chuck would be there, and he was. He didn't sit with her and Janey, which struck Laura as a little odd, since it would have been a natural enough thing to do. But after the meeting, he drew Laura aside, and after a few words of small talk, he said, "Why don't you and I go to dinner?"

He must have seen the guarded look in her eyes because he quickly added, "We can eat early and go to a meeting afterward."

Laura had the peculiar but distinct feeling that Chuck was avoiding Janey; she was now walking toward them, and he seemed rather ill at ease.

This was the thing she'd both dreaded and hoped for. Her mind went blank for a moment. Then she said, "Let me think about it. Call me tomorrow, all right?" She gave him her phone number and said good night.

In the car with Janey, Laura felt more confident and optimistic than she'd felt since leaving treatment.

"Janey?"

"Uh-hmm?" Janey was watching a traffic light about to go green.

"Will you be my sponsor?"

Janey looked at her, then back at the light. As it turned green and they moved off, she said, "Let's stop for another cup of coffee."

A sinking feeling hit Laura's stomach. She hadn't really considered the possibility that Janey might say no, but it looked as if this might be what was going to happen.

They pulled into a fast-food restaurant that had a drive-up window and ordered coffee. Then Janey pulled over to the side of the lot and parked.

"The answer is yes, I'll be your sponsor, if you still want me to be after you hear what I have to say."

The premonition that Janey was going to refuse to sponsor her was replaced by anxiety over what Janey might say next.

Janey sipped her coffee for a moment before continuing.

"Chuck's been trying to make out with you, hasn't he?" Janey asked finally.

"Well — I don't know if that's exactly the term I'd use. He gave me a ride home the night you couldn't go, and he's asked me to go to dinner with him — early, before a meeting. That seems pretty innocent to me."

"They told you in treatment about the risks in intimate relationships your first year of sobriety." Janey obviously wasn't phrasing this as a question.

"Yes, but to go out to eat with someone —"

"Laura, I don't believe in gossiping in AA and I don't talk about other members casually, but you've asked me to be your sponsor.

"That makes it a different situation. So I'm going to talk about Chuck for a bit.

"Chuck is as attractive and charming on the surface as he can be. I've known him for a while, not well, but well enough to see him operate."

" 'Operate'?"

"Chuck is what we in AA call a 'Thirteenth Stepper,' " Janey said. "He moves on new women in the program."

She looked at Laura very directly. "I know you've been feeling pretty down, Laura. Alcoholism affects us in the sense of who we are, sexually.

"When I was first sober, I couldn't get out of my mind the way I must have looked to my husband when I was drinking — sloppy and unattractive, even repulsive. I know you lost your husband...." She held up her hand when Laura started to speak. "And you've been telling yourself that it was probably the best thing, that it never would have worked out. But your pride has been mauled pretty hard."

Janey paused, tapping lightly on the steering wheel in an unconscious gesture of emphasis. "I've watched you since we've been going to meetings together. You're not too comfortable with other women. I know that feeling. I'd felt for a long time that women in general were more rivals than potential friends. Our mothers, bless their hearts, were brought up in a day when women based a big part of their identity on their relationships with men. We pick that up and our alcoholism exaggerates it, the way it does most things."

"I suppose all that's true, at least to some extent," Laura said. "But what's it got to do with my going to dinner with Chuck before an AA meeting?"

"I don't think Chuck's some kind of monster," Janey said. "I doubt that Chuck and guys like him sit down and work all this out before they make their moves on newly sober women.

"But alcoholic men have their insecurities too. A lot of them, including Chuck, I strongly suspect, use relationships with women as a way of dealing with those insecurities. In their own way, you see, they're a great deal like us."

"You're saying that you think Chuck is trying to run some kind of number on me as a way of feeding his ego, right?" Laura asked. "I've met guys like that, but Chuck doesn't seem to me to be that way."

"I know," Janey said with a rueful smile. "You, of all people, should know how charming and plausible alcoholics can be."

Laura thought of her manipulations of people. Her supervisor on her last job, a male, had been manipulated to keep her on far after she should have been let go. She nodded, a little grudgingly.

"And some alcoholics, like Chuck especially, are capable of even greater charm when they're sober," Janey said. "I don't think Chuck rubs his hands together and laughs with villainous glee while he plots the downfall of some newly sober female AA member.

"But he knows, intuitively, that women like yourself are vulnerable, and he knows exactly how to play on that. In fact, I'll bet he has some dandy rationalizations, for his own benefit, about how he helps new women regain their sense of identity and sexual attractiveness — by having affairs with them."

"Well, what's so wrong about wanting to feel sexually attractive?" Laura demanded. "This isn't the Victorian era. And I'm not some dewy-eyed virgin."

"Laura," Janey said, and there was a toughness in her tone that Laura hadn't heard before. "Let's get one thing straight. I'm not concerned about sexual morality, yours or anyone else's. For one thing, it's none of my business. For another, despite being an old married lady, I'm not a prude. I haven't always been the greatest example of sexual propriety myself.

"It's your *sobriety* I care about, not what you do with whom. If I'm going to be your sponsor, then I expect you to listen to what I have to say and keep an open mind. If you don't, then there's no point in my sponsoring you."

It was, for all practical purposes, an ultimatum. Laura felt her resentment of authority rising up, the desire to be in charge of every important detail of her life.

How well have you done in the past? came an unbidden voice from somewhere inside herself. "I'll listen," she heard herself say to Janey.

"Good," Janey said. "Look, let's be realistic and basic. It's not sex in itself that gets people drunk, it's the emotional stuff that goes on around sex that's dangerous. Newly recovering alcoholics are people with a lot of very strong, deep emotions. Ask yourself right now, how well would you deal with all the emotional stress that comes with a love affair?"

"Probably not very well at all," Laura admitted after a long moment. She was grateful for the self-honesty that she had begun to develop in treatment. There had been a time when she would never have admitted to any weakness or vulnerability.

"Chuck-baby has an AA fling or two a year," Janey said, "depending, of course, on how many attractive, unattached females come into the program in the area.

"He's very concerned, of course, if the girl gets drunk as a result of her fling with him. He then plays Mr. Good Guy and tries to get the women in the program to help the poor girl, and he applauds as hard as the next member if the girl picks up another white chip.

"If she doesn't get drunk, and begins to hang in there and grow in her own sobriety in spite of her relationship to Chuck, he drops her and finds another pigeon. Staying with a woman who's getting back her self-respect and independence doesn't fit in very well with Chuck's needs over the long run. Incidentally, guys like Chuck aren't immune themselves from getting emotionally messed up from affairs and getting drunk. Chuck's been around AA for a good while, but he's had a couple of trips out into the weeds."

"But. . .I thought you could trust people in AA!" Laura said.

"You can, if they're practicing the principles of AA in *all* their affairs, if you'll pardon the pun.

"The Thirteenth Steppers aren't doing that — they're using people, just the way they undoubtedly did when they were drinking."

"But how do I know the difference in people?" Laura asked.

"It takes time and experience in AA to begin to be able to tell the difference," Janey said. "That's one of the things sponsors are all about, to help you gain that kind of knowledge." Janey patted Laura's shoulder. "You're a lovely woman, Laura, and you won't have to join a convent to stay sober. But it's all too easy to use relationships with men in the same way we used booze, to avoid getting to know ourselves, so that we can grow to accept and like ourselves. And that's what that rule-of-thumb about relationships the first year of sobriety is all about."

When Chuck called her at her mother's house the next day, Laura put aside all the sarcastic and cutting things she'd had to force herself to stop rehearsing and simply said, "Thanks, Chuck, for asking me out, but I don't think I'm ready right now."

There was a long pause at the end of the line.

"Got yourself a black-belt AA sponsor, have you?" he asked finally, the flip words not quite covering a resentment in his voice.

"Yes, I guess I have," she said quietly. As she put down the phone, she realized that she'd been right in thinking that Chuck was avoiding Janey at the meeting the night he asked Laura out.

In the next few days Laura found herself feeling more pity than anger or indignation when she thought of Chuck. At a meeting a few nights later, when she and Janey saw Chuck chatting with an attractive, young newcomer, Laura returned Janey's droll wink with no feeling of jealousy or envy at all.

Business Meeting

In a way, Ken thought, *it was like any other meeting, at least before the start.* People were sitting and standing around, drinking coffee, smoking, and making small talk. If he forgot it was a Monday night, a night on which the Step-by-Step group of Alcoholics Anonymous didn't normally hold a meeting, he could imagine that it was like any other.

Ken had been a member of the Step-by-Step group for some time now, but this was his first business meeting.

At first, he had not known how to go about joining the group. The only requirement to join AA was a desire to stop drinking, but he hadn't known how a person got to be a member of a particular AA group.

He'd felt a little foolish, but relieved, when he learned that all he had to do to become a member of the Step-by-Step group was to simply say he was a member. He'd worried about the possibility of being rejected; he was grateful for this easy acceptance.

When Richard, who was the group chairman for the year, called the meeting to order, he dispensed with most of the usual routine for opening meetings.

"Welcome to the quarterly business meeting of the Step-by-Step group of Alcoholics Anonymous," he said. "I'm Richard and I'm an alcoholic. I'm also the person you chose to be the group chairperson for this year and that's why I'm conducting this meeting.

"We refer to these as 'business meetings'; in some areas, they're called 'group conscience meetings.' We use the *group conscience* — meaning we let a simple majority rule when we vote on things — to decide how we're going to handle the various issues affecting the group."

The Step-by-Step group, Ken had learned, held business meetings four times a year. The business meetings were held on Monday nights, since Mondays were not regular meeting nights and therefore posed no conflicts.

There had been announcements for this meeting at every regular meeting for the last two weeks. Ken had heard that it was important for members to attend the group's business meetings and he was anxious to do what he was supposed to do in AA. A trip back out into the weeds requiring a stay in a treatment center had come about for Ken, partly because of not heeding AA advice about getting a sponsor. Ken was now determined to follow the suggestions of those in AA he had found trustworthy.

Richard asked Annette, whom Ken took to be group secretary, to read the minutes of the last business meeting. When she finished, he asked if everyone accepted the minutes as read. Evidently everyone did, for there was no objection.

Richard called on John, who was group treasurer, for the financial report.

"We're current on all expenses," John said, by which Ken understood that all bills were paid up. "We have a surplus of seven hundred and fifty-five dollars and some odd cents — the figures are on the copy of the statement I've pinned up on the bulletin board. The whole statement is there; everyone's welcome to look it over and ask if you have any questions." *Quite a thing,* Ken thought, *for John, the one-time "low-bottom" drunk, to have the responsibility of handling the group's finances.*

"All right," Richard said when John was finished, "before we start on new business, is there any old business from the last meeting that we need to take up?"

"Yes," said Phil from the front row, "last time we said we were going to have somebody check into getting exhaust fans to clear the smoke out of meetings. Has that been done?"

Richard looked at young Buddy. "Buddy was going to talk to a heating and cooling contractor about that. How about it, Buddy?"

Buddy looked a little embarrassed, but Ken had learned that was Buddy's usual expression; he was a friendly but rather shy young man.

"It'll cost us a couple of hundred to get two exhaust fans installed," Buddy said. "That's at cost; the guy I talked to said he wouldn't take a profit on the job." Buddy, a construction carpenter, knew a lot of people in the building trades.

"Why don't we go ahead and spring for it, then?" Phil asked. "John, can we afford it?"

"I don't see why not," John said. "The group has asked me to keep a prudent reserve of five hundred dollars; we've got two hundred fifty over that."

"Well, does someone want to make a motion?" Richard asked. Phil began to speak. "I move that we —"

"Do we really *need* this exhaust fan?" Brad interrupted. A small, white-haired man in his sixties, he spoke with a hint of belligerence in his tone.

"You were out of town when we held the last business meeting, Brad," Richard said. "We discussed how the group is growing in size and about how the smoke has started to get pretty thick at meetings, what with more people attending, especially on speaker meeting nights."

"I never knew a real AA member who objected to a little smoke," Brad said, drawing on his pipe.

"I'm Joe and I'm a real AA member," said the big bearded man from the front. "It's getting to be more than a 'little' smoke, Brad. I'm a smoker —" Joe dragged on his unfiltered Camel by way of illustration. "And the smoke bothers *me* sometimes."

"Let's hear from some more people," Richard suggested.

"I'm Annette and I'm an alcoholic." Annette's normally light voice was firm. "I think we should have the extra exhaust fans. And I think we should consider having at least one nonsmoking meeting."

Two or three people murmured yes, while a couple of diehard smokers snorted.

"Hold that thought, Annette," Richard said diplomatically. "We'll finish with this issue and take up the nonsmoking meeting as a part of new business."

"I thought we had the heating and cooling fans rigged up to work on just a ventilating cycle," said Henry in his Brooklyn accent.

"We do," John said. "But they're not designed for clearing the air for the whole room, just for circulating heat and cooled air. They're not up to the job of exhausting the smoke when the room's nearly full of people."

"Well, how do we know these new fans will work any better?" Brad asked. "We could spend a lot of money and not be any better off." Ken felt himself getting irritated with Brad; the older man seemed to simply be negative.

"What did the heating and cooling contractor say about that, Buddy?" Richard asked.

"He, uh, said the fans would take care of the smoke," Buddy said. He was clearly uncomfortable with the direction the discussion was taking.

The discussion went round and round. Opinions seemed equally divided between going ahead with the new exhaust fans and not spending the money.

Finally Richard said, "Does someone want to move that we investigate it a little more and bring it up again at the next business meeting?"

Everyone looked relieved — the motion was made, seconded, and approved, and they went on to the next item of old business.

"There was the question last time as to whether to have some — or all — of our regular meetings be closed meetings," Richard said. "Attendance was small at the last business meeting, and we said we'd wait until this meeting, with more members present, to discuss the idea further. I believe that Wade brought up the idea of closed meetings, right?"

"Excuse me, Richard," said old Tom. "Maybe we ought to say for the benefit of anyone who's new, exactly what we mean by 'closed' meetings." Big, leather-handed Tom was one of the group's most respected members.

"Good idea, Tom," Richard said. *"Open meetings*, which all of ours are at present, mean that anyone can attend — not just people who identify themselves as alcoholics. Of course, we have the men's and women's meetings, but those aren't closed to nonalcoholics, just limited to that gender.

"Closed meetings mean that only people who identify themselves as alcoholic or powerless over alcohol, or with a desire to stop drinking are supposed to attend. I say 'supposed' because I've never heard anyone at an AA meeting make a big point of throwing a nonalcoholic out of a closed meeting." Richard looked at the tall, dark-haired man sitting about halfway back and near the coffeepot. "Why don't you kick off the discussion now, Wade, since you suggested the idea of closed meetings at our last business meeting?"

"I think we may be making a mistake by holding all open meetings," Wade said. His big droopy mustache gave him a *bandido* look; he wore aviator-style glasses with metal frames and lenses that were tinted on their upper halves.

"We may be keeping away some people who're afraid of breaking their anonymity, or at least be making them uneasy about taking part in discussions," Wade said. "As it is now, people bring wives and husbands, girlfriends and boyfriends, and God knows who-all to our meetings. Some 'earth people' are okay, but I've seen cases where some nonalcoholic has gone out and told people on the outside who they've seen and what they've heard, and it hasn't been very good."

Bonnie raised her hand and asked, "Do you know of any cases like that here in the Step-by-Step group?" She noticed

Wade's unfriendly look and added, "I haven't been here long; that wasn't a sarcastic question."

"Not that *I* know of," said Nick.

"Whether or not there's a specific incident that somebody remembers isn't the point," Wade said, an edge of impatience in his voice. "The group I belonged to before this one had a big Al-Anon problem. Some guy's wife who was with him at an AA meeting saw a man pick up another white chip after he'd been out drinking again. She saw the man's ex-wife at an Al-Anon meeting and told her about his slip. The ex-wife began giving him a lot of grief, not wanting to let him see their kids and so forth."

"Well, I can tell you we don't have that kind of Al-Anon problem *here*,'' spoke up Kay, a big-boned woman in her early forties with prematurely grey hair. Kay was a member of Al-Anon as well as Alcoholics Anonymous. "Our Al-Anon members know how to keep anonymity and confidentiality as well as AA's do." Kay was also not reluctant to let others know her opinions.

"They may know how, but do they do it?" Wade asked rather sarcastically.

"You're damn right they do," Kay answered.

"Nick, did you want to say something?" Richard said quickly, obviously heading off the confrontation between Kay and Wade.

Nick, a husky, dark-haired man in his late thirties, was relatively new to the group.

"Having closed meetings would be hard on some of the new people who've lost their driver's licenses," he said. "A lot of people who've gotten DWI's have to depend on their spouses or family members for rides to meetings. If the person driving can't attend the meeting, he or she would have to sit out in the car or else leave and come back for the alcoholic. Either way, it could be a hardship."

"Well, too bad," said Wade. Ken thought Wade had a sneering tone in his voice. "If they hadn't driven drunk in the first place, they wouldn't have lost their licenses. If they want AA badly enough, they'll find a way to get to meetings. Let 'em work it out themselves."

Ken noticed Nick tense — he guessed that had Nick been drinking on an occasion like this, he would have probably challenged Wade, maybe to a fistfight.

As the discussion went around, it began to calm down. Most people spoke in favor of leaving the meetings the way they were, open. A few — Wade, of course, and Chet and Wylie and Frank — spoke in favor of closing the meetings. Finally Richard asked for a motion.

"I move that we have closed meetings," Wade said.

"I second it," said Wylie.

"All in favor?" Richard asked. Wade, of course, raised his hand. So did tiny, red-haired Wylie. Surprisingly, neither Chet nor Frank voted in favor of closing meetings, although they'd spoken in favor of doing so.

"All opposed?"

Most of the people in the room raised their hands.

"Motion doesn't carry," Richard said. "Meetings will continue to be open." He glanced at Annette, who was keeping the minutes; she nodded as she recorded the result.

"Any other items of old business?" Richard asked.

"I'd like to ask a question," said Chuck. "What's this 'prudent reserve' that John mentioned?" Ken thought it interesting that Chuck had kept this question in mind all through the debate about open versus closed meetings.

"John, you want to explain that?" Richard asked.

"Sure," John said, looking at Chuck without a great deal of enthusiasm. "Thirteenth Stepper" Chuck wasn't well-liked by every member of the group.

"The group has asked me, as treasurer, to keep a certain amount on hand in the group's bank account to cover expenses, in the event that our receipts from contributions should fall off or we have some unexpected expense. The group's conscience on this was that we'd keep enough for two months' regular expenditures in reserve; that works out to five hundred dollars, rounded off. That would cover electricity, water, rent, coffee and supplies, AA literature — the regular ongoing expenses. Anything over that we divide up between the group's intergroup contribution and a contribution to the AA General Service Office in New York."

Laura, a newcomer who Chuck had unsuccessfully tried to "Thirteenth Step," raised her hand. "Why don't we accumulate more?" she asked. "I mean, is there a reason why we send most of the money over the reserve to these other places instead of keeping it for the group?"

"That's a good question, Laura," John said. "It's good that you asked, because there might be some other people who're new in the group wondering the same thing.

"The reason we don't try to accumulate more is that over the years it's been found that AA groups that grow fat financially often wind up with serious problems.

"If there's a lot of money in a group's treasury, then there begins to be suspicion and anger and resentment over who controls it and what's done with it, and so on.

"That's the reason why it's not recommended that an AA group own property — a meeting room, for instance — or have a large amount in a bank account. It's recommended that an AA group accept *no* money from any individual or group outside AA itself. And a group is not to accept more than five hundred dollars in a year even from an AA member — and that's even in the case of a bequest left to an AA group in a member's will. Keep It Simple seems to work for AA groups as well as individuals, and 'staying poor' seems to work best for AA groups."

"Thanks, John," Richard said. He glanced at his watch. "Is there any other question, or any other old business?"

Ken looked at his watch; they'd already spent the better part of an hour and hadn't even gotten to new business yet. He was seeing a side of AA he hadn't expected at this business meeting.

"Our group service representative has a report on the GSR meeting she attended as part of the intergroup get-together recently," Richard said. "Janey?"

"For newcomers let me say what intergroup is and what your group service representative does," said Janey, a petite woman in her forties.

"*Intergroup* is sort of an association of the individual AA groups in an area. An intergroup usually maintains an answering service for people needing help or wanting information about AA. Ours publishes a newsletter that tells about AA events in our area, things like combined meetings where two or more groups go in together to have covered-dish dinners and things like that. An intergroup also often helps the individual AA groups coordinate their efforts to do things like set up meetings in prisons and the like.

"The *group service representative* — which I am this year — meets with GSR's from other groups at intergroup meetings to talk over the various concerns AA as a whole in the area may be having. GSR's also attend regional AA conferences — again, to talk about common concerns and the good of Alcoholics Anonymous on a regionwide basis."

Janey paused and looked at her notes. "These are some things I learned at the latest intergroup meeting.

"The AA answering service needs some first names and phone numbers. It works this way: when someone calls the AA answering service asking for help, the person answering the phone gets their number and then contacts an AA volunteer in the caller's area. That AA volunteer then calls the person to see if he or she can be helped. The answering service does not give the volunteers' phone numbers to the callers."

There was a chuckle in the room at this; many had visions of being repeatedly called by drunks who had latched on to their home phone numbers.

Janey gave a brief report on the other topics discussed at the last GSR meeting and what they might mean to the Step-by-Step group.

"Thanks, Janey," Richard said when she had finished. "Well, I guess we're ready for new business."

Buddy raised his hand. "I'd like to see if we could offer a thirty-day chip for people who're new in AA. We have chips for ninety days and six and nine months, plus the blue chips for anniversaries, but some groups have started giving out an aluminum chip for the first month of sobriety. I think it would mean a lot to new people."

"Good thought, Buddy," Richard said. "Let's hear from the group."

Tom spoke up again. "I know that a lot of groups have started giving out the thirty-day chip," he said, "but I'm not convinced it's such a good idea." Ken knew that Tom was Buddy's sponsor; he thought that Buddy looked disappointed at Tom's disagreement with his proposal.

"A lot of people can 'pull a sober' for thirty days," Tom went on. "That's what my first sponsor called stopping for a short time — pulling a sober, rather than pulling a drunk.

"If a person stays sober for three months, he's got a pretty good start on recovery. But thirty days — it seems to me that a lot of people would white-knuckle thirty days, get the chip thinking they'd really done something, then go get drunk."

Laura raised her hand. "It really meant a lot to me when I made my first month sober," she said. "I think I'd have been really encouraged to have been able to pick up a thirty-day chip."

"But you didn't take a drink," Tom said to her with a smile. "The white chip, the one that gets a person started, is the most important one. I don't think it hurts a person to hang in there for three months to get the next chip."

Ken found his own hand in the air. "I think chips are very important, especially for new people," he said. "When I had to go through treatment after my big relapse, it would've meant a lot to be able to get a chip right after being discharged."

"I agree with Tom," Wade said. Ken had thought that maybe having his closed-meeting idea shot down might've quieted

Wade, but evidently the effect had only been temporary.

"I think that if we have thirty-day chips," Wade said, "we'd just have a bunch of people bouncing into and out of AA, accumulating a drawerful of the damn things." Wade's voice was abrasively hostile; *he was still smarting over the closed-meeting issue,* Ken reckoned.

"Nowhere in the Big Book," said Frank, shaking his smooth, bald head slowly for emphasis, "does it say anything about chips, at least to my knowledge." Thickset Frank had a smug tone, and Ken began to feel very irritated.

"We have a chip system that's been working for years," intoned big, silver-haired Chet, his hands folded across his big belly. "If it ain't broke, don't fix it."

Richard looked around the room. "Does anyone else have anything they'd like to add about the idea of thirty-day chips?" No one responded, and Richard said, "Buddy, would you like to make the motion that we begin giving out thirty-day chips?"

"I, uh, move that we start giving out thirty-day chips," Buddy said. He looked and sounded as if he wished he hadn't brought up the idea in the first place.

"Do we have a second?" Richard asked.

"I second," Ken said.

"All in favor?"

Ken raised his hand and he noticed that there were a lot of other hands up also.

"Opposed?" Fewer hands this time — Wade and Chet and Frank and old Tom and little Wylie.

"The motion carries," Richard said after he and Annette both counted hands and agreed on the numbers. "John, can you see about getting us some of those aluminum chips?"

John nodded and made himself a note. Wade got up, his face red, and walked out, closing the door a little harder than was absolutely necessary. A few people exchanged glances, but no one said anything about Wade's early departure.

"More new business?" Richard asked.

"Yes," Annette said. "The nonsmoking meeting?"

"Oh, right. Well, I guess first we ought to discuss which meeting or meetings we'd be declaring nonsmoking. What were your ideas on that, Annette?"

"I was thinking of the speaker's meeting on Wednesday night, when we have the largest crowds and the smoke is the thickest."

"I don't think that's such a good idea," said Henry in his Brooklyn accent. His words came out in a torrent. "The speaker meeting is when we get a lot of newcomers. Some of them are trying to put together their first day or two without a drink. Telling them they can't smoke would stress them a lot; a lot of them wouldn't stay for the meeting."

"What meeting, then?" Richard asked.

"What about the Big Book study group on Sunday mornings?" Janey asked.

"I don't think trying to stop smoking at *any* AA meeting is a good idea," said Brad. His pipe sent curls of smoke around his white hair. "I mean, drinking coffee and smoking — how much more traditional can you get when it comes to AA?"

"A lot of people are more health conscious today," Annette said. "Alcoholics included. Breathing someone else's smoke is almost as unhealthy as smoking yourself."

"I don't think that breathing a little smoke for an hour at a time is going to send anyone to an early grave," Brad said with a laugh that was as much snort as chuckle.

Richard looked around the room again. "Maybe we could get some input from people we haven't heard from yet," he suggested.

"Well, I'm not a smoker," said Doris, who was usually quiet. "I sometimes get a sore throat as well as burning eyes from the smoke at meetings, depending on where I'm sitting and who's sitting near me.

"But the thing that bothers me worst is my clothes. When I come home from a meeting, I have to hang the clothes I've been wearing outside. None of my family smokes, and the smell on my clothes is so strong that it bothers everyone." She paused.

"But. . .I can't honestly say that I think we ought to tell people they *can't* smoke. I mean, if a person's a smoker and trying to quit drinking, trying not to smoke at the same time would be maybe too much extra stress."

"Thanks, Doris," Richard said, looking around the room. "Fran, did I see your hand up?"

"Yes," Fran said. She was a slightly older version of Annette, with the same short, dark hair and small frame.

"I think that tobacco is an addictive drug, just like alcohol," Fran said. "Granted, it doesn't make people do the crazy things we do when we're drinking, but there're some treatment centers now that insist on abstinence from tobacco as well as from alcohol and other drugs when a person comes in for chemical dependency treatment.

"I don't think there'd be anything wrong with asking people to not smoke during a meeting. After all, we're not asking them to quit, just abstain for an hour or so."

"I don't care what the treatment centers are doing," said Brad. "You start telling people they can't smoke, and they'll start staying away in droves." Brad, like some of the other older members, was not known for his admiration for treatment centers.

"Well, is it time to ask for a motion?" Richard said.

"I move that we declare the Wednesday night speaker meeting a nonsmoking meeting," Annette said.

"I second the motion," Fran said.

"All in favor, please raise your hands," Richard said.

Only Annette and Fran raised their hands.

"All opposed, the same."

Most of the group raised their hands, Brad the first among them. A few members abstained from voting.

"The motion does not carry," Richard said. "Does anyone have another motion regarding a nonsmoking meeting?" No one did.

"I have a thought," Richard offered. "Since Wednesday nights seem to be the worst for smoke, that night we could ask people to try to keep their smoking to a minimum, to try and not smoke at all if possible. That would put a sort of courtesy monkey on people's backs."

Brad spoke up promptly. "I move that the person chairing the Wednesday night meeting request that smoking be kept to a minimum,"

"I second the motion," Henry said.

"In favor?" asked Richard. Everyone raised his or her hand. Ken was surprised, to say the least. Brad had gone from a stubborn opponent of a nonsmoking meeting to a supporter of asking people not to smoke.

This business meeting was turning out to be quite a surprise for Ken. He was seeing a different side of some AA members he had thought he knew fairly well. He wasn't altogether pleased with what he was seeing.

Horace, a husky, fiftyish man with thick-lensed glasses and a raspy voice whom Ken didn't know very well, spoke up. "Richard, I think we need to discuss the kind of language we use in meetings. I know we're not a bunch of choirboys or Sunday school teachers, but there was some pretty rough language used in a recent meeting."

"Ah, yes," Richard said, shaking his head. "For the benefit of anyone who wasn't at the speaker meeting a couple of Wednesday nights past, a young man who came from another town to tell his story got a little carried away and used some language that was, let's say, a little more colorful than we're accustomed to hearing in the Step-by-Step group."

"He did indeed," said Phil. "Not only did he use four-letter words, he used a big twelve-letter one that you hear a lot on the street."

"The young man belonged to Narcotics Anonymous as well as AA, I believe," Richard said. "I understand that in NA, the language is sometimes a little more — gritty, shall we say?"

"The guy got all carried away in addition to being nervous," big Joe said. "That was the first time he'd told his story to a group other than his own; he didn't even realize he was using some of the words he laid on us. I was the guy who asked him to come speak to our group. He told me afterward that he wasn't even aware of saying the words that upset some people. He was really embarrassed; he asked if he should come back and apologize to our group. I told him, no. I told him —" Joe paused to look around, half-defensively, half-challengingly — "I told him that not only had most of us *heard* that kind of language before, most of us had *used* it at one time or another, at least when we were drinking."

"I still don't think it's right," Horace said. "There were husbands who'd brought their wives to that meeting; one lady had her eleven-year-old daughter there. I wouldn't want my wife and family to have to listen to that kind of language."

"You mean you never did any cussing and carrying on around your family when you were drinking, Horace?" big Joe asked with a grin.

Horace looked at Joe, and Ken could tell that only Joe's six-feet, four-inch height and two-hundred-forty-plus pounds kept Horace from lashing back.

"I still don't think it's right," Horace muttered.

Ken wasn't envying Richard his role as chairperson for this meeting. Ken had already seen more hostility and resentment and anger than he had imagined could exist in an AA group.

"Joe," old Tom spoke up, "I hear what you're saying. Most of us, guys and gals alike, have used our share of colorful and salty talk when we were drinking. I still do, on occasion, although I don't seem to find it necessary as often as I used to.

"But I see Horace's point too. I don't think the kind of talk that young man used at the speaker meeting is appropriate for our meetings."

"I agree," said Phil. "I'm not a goody-two-shoes myself. I was a college student in the sixties when everyone was for expressing their right to free speech by using words that would shock the Establishment.

"Well, I guess now that I'm part of the Establishment, I don't find it necessary, as Tom says, to talk as roughly as I used to.

I've decided that exercising my right to free speech isn't worth the trouble it causes most of the time."

"The young man just forgot himself," said Anna, the most senior of the women present. "He used the street language because he was nervous — I talked to him before the meeting, and he told me about it being his first time to speak in front of a group other than his own.

"Speaking personally, his language didn't offend me, but I can see how some people might be turned off by it."

Having Anna — middle-aged, impeccably groomed, the definition of ladylike — *come to the young man's defense was very effective,* Ken thought, *even more so than big Joe.*

When everyone who wished had given some opinion or thought on the incident of the rough-talking speaker, Richard asked, "Should we have some sort of rule about avoiding the use of offensive language in the future? Can we even define the word *offensive?*"

"I don't think we have a problem in regular discussion meetings," Horace said. "I mean, we hear a 'damn' or 'hell' now and then, but that's nothing you don't hear on network television these days. Maybe if we could just tell the speakers, if they're from outside this group, that we don't like unduly rough or profane or obscene language?..."

"Do you as a group feel this should be done as part of our regular meeting opening, or simply one-on-one between a speaker and someone from this group?" Richard asked.

"I think it could be done one-on-one," Tom said. Murmurs of agreement swept through the room.

"And would we say that the person chairing the Wednesday night speaker meeting would be the one responsible for telling the speaker about this?" Richard asked.

"I think that's reasonable," Joe said. "You can bet your...you can bet that I'll tell speakers I ask from now on!"

A general laugh at this broke much of the tension in the room. "Do we need to have a motion about this?" Richard asked, looking around. No one replied, and he said, "All right, the minutes will just reflect that we talked about this and there was an informal consensus about what we've agreed.

"Any other new business?" Richard asked. No one spoke up, and Ken found himself relieved — it seemed that this meeting was dragging on forever.

"We do have the matter of a slate of officers for the group for the coming year," Richard said. "We're not due to vote on new officers until the next business meeting, but the steering committee has prepared a list of candidates for each position. I'm going to pass out copies of that list to each of you so that you'll have plenty of time to look it over before the next business meeting."

Richard handed a stack of sheets to Joe, who took one and passed them along.

"All of the people on this list have agreed to serve if chosen," Richard added as the copies of the candidate list were passed around the room.

"Just a minute," Henry said suddenly after he had gotten his copy and looked it over briefly. "How come we don't get to choose candidates ourselves? How come this steering committee does that?" Again Ken heard the note of hostility.

"The group does have a chance to choose candidates," Richard said. "At the next meeting we'll give everyone a chance to make nominations for each position."

"Then how come this list?" Henry asked. "And exactly what is this 'steering committee'?"

"I'll answer your last question first," Richard said. "The *steering committee* is a group of five people — by our group conscience those are the group chairperson, the group treasurer, the group secretary, and two other group members. These people are available to make decisions and policy when there isn't time, or when it would be too awkward to call a business meeting of the whole group.

"For instance, last winter our heating unit broke down. John as treasurer is responsible for making purchases and paying for services for the group, but he hesitated at making the decision to spend money to have our old heating unit repaired or buy a new one. He was able to get together with the steering committee in a matter of hours. It was something that *had* to be decided right away, since the weather was below freezing and not only could we not hold meetings with no heat, our plumbing could have frozen and burst.

"To answer your first question — we began preparing a list of people for group offices several years ago when we'd started to get bogged down in the process of nominating candidates.

"Oftentimes, someone would nominate another group member at the business meeting when the nominee wasn't present — we'd have no way of knowing whether the person being nominated would be willing to serve. Sometimes the persons nominated would decline right on the spot, and there'd be no other nominations for that position. It got to be a regular circus at times.

Richard paused and sipped the coffee remaining in his cup, making a slight face, for the coffee had gotten cold.

"So, we had a group conscience decision to have the steering committee get together a list of prospective new group officers. The committee would make sure each person on the list is willing to serve if elected. Then, at the meeting where the actual election takes place, members can either accept the list of persons recommended by the steering committee, or individual members can nominate anyone they choose from the floor for any position. We do ask that if anyone plans on nominating someone from the floor, they make sure that person is willing to serve before nominating them." Richard paused to let all that soak in. "By the way," he added, "the two steering committee members in addition to the group chairperson, treasurer and secretary, are candidates on the list in front of you, too, as you can see." He waited again, then asked, "Does that make sense to you, Henry?"

"Yeah," Henry said. He sounded as if he accepted the practice Richard had just outlined, although he wasn't wildly enthusiastic about it. Ken remembered the brief time he'd worked at a unionized plant as a young man; the union members often seemed to have this sort of generally suspicious attitude. Ken was glad he wasn't in Richard's shoes as chairperson of this meeting. Ken's dislike of having to take part in group decisions was one reason he was now self-employed.

"Any other questions about the list of candidates?" Richard asked.

"Richard," Fran said, "I see only one woman's name on this list of proposed group officers. Why don't we have a female nominated for group chairperson? Or one of the other important offices? The only female's name is beside one of the steering committee positions."

"If you'll notice, Fran, Annette's name is up again for group secretary. But as for your overall question — I'm not sure why there aren't more women's names there. You can nominate any woman you wish when we have the election at the next meeting. Please just make sure that any person you nominate is willing to serve." *Richard handled that well,* Ken thought. The truth was that the Step-by-Step group had more male members than females, and there was undoubtedly a bit of unconscious male chauvinism among the majority. Still, with women like Fran and Annette in the group, the men weren't going to get away with too much in the long run.

"Well, we've gone over a lot of things," Richard said, glancing again at his watch. "It's getting fairly late, but if anyone else has anything they'd like to bring up. . . ."

Ken held his breath; he suddenly wanted to be *out* of this meeting.

No one had anything else. Ken thought the faces of most of the other people in the room looked as relieved as he felt when Richard asked them to join in the Lord's Prayer and the business meeting was over.

Ken hurried out. He noticed that there didn't seem to be the tendency tonight for people to stay after the meeting. Most of the others were quickly heading for their vehicles.

Ken felt some uneasiness about what he'd seen and heard at his first AA business meeting, and perhaps even more uneasiness over some of the feelings he'd had.

He'd come to see Alcoholics Anonymous meetings as a place to escape the everyday pressures and conflicts of the outside world, with its competition and stress and ill-will among people. But at the business meeting of the Step-by-Step group, he'd seen ego running riot, anger, resentment — all things he'd come to see as detrimental to sobriety and serenity.

Ken did what he'd learned, the hard way, to do when something was bothering him — he called his sponsor. As it happened, his sponsor, having been the chairperson, was in a good position to understand Ken's feelings about the business meeting.

"So the business meeting shook you a little?" Richard asked. He'd stopped off at Ken's auto repair shop. The workday was over, at least as far as the shop being open to the public; Ken and Richard sat in two battered chairs in Ken's little box of an office in one corner of the shop. An old automatic coffee maker on top of Ken's file cabinet wafted aromatic steam into the air.

"I wished, after it was over, that I hadn't even attended," Ken said.

"I understand," Richard replied. "There were times when I wished I hadn't agreed to be the group chairperson.

"Still, it's a necessary part of really belonging to an AA group. It's kind of like sticking with your family even when its members aren't getting along very well."

"But I've never heard the arguing and anger and all in regular AA meetings," Ken said.

"Believe it or not, Ken, not every business meeting is like the one last night. The Step-by-Step group's business meetings, more often than not, go pretty smoothly."

"I couldn't believe all the sensitive-ego business last night," Ken said. "And I can't get over how different some of the members seemed last night from what I'd thought they were really like."

Ken brought Richard a cup of coffee. "I guess it has to do with AA's primary purpose," Richard said. He sipped thoughtfully on his coffee and continued. "At regular meetings, we're there to try to stay sober and help other alcoholics. But the aims of business meetings are a little different, at least in the short run. Business meetings are about group decisions and whose way of doing things is better, and about who gets listened to. There's built-in potential for friction in those circumstances."

"But. . ." Ken didn't know exactly how to say what was bothering him. "It seems that I hear people in AA meetings *talking* about practicing AA principles in all their affairs, but some of those same people didn't seem to be practicing AA principles last night."

Richard stroked his beard. "It says in 'How It Works' that 'no one among us has been able to maintain anything like perfect adherence to these principles.' Right after that it says, 'We are not saints.' "*

"I know," Ken said. "I guess the fact that I got angry and resentful along with some of the others bothers me as much as anything."

"Tell me about it."

"Well, when Wade got angry and walked out of the meeting like a spoiled kid, I felt like going after him and telling him what I thought of him, if not worse."

Richard sighed. "Wade's a sort of special case, not because of his argumentativeness, but the lengths to which he carries it."

---

*From *Alcoholics Anonymous*, 3rd ed. (New York: Alcoholics Anonymous World Services, Inc., 1976), 60.

Richard paused. "I don't approve of gossip about AA members, but it's hardly a secret that Wade has jumped from one AA group to another all over the area in the last few years.

"It seems to be a pattern with him. He'll join a group, take part in group activities for a while, then get angry over something or other and stalk off and join another AA group."

"He's been sober quite a few years, hasn't he?" Ken said.

"Let's say that he hasn't apparently done any drinking for a time," Richard said. "The distinction between being sober and being dry probably applies in Wade's case."

"I wonder how he manages not to drink?" Ken said. "I think that if I was as angry all the time as Wade seems to be, I'd probably end up on another drunk."

"Anger seems to be a sort of drug in itself to some people," Richard observed. "Being angry changes the body's chemistry. If a person's depressed, getting angry can temporarily relieve the depressed feelings. I emphasize the word *temporarily;* the problems from chronic anger accumulate just like the problems from alcoholic drinking."

"Now that you mention it, I've caught myself almost deliberately getting angry sometimes when I've felt down," Ken said.

"I don't have any scientific proof of this," Richard said. "But I suspect there are people who get hooked on their own anger, using it like a drug to deal with other feelings they don't feel equipped to handle."

"Well, at least there won't be another business meeting for three months," Ken said.

"Yes, there's that." Richard laughed.

"To be honest with you," Ken said, "I may not attend the next one. Not if there's likely to be the kind of ill-humor and friction I saw at this one."

"Well, that's your choice, Ken," Richard said. "But remember the sign that hangs over the chairperson's desk in the meeting room? It says, 'When anyone, anywhere, reaches out for help, I want the hand of AA always to be there. And for that: I am responsible.'"

"I figured that meant talking to people who are trying to get sober and greeting new people at meetings, stuff like that," Ken said.

"It also means being part of an AA group and helping that AA group survive and thrive. Sure, talking to drunks trying to get sober is important, and greeting newcomers is important, as is telling our stories and sharing our experience, strength, and hope at discussion meetings. But...," Richard said, pausing to give his next words added emphasis, "so are the down-to-earth, nitty-gritty kinds of things.

"Things like a place to hold a meeting, electricity for light and heat in the winter and coffee and AA literature and all the rest of the simple, physical stuff. That kind of thing isn't what we deal with at regular meetings, where we say our primary purpose is our own and others' sobriety. A regular meeting isn't the place to talk about things like who's going to keep the meeting room clean. But at some point we have to concern ourselves with such things if we're going to be able to continue to meet."

"I see your point," Ken said. "I guess I hadn't looked at it quite that way."

"Incidentally, one of the guys who's the most argumentative is also one who does at least half the janitorial work for the meeting room — for no pay, of course, strictly as a volunteer."

"No kidding?"

"Yes — old Brad, with his snide remarks about 'real' AA members. He comes in at least twice a month, strictly of his own volition, and vacuums the meeting room and cleans the toilets, dusts everything, washes out the ashtrays. He's been doing it for a long time, with no complaint and no bragging and no demand for recognition."

"That puts him in a different light," Ken said.

"And Wade — as crotchety and irritable as he is — he's done a lot of Twelfth Stepping, volunteering for the Intergroup answering service. He's probably talked to hundreds of drunks on the phone in his time."

143

"So maybe I'm being a little judgmental, eh?"

"It's human," Richard said.

"I guess this kind of thing goes on in every AA group, then, at business meetings."

"Well, it depends on what kind of business meetings AA groups hold. Some groups don't even bother to have separate meetings to discuss business matters. They just take a few minutes before, after, or even during a regular meeting to decide who's going to chair which meeting, or whatever. Some groups may schedule a short business meeting on a monthly or quarterly basis that way; others just hold a business meeting whenever they feel one's needed."

"That sounds like a pretty good idea," Ken said.

Richard adjusted his glasses, then continued. "Well, if you have a group that meets in a church, say, or in some other place where the only responsibility to the landlord is to straighten up after meetings, that informal kind of business meeting can work out all right.

"But the Step-by-Step group leases its meeting room, like a private business might lease office space. We're responsible for paying each of the utilities and the rent, buying supplies, performing janitor service, replacing locks...."

"Replacing locks?"

"Yes." Richard grinned wryly. "It's a fairly regular thing. The persons chairing the individual meetings have to be given keys to the meeting room, right? If they have to be late, or absent, then they have to get someone else to take over the meeting. So they pass the key along to that person, who may or may not remember to return it.

"After a while, we have a lot of keys out and we don't know who's in possession of all of them. So, we change the locks and start over."

"It's becoming obvious to me that there's more to being a member of an AA group than just showing up at meetings and shaking hands and helping clean the coffeepot," Ken said.

"Right. It means taking on duties as a group officer when we're asked — something I didn't particularly want to do when the steering committee asked me last year about being group chairperson. But AA has given me life; I feel I should give something back."

Ken arched a brow. "The Step-by-Step group waits until people have some length of sobriety before asking them to be officers and chair meetings and so forth, right?"

"Right. A couple of reasons for that: One, we don't want to give a newly sober person too much to handle at first — just staying off the booze can be a full-time job in the beginning. And two, we need, realistically, to see if a person's going to stay sober before we start relying on that person."

"Well, I guess I'll come to the next business meeting, then," Ken said, "even if I have to do a little bit of tooth-gritting beforehand.

"I was like you," Richard said. "I was shocked the first time I heard members yelling a little at each other at my first business meeting. But since then I've learned that being a part of an AA family may mean dealing with some conflict once in a while. I have to deal with conflict without drinking in my everyday life sometimes, anyway, as part of my recovery. Dealing with a little of it in AA is good practice."

They finished their coffee, and Richard left shortly thereafter. Ken thought about what Richard had said about AA family. At this point in his life, separated from his wife, living alone, Ken needed all the family he could get. He thought about some of the royal fights he and his wife Mary had had while he was drinking. He compared those to the bit of rancor he'd witnessed at the business meeting the previous night. He had to admit that the business meeting had been mild by comparison.

Ken realized that he'd probably come to a new point in his relationship with Alcoholics Anonymous. He was now seeing AA for what it really is: A group of individual men and women sharing their experience, strength, and hope. A group that acknowledges freely that its members aren't saints, aren't perfect. A group that acknowledges while not everyone is going to like everyone else, there is a special kind of love of one alcoholic for another that is a strong adhesive, holding AA together.

The No-Addict Watchdogs

Joel's cramped office was in what had once been a storage room at the end of Skid Row.

The detox hall's official name was the Detoxification Unit. But some irreverent patient in the past had nicknamed it Skid Row, and the name had been passed along until it was now more or less accepted, even by the treatment center's administration.

Robbie had spent his first five days at the treatment center on Skid Row going through primary withdrawal. During this time, he'd learned he was at some risk of a seizure or convulsion or other such unpleasantness associated with stopping alcohol and other drug use. He'd since been moved to one of the regular rooms, of course. But since his assigned counselor had an office at the end of Skid Row, Robbie had returned here often during the almost six weeks he'd been in treatment.

"Come in, man," Joel said when Robbie tapped on the half-open door and stuck his head around it. "Got your aftercare plan yet?" Joel added in a tone that suggested he expected a yes.

Robbie hadn't liked Joel at first. To be honest, Robbie had, at times, hated the wiry, fortyish man, whose appearance was a curious blend of aging hippie and gym coach. Now Robbie considered Joel as much a friend as a counselor, although Robbie was careful to not let this get in the way when Joel was wearing his counselor's hat.

Robbie floated the paper clipped sheets of his aftercare plan down on top of the other papers that covered every inch of Joel's desk. Joel's office always looked as if a minor clerical disaster had just taken place. Stacks of files, legal pads with Joel's crooked handwriting on them, piles of professional journals and books on addiction and treatment and family dysfunction and recovery — all were jumbled together. Joel, nevertheless, moved effortlessly through the seemingly hopeless disorder.

"Umm," Joel grunted as he looked over Robbie's aftercare plan. Joel wore half-glasses for reading, and he tilted his head back a little to catch Robbie's work in them. Joel's hair was long enough to be caught in a ponytail at the nape of his neck. He wore a big mustache that covered his whole mouth and drooped like a tragedy mask at the corners. From the neck down, however, he had none of the old-druggie look. His compact, muscular physique wouldn't have embarrassed a Marine drill instructor.

"Looks pretty good," Joel said as he turned the pages of Robbie's *aftercare plan,* the method by which Robbie planned to stay clean and sober after his discharge from treatment tomorrow.

"So what's lacking?" Robbie asked. He'd come to know Joel well enough to sense the difference between when Joel was pleased with something and when he was underwhelmed.

"I notice you listed Narcotics Anonymous as your number-one support group," Joel said.

"Sure." Robbie shrugged. "I'm an addict, right?" He shifted his lanky frame in the chair across the desk from Joel. Robbie was twenty-five, tall and thin, with a bony but handsome face and shaggy blonde hair. He wore the unofficial "uniform" of the treatment center — jeans, T-shirt, and athletic shoes.

"Right," Joel said. "But I see that you're going to be staying with your parents for a while. They live in a small town, and I'm pretty sure there isn't a Narcotics Anonymous group there.

The nearest one's fifty miles away, here in the city, and you don't have a driver's license at present."

"Well, I'll go to AA when I can't get to NA meetings," Robbie said. He hated to be reminded of the loss of his driving privileges.

"Why did you list NA as your first choice?" Joel asked. "Haven't I heard you say that alcohol was usually your favorite mood-changer?"

"Well, sure," Robbie said. "But it was cocaine that got me all screwed up financially, and I smoked grass all during high school and screwed up my grades. And it was grass that got me the possession charge too."

"Uh-hmm," Joel said with what Robbie recognized as a "gotcha" expression on his face. "And you think Narcotics Anonymous is a lot cooler than AA, right?"

"No, I . . ." Robbie stopped. He'd learned a few things in the last forty-one days about honesty. "Okay," he admitted, "that's got something to do with it. I mean, there are a lot of old guys in AA. The people in Narcotics Anonymous are younger, and —"

"And more hip, right?" Joel interrupted. "And there're more chicks in NA, and NA's hug instead of shaking hands — I know all about that, pal."

"So what's wrong with those things?" Robbie asked. "There's nothing wrong with enjoying going to meetings, is there?"

"Nothing wrong with enjoyment, but enjoyment's not the reason you should be going."

"*You* go to NA," Robbie pointed out.

"Sure — because there're several NA meetings right here in the city. I also go to Alcoholics Anonymous meetings; I belong to AA as well as NA."

"But I've had problems with drugs other than alcohol," Robbie persisted.

"Don't misunderstand me," Joel said. "I think Narcotics Anonymous is great; NA has saved a lot of chemically dependent people. But belonging only to NA has some limitations, especially for people like yourself."

"Such as?"

"One — NA hasn't been around as long as Alcoholics Anonymous, and it isn't in as many places as AA. Like your parents' hometown, for instance.

"Two — On the average, NA members don't tend to have as much length of recovery as AA members. It's not unusual to find AA members with ten or fifteen or more years of sobriety. In some NA groups, a person with a year's clean and sober time is an 'old-timer.'

"Three — NA and Al-Anon and Overeaters Anonymous and Gamblers Anonymous and other groups have borrowed the Twelve Steps of Alcoholics Anonymous and adapted them. When you go to AA, you go to the source."

"I know," Robbie muttered.

"But?"

"But AA seems so — *dry* — or something."

"You mean they don't use the latest slang and street talk, and they don't use the colorful four-letter words as often as you sometimes hear them in Narcotics Anonymous, right?"

"Well, that's one thing," Robbie said. "I mean, a person should be free to express himself."

Joel sighed.

"I'm going to pull an old-guy number on you," he said. "There've been some people over the centuries who've done a pretty fair job of expressing themselves with hardly a word of street talk — William Shakespeare comes to mind among others. Street talk can be just buzzwords, a way of talking without really saying anything.

"You've heard me use some pretty salty language on occasion, I admit. But I found early in my recovery that the four-letter words were most likely to pop out of my mouth when I was on some kind of ego trip or resentment binge or self-pity party."

Robbie thought about this. "I guess I see your point," he said. "I can make myself angry just by going into a big-time cussing mode."

"There you are," Joel said. "And AA's aren't goody-two-shoes people. Most of them have used, as well as heard, most of the street words. It's just that they don't usually choose to use that kind of language in meetings. And being able to choose is a big part of what recovery is all about."

"Okay, okay," Robbie said, throwing up his hands in mock defeat. "I hear what you're saying — I'll go to AA."

To his surprise, Joel didn't fall into a lighthearted mood.

"I'm serious about this, Robbie," he said. "I've seen a negative attitude toward Alcoholics Anonymous get a lot of multi-addicted people back out into the weeds."

"But I'm *not* just an alcoholic," Robbie said. "I consider myself powerless over marijuana and cocaine and uppers and downers — all drugs, not just booze."

"Good," Joel said. "But that's not the test for AA membership. AA doesn't require you to not be powerless over drugs other than alcohol. It just asks that you have a desire to stop drinking."

"Well, I have that," Robbie said. "Or, the desire to not *start* drinking again."

Robbie knew that his voice sounded sincere, and he was, in fact, sincere. But he also knew that a part of him was wanting to say what Joel wanted to hear so this session with his counselor could end.

Joel sat slouched comfortably on the other side of the desk, studying Robbie's face over the tops of the half-glasses. "All right," he said at last. "Tomorrow you go back into the real world. We'll see what we'll see."

And with that, the session was over. Robbie went back down Skid Row, past the nurse's station, and down the hallway of the men's section. He felt uneasy. He'd done a bit of complying with Joel at the last, saying what he thought his counselor wanted to hear rather than what he fully accepted himself. He had the feeling that he hadn't gotten away with anything.

Everyone who'd been at the Step-by-Step group's last business meeting was greatly relieved at how smoothly this one was going.

The last business meeting had seen members snapping at each other, one walking out in anger. This meeting had thus far gone so smoothly that in forty-five minutes almost all the necessary items of business had been taken care of, including election of group officers for the coming year.

"Is there any more business?" Richard asked. He was the chairperson for this business meeting.

"I think there's something we ought to discuss before we close," said Brad. One of the group's oldest members, Brad had been one of the most argumentative at the last business meeting.

"We're getting a lot of new people coming into meetings," Brad said. "A lot of them are from *treatment centers* —" He mouthed the term as if it had a slightly bad taste. "And I guess a lot of them have done drugs. I suspect that some of them don't even have a problem with alcohol. I think we ought to have some sort of policy about 'drug addicts' at our meetings."

"What kind of policy are we talking about?" asked big Joe. With his long hair and beard and cycle clothes, Joe had the look of a man who, while he'd certainly done his share of drinking, wouldn't have turned up his nose at other drugs in his pre-AA days.

"I think we need to make it clear that we stick to AA principles regarding people who have problems other than alcohol," Brad said.

Phil, dressed in a business suit in stark contrast to Joe, spoke up. "We say in the opening of our meetings that our primary purpose is to stay sober and help other alcoholics achieve sobriety. Isn't that sufficient?"

"Well, I'm not so sure," Brad said. "Some of these new people coming in may not even *be* alcoholics."

"Very few people who don't have a problem with booze show up at Alcoholics Anonymous meetings," Annette, the group secretary, observed dryly.

There were some chuckles in the room at this comment, and Brad's face grew a little red.

"My point is that we need to stick to AA's primary purpose," Brad said doggedly. "We're not here to help people with marijuana problems, or heroin problems, or cocaine problems. There's Narcotics Anonymous for that."

"That's right," spoke up Chet, another older group member.

"I agree with Brad," said tiny, deep-voiced Wylie.

"There's no NA meeting for fifty miles," big Joe said. He was probably one of the few people in the room aware of that fact. "What do we do, just tell people to go try to make it on their own?"

"We need to stick to our guns," Brad said. "We're responsible for seeing that AA doesn't get overrun with every Tom, Dick, and Harry who has some other kind of problem."

"Is it really that big a problem here?" Phil asked.

"It *could* be," Brad said ominously.

"Well," Richard said, breaking in, "let's hear from some of the other members of the group. Tom?"

"I don't think it's a problem now," Tom said, "but I think Brad has a point." Tom was about Brad's age, and his years in AA and his low-key common sense made people listen to him. "We need to make it clear that we're here to stop drinking and stay sober. Now, it doesn't matter if a person has other problems; the early AA members decided that if a person wanted help in staying sober, no matter what other problems he had, he wouldn't be turned away."

To Richard's surprise, quiet young Buddy raised his hand.

"I'd hate for anyone to feel unwelcome in AA," Buddy said. "The problem that got me to AA was my drinking, but I fooled around with pot and other drugs some too. Alcohol was always my favorite high, but I know I can't safely use any other drug."

"We're not saying we wouldn't welcome a person who's used other things as well as alcohol," Tom said. "We're just saying that at an AA meeting, our purpose is to stay sober and help others who want to stop drinking. It simply means that we don't talk about problems other than alcohol and staying sober at AA meetings."

There were a few more comments from various members, some for sticking to AA's primary purpose and others for not simply rejecting people because they had additional problems.

Finally, Richard said, "Well, do we need to have a motion to do something different than what we're doing now?"

Brad spoke up. "I move that we have a statement at the opening of each meeting that people should confine themselves to remarks concerning alcoholism."

"I think we should add, 'And to problems with living sober,'" Buddy said.

"How do you feel about that?" Richard asked Brad.

"Sounds all right," Brad said.

"Okay, let's say that we have a motion to have each meeting chairperson read a statement at the beginning of each meeting. It would read, 'Persons should confine their discussion and comments to problems pertaining to alcoholism and living sober.' Is that acceptable as a motion?" No one disagreed. "Is there a second to that motion?"

Phil seconded it. A show of hands passed the motion almost unanimously. Only big Joe abstained from voting. There being no further business, Richard closed the meeting.

The bronze medallion, the size of a half-dollar, felt heavy in Robbie's hand. On one side there was an engraving of a butterfly, on the other the words *freedom* and *growth*. Robbie leaned down for C. J.'s hug after she presented him with the medallion. C. J. wasn't much over five feet tall, a middle-aged woman who reminded Robbie of his fifth-grade teacher.

An exceptional woman, C. J. handled the job of director of the treatment center with the finesse of a diplomat and the strength of a staff sergeant.

"Well, Robbie," C. J. said, "you know by now that it's customary for patients completing treatment to say a few departing words."

"Right," Robbie replied with a nervous grin. He stepped up to the lectern from which C. J. had called him to receive his medallion. The entire patient population had gathered for morning assembly in the treatment center's big main meeting room.

"It's been forty-two days since I came through the front door of this place," Robbie said to the thirty-odd patients. "I won't say 'walked through' the front door," he added. "More like lurched — I'd had a six-pack and a couple of joints on the way here to keep my courage up."

Most of the other patients laughed at this — quite a few of them had entered in more or less the same condition.

"I didn't have the slightest idea of what to expect," Robbie went on. "That's why I had to get ripped before I had nerve enough to come here in the first place.

"For my first week here I was in a pretty dense fog. I do remember wanting to leave, really bad. The staff persuaded me to stay; I'm glad they did."

Some of the faces looking back at him this morning were those of friends, people to whom in his stay here he'd become closer than to almost anyone else in his life.

Other faces held other expressions — some had that sleepy, dopey look he knew he'd had during detoxification; others held defiant expressions that suggested the denial and resentment common for newcomers in treatment for chemical dependency.

"In my second week," Robbie said, "I was into denial in a big way. After all, I'd only drunk some beer and liquor and smoked some weed and popped a few pills and done a line now and then.

"But after that second week, I began to see that what I'd believed were just good-time, partying kinds of drinking and using were actually robbing me of the most valuable thing I owned — myself."

Robbie knew that some of these patients would never grasp the seriousness of chemical dependency, at least as it applied to themselves. Others might, eventually, but only after having to do more drinking and using to prove their addictions to themselves.

He almost hadn't gotten hold of the idea himself. He'd begun complying with the treatment center's program in his second week, telling himself he was using good sense in following his attorney's advice. He'd put in his time in treatment to favorably impress the judge when it came time to receive his sentence for driving while impaired and possession of a controlled substance.

But the program had, it seemed, taken hold of him before he took hold of it. He'd slowly but surely begun to see the truth of how alcohol and other drugs were taking him down a dead-end road.

"I just hope that anyone who's feeling like I did in the beginning will keep an open mind," Robbie said. "Addiction is serious business. I'm so convinced of that, that I've already made arrangements to go to an AA meeting tonight after I get home." He paused for a second, decided he'd said enough, and closed by simply saying, "Thanks to all of you."

All but the newest and most hostile patients applauded. After the assembly was over, Robbie went through the details of being discharged — signing out his valuables, packing his clothes, and saying good-byes to the nurses and counselors. He was excited about going home, but there was a sense of sadness at leaving this place where his life had so radically changed.

His father was waiting for him in the front lobby at 11:00 A.M., discharge time.

Robbie saw his father in a different light now, after the center's Family Week program. Robbie had been amazed when his father actually took a week off from his successful real estate business to take part in the five-day program for family members.

Robbie had always seen his tall, distinguished father as a sort of benevolent dictator, a man who was pleasant enough most of the time but who'd had little time for his children as they grew up. Now Robbie knew that his father's compulsive work habits had similarities to an addiction, to Robbie's chemical dependency.

His father held out his hand as Robbie approached, but Robbie stepped past the hand and embraced his father. After an instant of stiffness, surprise at this uncharacteristic gesture on the part of his son, his father returned the hug, beating Robbie on the back in the way of males showing affection.

In his father's new Cadillac — his father bought one every year — the ride home was smooth and silently pleasant. The silence extended to father and son; Family Week had opened some lines of communication, but years of gradually growing apart weren't to be overcome immediately.

It was just under an hour's drive from the city to the small town and his parents' home on the quiet, tree-lined street. A solid brick house, it was as respectable and discreetly prosperous in appearance as Robbie's parents themselves.

His mother met them, trying, Robbie knew, not to make a fuss over him. His mother still had a youthful attractiveness despite the grey in her dark-blonde hair and the lines in her face. She was still as slender as either of his sisters, and her clothes had the tasteful, low-key elegance befitting the wife of a successful businessman and pillar of the community. Robbie could imagine only too well how his drinking and other drug use and legal troubles must have shamed his parents.

His mother had refused to let Mrs. Thompson, the housekeeper, make lunch for her menfolk on this special day. She prepared the meal herself, and made an obvious effort to avoid hovering over Robbie as he ate. Robbie was grateful for his parents' welcome and their interest in him. But he was also grateful when lunch was over and he could gracefully escape to be alone for a while.

He went out to the big garage behind the house and found his ten-speed bike at the rear, among the odds and ends accumulated over the years of three children growing up. He might buy a moped — a "drunkmobile," he'd heard such a vehicle called by others in treatment — for the year he'd be without his driver's license. To buy a moped, however, he'd have to get a job and earn some money; he would not ask his parents for a loan. For now, though, the trusty old bicycle would get him around the neighborhood and downtown to AA meetings.

It had been an inevitable and unfortunate chain of events. He'd cracked up his new Camaro; this had led to the highway patrol's discovery that he was driving while impaired; this had led to the search of his car and discovery of the marijuana. He'd told himself many times how lucky he'd been that it had been grass and not coke; now he tried not to beat himself up with guilt and anger as he pumped up the bike's tires and checked it over.

One tire needed replacing. His father had gone back to his real estate office after lunch, and Robbie had to ask his mother to take him to the bicycle shop to get a new tire. Back at the house, he spent the rest of the afternoon replacing the tire and going over the bike with an oilcan and adjusting tools.

That evening, he politely but firmly refused his parents' offer to take him to the AA meeting. It took him less than twenty minutes' riding time to reach the room behind the office building on Main Street, where the Step-by-Step group of Alcoholics Anonymous met.

He chained his bike to the lifting handles of the big Dumpster that squatted in the alley near the door to the basement meeting room. The ten-speed looked absurdly spindly and kidlike beside the big Harley-Davidson motorcycle parked near the door.

Inside the meeting room, he found a couple of dozen people talking, drinking coffee, and smoking.

"Hi," said a young man about Robbie's age. "My name's Buddy," he added, sticking out a strong, callused hand.

Robbie introduced himself and said he was just out of treatment.

"Glad you came your first night home," Buddy said.

"Is this a speaker meeting, or discussion, or what?" Robbie asked.

"This is the men's discussion meeting," Buddy said. "The gals have a women-only meeting on Thursday nights. Tomorrow night is the speaker meeting."

Robbie now realized that all the people in the room were males. They seemed to be of just about all descriptions.

He and Buddy went over to the ever-present AA coffeepot and Robbie smiled to himself as he filled his cup to the brim. It had been a joke at the treatment center that the most powerful appeal of off-premises AA meetings was the "real" coffee; the treatment center served only the decaffeinated variety to the patients.

Buddy continued with his listing of the group's meetings: "Fridays we have a Step meeting; Saturday night is a regular general discussion meeting; Sunday morning there is a Big Book study group — we alternate between the Big Book and the Twelve and Twelve."

"I know what the Big Book is," Robbie said. "What's the Twelve and Twelve?" He'd been given a copy of *Alcoholics Anonymous*, what most AA members called the Big Book, while in treatment.

''*Twelve Steps and Twelve Traditions*,'' Buddy said. "It's a detailed look at each Step and Tradition. You can buy a copy here any time you want. If you don't have ready cash, the group will let you have it anyway, and you can pay for it when you get the money."

As he assured Buddy he'd be able to pay for the book, Robbie thought that so far things were looking all right as far as AA was concerned. He'd be able to attend a meeting every night except Mondays and Thursdays. The bike ride was short and pleasant enough.

A thin, rather unhealthy-looking man named John chaired the men's meeting tonight. As part of the opening, John said, "We ask that everyone who takes part in the meeting confine his discussion to problems with alcoholism and living sober."

After going through the opening, John asked, "Do we have any visitors or newcomers tonight?"

Robbie raised his hand and said, "I'm Robbie." After a second's hesitation from the group they said, "Hi, Robbie," in unison. Robbie realized that he'd forgotten to identify himself further after giving his first name. The question of his status — alcoholic or addict — was for the time being taken care of through omission.

"We're glad you're here, Robbie," John said. "Is this your hometown?"

"My folks live here," Robbie said. "I just got out of treatment this morning."

"Good for you, making a meeting so soon," John said. "Well, does anyone have a topic or problem for discussion?"

Typically, no one did. "Well," John said, "I was thinking on the way to the meeting about the One Day at a Time business. We talk about it a lot, but it's still a good topic, especially with new people in the meeting."

And with that the discussion began. Robbie found himself truly interested in what the various men called on had to say as they described their personal difficulties with, and strategies for, living in the present. He realized that he'd been doing some projecting ahead mentally to the time when he'd have a job, would know what his sentence was to be, would get his driver's license back. . . .

The year's driver's license suspension was mandatory. He might or might not get "active" jail time. He was, of course, hoping for a minimum sentence, and that suspended.

Sometimes, he felt optimistic — this was his first encounter with the law, and with his having completed treatment for chemical dependency, the judge might well be lenient. At other times, he feared the worst — weeks, perhaps months in jail, at least on weekends under this state's current sentencing practices. And with it, the depression of being locked up, of being treated as a criminal, not to mention the actual risk of being locked up with people who were truly dangerous!

He found it hard to think of himself as a criminal. He'd been extremely lucky that the drug he'd been caught with was marijuana and not cocaine. Like many addicts, he'd helped support his own drug use by some casual dealing to friends and acquaintances. It had seemed harmless enough at the time, and the risk involved had seemed rather romantic. Now he simply felt dumb.

By the end of the meeting, Robbie felt better. No one had said much about alcohol itself. Most of the comments had to do with living a sober life. The choice of drug seemed to be of relatively little importance. Robbie was beginning to realize what Joel had been talking about. He could have as easily been at a Narcotics Anonymous meeting tonight; even the talk, since this was a men-only meeting, had contained enough street language to provide a relaxed atmosphere.

Buddy gave his phone number to Robbie and told him to call anytime he felt he needed or wanted to talk. Buddy also offered Robbie a ride anytime he needed one; he'd seen Robbie's bike when they walked out after the meeting and guessed that Robbie was without driving privileges.

Robbie appreciated Buddy's friendliness. Although Buddy wasn't the kind of guy with whom Robbie would have socialized when he'd been partying, it was nice to know that he'd made a friend in AA.

At the end of the same meeting, big Joe sought out Richard. Richard had known the big man long enough to recognize a troubled look, despite the thick beard that covered most of the lower half of Joe's face. "I've been thinking about this anti-addict business," Joe said. "It's got me a little bit bugged."

"You mean, what happened at the business meeting last night?"

"Yeah. You know as well as I do, Richard, that there are damn few people under the age of thirty coming into AA who haven't used other drugs besides alcohol."

"That's true," Richard admitted. As a college professor, he was all too aware of the drug-using habits of young adults, in addition to his own experience with chemical dependency.

"If we have some kind of tough anti-addict attitude," Joe said, raking his hand through his hair, "we're going to scare off some people who need AA."

"We're simply making it clear that we ask people to stick to topics dealing with alcoholism at our meetings." Richard shrugged. "Surely that isn't too hard-nosed, is it?"

"You know how sensitive and thin-skinned people like us are," Joe said. "I'm afraid that what they're going to hear is that we don't want any drug addicts, whether they also have a problem with booze or not."

"That's not what we're saying."

"Isn't it? I don't mean you and me, Richard. But there are people in this group who really *don't* want any drug addicts to attend, no matter what."

Richard was inclined to agree with Joe, but as group chairperson he felt he had to appear impartial. He therefore didn't reply.

"And besides scaring people off, there's another thing that worries me," Joe went on. "We've both known people who were willing to admit to a problem with booze, but who didn't want to give up other drugs, like tranquilizers or marijuana. If we put all this exclusive emphasis on alcohol, and refuse to even mention other drugs, there are people who will take that to mean it's all right for them to do a little drugging, as long as they don't drink."

"I hadn't looked at it just that way," Richard said. "You may have a point. But this is a pretty traditional AA group, Joe. I don't think you'll sell most of the members on that idea."

"What is it with some of these folks, anyway?" Joe asked in frustration. "Do they think that they're going to catch drug addiction by sitting next to somebody who identifies himself as an addict?"

"I doubt that." Richard chuckled. "Although I'll admit there are people who act that way.

"But in the early days of AA, there was a real fear that the Fellowship's primary purpose might get lost in the shuffle of people bringing in other kinds of problems.

"It became obvious pretty quickly to the early AA's that they were onto something good. That was before groups like Al-Anon and Narcotics Anonymous and Gambler's Anonymous and all the other 'anonymouses' adapted the Twelve Steps to their specific problems. The early AA members saw that the *simplicity* of AA, which was probably its greatest strength, could get lost by loading it down with problems other than alcoholism. That's a big part of the reason for the custom of keeping AA strictly for alcoholics."

"I realize that," Joe said. "And I appreciate those concerns. But times have changed. We *do* have the other programs now. And AA itself is well-established, worldwide. So how does it hurt AA for somebody who identifies himself as an 'addict' rather than an 'alcoholic' to speak in discussion meetings? Or at least attend them?"

"On one side of the coin, you're probably right," Richard said. "On the other side, though, since there are now those other programs for other problems, there's no reason why AA shouldn't stick to its original purpose."

"We both know, though, that chemically dependent people can *smell* attitudes," Joe said. "And I'm afraid that there are some people in this group with some pretty narrow-minded attitudes."

163

Wednesday, Robbie spent the day looking through the help wanted ads in the local newspaper and registering at the state employment office in town. His parents certainly weren't pressuring him to go to work, but he felt a need to begin building some independence. Besides, being employed by the time he came up for sentencing wouldn't hurt anything.

Wednesday night, he rode his bike again to the Step-by-Step group's meeting room. Tonight was speaker meeting night, and there was a much larger crowd. He met many new people, including several nice-looking young women.

The speaker was a man named Pete, a little older than Robbie, wearing a wild head of hair that wouldn't have been out of place on a rock musician, and an earring. Pete had come from another town to speak here tonight.

"Part of my story has to do with drugs," Pete said after he'd given a brief sketch of his life up until the time of his first exposure to mood-altering chemicals. "I don't plan to dwell on drugs tonight in telling my story, but they are a part of it. I know that some people in AA don't like to hear about drugs, but if anyone's offended, jump on the guy who asked me to speak, after the meeting."

This little witticism drew some chuckles from people in the audience, but Robbie sensed that Pete hadn't been joking about the fact that some AA's didn't like mention of drugs other than alcohol.

Robbie identified a good deal with Pete's story. Pete's first experience with mood alteration was not with alcohol but with marijuana.

"I smoked dope 'cause I wasn't old enough to drink," Pete quipped, and the crowd laughed. Robbie himself had experienced the irony of finding grass easier to get, as a minor, than it was to buy beer before he was of legal drinking age.

Pete wasn't a world-class speaker, but he said what he had to say in a straightforward manner. Robbie didn't have to pretend enthusiasm as he applauded along with the others when Pete was finished.

After the meeting, Robbie talked with Buddy and Laura and Bonnie and several other members of the Step-by-Step group. He left feeling optimistic about AA and life in general.

Thursday, he answered several ads in the help wanted section and made another trip to the employment office. The day left him feeling tired and frustrated. The jobs he'd inquired about either required training and experience he didn't have, or were low-pay, entry-level jobs.

He'd hoped, of course, to connect with a decent job right away, although common sense had told him that might not happen. It was, he reminded himself, only his second full day out of treatment. He also reminded himself that his drinking and other drug use had kept him from earning his college degree and gaining experience in a better class of job. But this fact didn't make him feel noticeably better.

Thursday night was the women's meeting of the Step-by-Step group, so Robbie stayed home and watched TV.

After another frustrating day of job search on Friday, Robbie was more than ready for the evening's meeting. The Friday night meeting this week was chaired by a man named Brad, who was in his sixties, short, and white-haired. There was a smaller crowd than on Wednesday night. The group was discussing the Ninth Step, the one about making amends to people hurt by the alcoholic's behavior.

It came down to a few minutes before time to close the meeting. Everyone besides Robbie had spoken on the Step under discussion, and Brad called on him.

"I'm Robbie and I'm an alcoholic and addict," he said.

"Hi, Robbie," said most of the people. Robbie noticed Brad didn't join in.

"I don't really have anything to contribute," Robbie said. "I'm new in AA and I haven't gotten to the Ninth Step yet. I'm just glad to be here. Thanks."

Brad went immediately into the closing of the meeting. Robbie felt very uncomfortable. He had the definite feeling he'd committed some sort of blunder.

165

After the meeting, Robbie almost asked Buddy about what had happened, but he couldn't bring himself to admit his uneasiness to the young blue-collar worker.

At the Saturday night general discussion meeting, the chairperson, a woman named Janey, didn't call on Robbie. While there was a larger crowd here than on Friday night, and while he wasn't the only person to not be called on, Robbie couldn't help feeling some resentment that he hadn't been asked to say anything. He told himself that he shouldn't feel as if he'd been deliberately snubbed, but there was the definite suspicion that that was exactly what had happened.

Robbie went to the Sunday morning meeting and was called on to read a passage from *Twelve Steps and Twelve Traditions,* the Twelve and Twelve. This time, when he identified himself as alcoholic and addict, there didn't seem to be negative vibrations in the room; he'd noticed that Brad wasn't here this morning.

The following week started off with the employment office sending Robbie on a job interview. It wasn't a particularly exciting job prospect — a local woodworking shop was looking for a general-purpose worker.

Robbie had done some woodworking in high school shop classes and knew how to operate a table saw and band saw and other common woodworking machines. The shop's owner talked with him and had him fill out an application, but the man didn't seem very enthusiastic. Robbie thought that having listed his college work on the application might have been a mistake — it made him in a sense overqualified for what was an entry-level job. As he left, he told himself that it was no great job anyway, but his ego felt bruised nevertheless.

Tuesday, he went on another job interview, this one for "manager trainee." It turned out to be a job in a fast-food restaurant; "management training" started with filling orders behind the counter, what amounted to kid's work.

By Tuesday evening, he was badly in need of a meeting. He met Buddy when he walked into the Step-by-Step meeting room, and after a few minutes' casual conversation, Buddy said, "Uh, Robbie, I think there's something you ought to know. . . ."

Buddy was clearly uncomfortable with whatever it was he felt he needed to say. "This group. . ." He paused, raking a hand through his hair. "Well, some of the members aren't too fond of the word *addict*. I'm not trying to tell you what to do, but if you could just identify yourself as *alcoholic*. . . ."

"Sure," Robbie heard himself saying, "no problem."

But it was to be a problem. The more he thought about it as the meeting went on, the more his resentment grew — not at Buddy, but at this AA group. Brad was undoubtedly one of the ones who didn't like the word *addict*. Robbie was an alcoholic, he had no doubt of that, but he was also an addict. And who gave these people the right to tell him what to call himself? There was something about the idea that rubbed him very much the wrong way.

That evening he was called on and he identified himself simply as alcoholic, true to his word to Buddy. He didn't feel the uncomfortable undertone he'd sensed in the group when he'd used the word *addict*, but he did still feel irritated. He left as soon as the meeting was over, not stopping to talk to anyone.

Wednesday, Robbie didn't have any scheduled job interviews. He made the rounds of the few manufacturing plants in the area, having to ask his mother to drive him around. He put in applications for production jobs, sitting in personnel offices while secretaries and clerical workers talked among themselves, treating him — "just another job applicant" — as a virtual nonperson.

The speaker at the Wednesday night meeting was a man in his fifties who was a "pure" alcoholic; Robbie knew this because the man made the statement, "Thank God I never got involved with *drugs*." Robbie was sourly amused at the irony of a person who had been addicted to a very dangerous drug — alcohol — saying thanks for never being "involved with drugs."

Thursday, Robbie took a day off from job hunting. He was becoming discouraged with his immediate prospects. Even if he landed a job, it looked as if it would be some menial one.

He thought of his drinking and using days — like a goodly percentage of young adults who used heavily, he'd helped support his own drug use by doing some more or less casual dealing, mostly marijuana, to people he knew. He'd sold coke a few times to trusted acquaintances, but cocaine was a much more dangerous drug to deal than grass.

Even in the casual way he'd done his dealing, he'd made some pretty fair money. Of course, it had gone quickly to support his drug use, but he couldn't help thinking now that he'd made more money just dealing to a few friends than he'd make at most of the jobs it seemed he now had a chance of landing.

This was dangerous thinking, he realized, the old-life kind of thinking. He wished there was an NA meeting within his reach. Members of Narcotics Anonymous would understand the financial as well as mood-changing temptations of the drug scene. This AA group — he could never bring up these kinds of thoughts and feelings at one of *its* meetings.

Friday, he put in a few more job applications. One of the jobs, which would involve working for a small company that made engines for ultralight aircraft, looked more promising than the others. Robbie had always been handy with his hands, and this company was small enough so that a newcomer wouldn't be lost in the crowd, plus the work seemed as if it would be interesting.

At the Friday night meeting, they talked about the Tenth Step. Although Robbie had gone through just the first five Steps while in treatment, Step Ten was enough like his Fourth Step that he felt he had something to contribute. He again identified himself simply as an alcoholic and his few brief comments drew a nod or two of agreement from some of the others at the meeting. He left feeling better about both the day and Alcoholics Anonymous.

Saturday night, the good feelings were abruptly snatched away by an interchange that began between a newcomer and a group member.

The newcomer was a young man about Robbie's age who showed up for the Saturday night meeting.

Bonnie, a woman with reddish-blonde hair, was chairing the meeting. When she asked if anyone had a problem, the newcomer raised his hand.

"I'm Jim and I'm an addict," he said.

"I've been in a really bad place this week," he continued, not seeming to have noticed that no one greeted him. "I almost used this afternoon," he said. "I came this close" — he held up a thumb and forefinger a fraction of an inch apart — "and it scared the hell out of me."

Bonnie was looking extremely uncomfortable behind the chairperson's desk. She'd read the announcement about participants in discussion sticking to topics concerning alcoholism and living sober, but Jim had been in the rest room at the opening of the meeting and had missed this.

"I knew I needed to get to a meeting—" Jim was saying when Brad, who was sitting behind him, broke in.

"I think maybe you're in the wrong place, son," Brad said in his deep voice that carried all too well. "This is *Alcoholics Anonymous*," he said, putting heavy emphasis on *alcoholics*, "and we're here to not drink liquor. If you have a drug problem, you need to go somewhere else, like maybe Narcotics Anonymous."

There was an embarrassed silence in the room. Robbie was appalled. Despite his experience with the Step-by-Step group's general attitude toward drugs other than alcohol, he'd never expected to hear someone put down in public, the way Brad had put down Jim.

In treatment, it had been virtually drilled into Robbie and his fellow patients that going to a meeting was perhaps the best way of fighting off a relapse. But here was a young man who'd admitted almost having a slip that very afternoon, and a member of this AA group had more or less told him he wasn't welcome here tonight. To be sure, the young man may have meant a drug other than alcohol when he'd referred to "almost using," but to Robbie this seemed of secondary importance.

The silence was broken by the big man with the black hair and beard and cycle clothes.

"I'm Joe and I'm an alcoholic," he growled. "I'm also an addict, and I'm a member of this group, and I don't plan on getting out any time soon." He looked directly at Brad as he said this.

"I'm glad you're here, Jim," he said as he turned his eyes to the newcomer. "As far as I'm concerned, you're welcome."

"Of course you're welcome," said Bonnie quickly, from the chairperson's desk. "I'm glad you're here too, Jim. We do ask that people confine themselves to alcohol when discussing their drug problems directly, but I think that talking about what each of us might do if we're tempted to drink would be a very appropriate topic. Henry, could you start us off?"

Robbie guessed that Bonnie might've called on the stocky man with the Brooklyn accent because of what he had to say about AA and drugs.

"Although I'm an alcoholic," Henry said, "I also used and misused other drugs before I got into AA. I used uppers to get me started in the mornings when I'd have those godawful alcoholic hangovers, and tranquilizers to smooth me out when I couldn't drink booze or was going through some alcoholic withdrawal. I had to learn to live my life drug-free when I started trying to live sober. After I got into AA, I had the craving for a while, not just for booze but for the effects of other drugs too. . . ."

As the discussion continued, the tension in the room seemed to ease a little. A few people came out strongly for the idea that AA was for alcoholics, period. Chet and Wylie and Frank and Grady, all men of the same general age as Brad, talked along these lines.

In general, though, people stuck to talking about times they'd been tempted to drink. *Use,* Robbie thought. *What's drinking but using the drug alcohol?* Some had been successful in resisting relapse; others had had slips. In other circumstances, Robbie might have paid more attention and gotten more out of the discussion, but he was still too full of resentment at Brad and the others to more than halfway follow the talk.

After the meeting, there was an air of preoccupation among the members of the Step-by-Step group that Robbie might have noticed had he stayed around. As it was, he bolted for the door as soon as the meeting was closed.

"I guess I got in ol' Brad's face pretty strong," Joe said to Richard as they walked out. The rest of the people had left. Joe had given his phone number and an offer of help to the newcomer Jim.

"Well, you said what you felt," Richard said.

"I guess I might have been a little less hard-nosed, but Brad was pretty hard-nosed himself with the new guy."

"I know," Richard said. "I wouldn't have handled it the way Brad did, but he does have a right to his own point of view."

"I know," Joe said. "And each of us speaks for himself, not for AA as a whole. But practically telling the guy to get out — I'd hate to think what I might have done when I was new in AA if somebody had told *me* to get out!"

Richard grinned up at Joe, who towered half a head over him. "You won't ever have to worry about me telling you to get out, Joe," he said.

"Aw, I guess I am still kind of a roughneck," Joe said. "I didn't like the idea of seeming to bully a man as much older than me as Brad is, but I don't think what he did was right. He didn't have to humiliate the guy in front of everybody just because he identified himself as an addict and spoke of almost using instead of almost taking a drink."

"I tend to agree with you there, Joe. I have a suspicion that if Brad had had the whole thing to do over, he might have handled it a little differently."

"Yeah, jeez, it wasn't as if the guy was trying to get over on everybody with some junkie war stories. He just wanted help."

"Maybe Brad learned something about acceptance tonight," Richard suggested.

"I hope so. What do you think he might do? He didn't stay around after the meeting, I noticed."

"He might quit the group," Richard said, "although I doubt it. After all, he does have some people who agree with him about the addict issue. He may develop a more tolerant attitude, which would be great if it happens. Or he may just go on being one of the anti-addict watchdogs."

"Watchdogs," Joe repeated thoughtfully. "Yeah, I guess that's what guys like Brad are — watchdogs."

Monday, Robbie's father was going into the city on business, and, on the spur of the moment, Robbie decided to ride along.

They talked on the fifty-mile trip about Robbie's prospects for jobs in their little town, about times when Robbie and his sisters had been growing up, about relatives and sports and life in general. It was a more relaxed conversation than Robbie remembered having with his father in years.

Robbie asked his father to drop him off at the treatment center while his father took care of the business dealings that were the reason for the trip. The treatment center had an open-door policy for former patients to visit at any time during normal business hours.

Robbie said his hellos to the nurses on duty, to C. J., and to a couple of patients he knew. Then he made the trek down Skid Row to Joel's little office.

"So how's it going?" Joel asked, pushing a stack of paperwork aside and waving Robbie to the other chair.

"Well, I've kept my nose clean, but things could be better."

"A craving to drink or use?"

"Not yet," Robbie said, knocking on the arm of the wooden chair, "but I'm having a real problem with this AA group."

"What problem?"

Robbie told Joel about the cool reception he'd received when he'd identified himself as addict as well as alcoholic; about dropping the "and addict" but not feeling good about doing so; about the speaker who'd implied that some AA's didn't like the mention of drugs even in a speaker's personal story; about the incident with the newcomer, Jim, and the ill feelings that had seemed to float through the room afterward.

"It sounds as if that's a pretty traditional AA group," Joel commented when Robbie finished.

"Traditional, ha!" Robbie snorted. "Try prehistoric!"

Joel laughed. "It's something you're bound to run into sooner or later in AA. It's just as well that you're getting the chance to learn to deal with it now."

"You make it sound like some great opportunity," Robbie said. "What's the matter with those guys, anyway? You explained here at the center that alcohol is a mood- and mind-altering drug, just the same as marijuana or heroin or cocaine or whatever. But some of those people in that AA group act as if they want booze in its own special little category, with nothing else allowed in there. It's almost as if they want to make a shrine to alcohol!"

"Take it easy," Joel said. "There's no need to go off the deep end over the narrow-mindedness of a few individuals."

"But it's not right!" Robbie said, more loudly than he'd realized he was going to speak.

"And if there's one thing that we chemically dependent folks are capable of recognizing, it's injustice, right?" Joel stared at Robbie over the tops of his half-glasses until Robbie laughed in spite of himself.

"Okay," Robbie admitted, "I did get a little carried away. But it really doesn't seem right to me."

"Well, if you look at it strictly from a cold, medical and pharmaceutical point of view, it isn't *correct*. A drug is a drug is a drug."

Joel planted a sneaker-shod foot on the edge of his desk and clasped his hands around his knee. "But there's a good deal more than just facts involved in this. There's a lot of emotion around the relationship of alcohol to other drugs and to society, even before you consider AA's relationship to the issue."

"It seems to me that some AA members want to feel superior to 'drug addicts,'" Robbie said.

"And there may be some truth in that," Joel said. "After all, AA members are part of society, and society has tended to accept alcohol while it condemns other drugs."

"It seems to be a more personal thing than that with some of the AA members I've heard talk about addicts," Robbie said.

"And that too may well be in some cases. It's human nature, after all, to want to be on the other side of a situation that has caused embarrassment and humiliation and emotional pain.

"Most alcoholics have been looked down on by other people because of their drinking and their alcoholic behavior. Then, they get sober. Then, there comes the chance to reject, or at least feel superior to, another group of people — drug addicts. The alcoholic can say, 'I may be a former drunk, but at least I wasn't a dope fiend.' And the alcoholic who does that sometimes uses the idea of defending Alcoholics Anonymous as an excuse for discriminating against addicts."

"That's not a very pretty picture of AA members," Robbie said.

"Remember, I'm talking about individuals, Robbie, not Alcoholics Anonymous itself. AA isn't a prejudiced fellowship — but that doesn't keep individual AA members from being prejudiced over some things. Remember, it says in 'How It Works' that 'we are not saints,' talking about AA members as individuals."

"You lead us patients to believe that AA was the greatest thing since sliced bread," Robbie said.

"And I wasn't being at all hypocritical," Joel said. "I firmly believe that AA is the greatest thing that's ever happened for the alcoholic. But that doesn't mean that AA members as individuals aren't capable of being less than perfect. The founders and early members of AA recognized that; that's why they set things up so that no one individual — or AA group, for that matter — could mess things up too badly."

"Great, but what about people in my situation?" Robbie asked. "I have access to only the one AA group right now because of not being able to drive. And this particular AA group seems to me to be pretty discriminatory."

"Robbie," Joel said. It was the tone he'd used when Robbie was in his second week of treatment, the voice that had jarred Robbie out of his insincere compliance. "You know what I'm seeing in you right now? I'm seeing a man who's building a grudge and riding it toward a relapse."

That stopped Robbie cold for a moment. He stared blankly while he took a look mentally at his own attitude instead of at the attitudes of others.

Joel let him think for several moments, then asked, "What exactly is it about this particular AA group that would keep you from staying clean and sober by attending its meetings?"

"Well — nothing," Robbie admitted. "If you mean is there anything that would *cause* me to drink or use."

"Aha," Joel said, "but your attitude could cause you to relapse. Remember that the part about accepting the things we can't change in the Serenity Prayer comes before anything else. You're probably going to have to accept that some AA members are always going to have a negative attitude toward drugs other than alcohol, and toward people addicted to those drugs."

"That's true," Robbie said. "But it seems to me that my personal integrity is being compromised. I mean, if I just accept the way some of those people look at addicts, to the extent of identifying myself only as an alcoholic, won't I be dishonest?"

"Let me tell you what happened with me," Joel said. "I was a multidrug user. I always seemed to start with and get back to alcohol, but in between I did weed and uppers and downers and coke and some hallucinogens and even did some heroin while I was in Southeast Asia.

"I don't say all this to try to make myself out to be some big-time doper; it's just the way it was with me. I say it to indicate why it was hard for me to identify myself as just an alcoholic when I got to Alcoholics Anonymous.

"I didn't have any problem with being powerless over alcohol when I got into recovery; alcohol always seemed to do the most for me, and even if it hadn't, drinking it was sure to get me back on some other drug — so either way I was powerless over booze, because using it meant losing control of my life.

"But when I first got into Alcoholics Anonymous, I didn't figure myself for some garden-variety juicer. I actually felt superior, in a sick kind of way, to the people who'd just drunk booze. Just like some of the 'pure' alcoholics seem to feel about users of other drugs.

"Like you, I had a problem identifying myself as just an alcoholic. I wanted, by God, to let people know what a colorful history of substance abuse I'd had — that I had some *real* war stories!

"Fortunately, I got a sponsor who pointed out to me just how unhealthy that kind of thinking was. He told me that AA doesn't require people to identify themselves as alcoholics — doing so is a custom, but not a requirement. The same is true for Narcotics Anonymous, incidentally — saying, 'I'm an addict,' in NA is just a custom too.

"So, my sponsor suggested to me, why create problems I didn't need? If following the custom of AA and saying I'm an alcoholic makes things simpler, then why not do so? Especially since it's true, according to every guideline I've ever heard. Simply saying, 'I'm an alcoholic' when identifying myself at an AA meeting is no more a cop-out than saying, 'I'm an addict' at an NA meeting would be."

"I hadn't thought of it quite that way," Robbie said. "But it still seems to me that NA is a lot more liberal than AA when it comes to this kind of thing. Narcotics Anonymous recognizes alcoholics as being addicts — people addicted to the drug alcohol. People in AA don't seem to return the favor."

"NA is a pretty accepting fellowship," Joel agreed. "But don't kid yourself — there are NA members who're capable of discrimination too. Some NA's look down on the 'pure' alcoholic as being square and wimpy — the term *juicer* is one I first heard at an NA meeting.

"The point is, Robbie, not to limit yourself in the support groups 'appropriate' for you. Copping a bad attitude toward AA because of the actions or attitudes of a few individuals isn't going to hurt anyone but yourself in the long run."

"That makes sense, I guess," Robbie said.

"And I'd be willing to bet that not every member of this Step-by-Step group is a rabid anti-addict hard-liner."

Robbie thought of big Joe and Buddy. Joel was right. Robbie could have his own understanding of what it meant to be an alcoholic and addict, just as he could have his own understanding of a Higher Power and the Steps and the other elements of recovery.

As Robbie was leaving Joel's office, the counselor slapped him on the shoulder and said, "Don't worry too much about some conflict in AA. It's not necessarily bad — learning how to handle conflict in a healthy way is a big part of recovery. And if you disagree with some of the group's members, join the group and attend the business meetings and let the other group members know how you feel. You could be an asset to the group; who knows, you might help loosen them up a little where multiaddicted people are concerned."

Robbie was at the next business meeting, by virtue of having joined the Step-by-Step group. At that meeting, it was moved that, in the interest of not appearing hostile to people with problems in addition to alcoholism, the announcement about limiting discussion to topics dealing with alcoholism only, be removed from the format of meetings.

It was a close vote. It was a majority, in fact, by only one vote. Robbie voted for the removal of the announcement, and when it carried, he was reminded of what Joel had said about the possibility of being able to be a part of change in his AA group.

My AA group, Robbie thought with a little surprise. It was in fact his AA group now; he'd only planned to attend AA while he was constrained from attending Narcotics Anonymous meetings. Since joining the Step-by-Step group, he had ridden into the city with Buddy to attend an NA meeting there. It had been a good meeting, but Robbie felt no sense of loss or incompleteness the next time he attended a meeting of his own group, the Step-by-Step group of Alcoholics Anonymous.

The Old Guard

It was Amy's last evening in the city. Her memories of this AA meeting room, once so happy, now seemed to bring her only sadness.

The meeting room was in a freestanding building across from the main hospital complex. The AA group rented the room for a modest fee. In keeping with AA traditions, the group wasn't affiliated with the hospital, although many of its members, Amy among them, had gone through the hospital's chemical dependency treatment program.

The meeting room had large windows on two sides, open this evening in late summer to let the breeze blow through. A thunderstorm had passed through at about six o'clock, bringing with it cooler air and relief from the day's heat.

Amy had arrived early on this, her last night as a member of this AA group. She'd set up the coffeepot and hot plate, put out the tea, decaffeinated coffee, and hot chocolate as well as cups, sugar, creamer, and spoons. She'd hung up the two scrolls with the Twelve Steps and Twelve Traditions on them. She'd put out the AA literature but no ashtrays — this was a nonsmoking meeting.

The hospital's administration could probably have been persuaded to make an exception for AA meetings to the blanket no-smoking rule that covered all the hospital's buildings. But the group had decided to make this a nonsmoking meeting.

It wasn't the first AA group in the city to do this, but it was still in the minority.

At seven-forty-five, Tod ambled in.

"How's it going?" he asked.

"I've been better," Amy said.

Tod looked at her closely. Her normally cheerful face held a sad expression.

"Going-away blues?" Tod asked. He was a tall, gangly man of about thirty, a couple of years older than Amy. He had an attractively lopsided, boyish face.

"I guess," Amy said. "I thought I was going to get away clean, but now that I'm all packed and ready and tomorrow's the big day, it seems to have hit me all at once." Sadness on Amy's face was perhaps more noticeable than on the faces of other people. Her red hair and short nose with its dusting of freckles and her brilliant blue eyes seemed to radiate optimism and good humor most of the time.

Tod gave her a brotherly hug, patting her back gently. More people were beginning to arrive now, singly and in small clumps.

Megan, Amy's sponsor, came in and gave her a hug. A fair number of the members of this AA group also attended meetings of Narcotics Anonymous, and NA's custom of hugs rather than handshakes had carried over to this AA group.

"I've lost another five pounds!" Megan whispered excitedly to Amy. "I know we're not supposed to be scale-watchers, but I hadn't weighed in a couple of weeks, and was it a nice surprise!"

Megan, a tall, big-boned brunette in her late thirties, was married and the mother of two children. Megan and Amy both attended meetings of Overeaters Anonymous as well as AA. In fact, it was OA that had led to their becoming friends and Amy asking Megan to be her AA sponsor. Keeping their AA anonymity in OA and vice versa had drawn them together.

"Hi," said Louise breathlessly to Amy and Megan. Louise was a short, energetic young woman who always gave the impression that she was trying to catch up to herself. "Are either of you going to ACoA tomorrow night?" she asked Amy and Megan. "I'm supposed to be chairing the meeting and I've got to work late...."

Megan assured Louise that she'd open the Adult Children of Alcoholics meeting for her. Amy faced losing more than one support group by moving from the city to a small town. A lot of the members of this AA group belonged, like Megan, Amy, and Louise, to other Twelve Step groups like NA, OA, ACoA, and Al-Anon. There was even a mild joke going around about starting a support group for people who belonged to support groups. But it was a joke — everyone Amy knew valued their recovery too much to take any group for granted that was helping them.

As she watched the room filling up with the people with whom she'd shared so much, Amy began to feel her eyes sting with unshed tears. She went to the rest room before the meeting started, dabbing at her eyes and regarding herself in the mirror. Although she was still not as thin as she wished to be, she no longer had to take fat jokes so personally. Red hair and freckles might not have been at the top of the list of component parts she'd have ordered had she been able to design herself. But she liked herself immeasurably better now than she had a little over a year ago.

Tod was chairing the meeting. After he'd called it to order and gone through the opening formalities, he said, "This is a discussion meeting. Does anyone have a problem they'd like to share with the group?"

Amy raised her hand and said, "I'm Amy and I'm powerless over alcohol and other drugs."

An enthusiastic "Hi, Amy," came from the group.

"As some of you know," Amy said, "I'm being transferred by my employer to a small town about fifty miles from here. In fact, this is my last night as a member of this group; the movers are coming in the morning.

"This transfer means a promotion and a raise, and I thought I was doing great. But I've discovered this evening that not only am I sad at leaving all of you — I'm scared.

"This is the place where I first got sober, where I joined AA and got into recovery. This is the only AA group I've ever belonged to, and..." Her voice cracked and, dabbing at her eyes again, she stopped speaking. "That's all, I guess; just — thanks! — all of you."

After a brief silence Tod said, "I left my first AA home group when I was about eight months sober. I was scared to death; I didn't care what people told me about my AA program being portable and how AA is almost everywhere. I didn't think I'd ever find another group of people, even other recovering alcoholics, that I could trust and share with the way I had my first AA group.

"I was lucky, though. I found a new AA group that, within a week, had me feeling as comfortable as I'd felt in my first group."

He stopped and looked around the room. "What about *change* as a topic?" he asked. "I know from personal experience that change — almost any kind of change — can be very unsettling to us alcoholics. A change of jobs, a change of AA groups, a change of towns, whatever. Somebody please volunteer to kick off the discussion, and when you're through, pass it along to someone else."

Jack, a short, husky young man in jeans and cutoff sweatshirt, was the first to speak.

"I'm Jack and I'm a drunk and a dope fiend," he said, and there were some chuckles at this reference to some of society's traditional notions about alcoholics and other drug addicts.

"I can identify with what you're feeling," Jack said to Amy. "What town are you moving to?"

She told him the name of the town, and he said, "I've been to a few AA meetings there. The Step-by-Step group has the most meetings there; it's a pretty traditional sort of AA group, but it seemed all right to me."

Jack paused for a moment, thinking. "I guess the biggest problem I've had when it came to changing AA groups was identifying myself as both an alcoholic and addict. Some of the more traditional groups don't care much for the word *addict*. I've learned to Keep It Simple; if a particular AA group objects to using the term *addict*, then I just identify myself as alcoholic and let it go at that. But if something a group does bothers me too much, I just find another group."

Amy had had no problem identifying herself as an addict as well as alcoholic; in fact, the reverse had been true. She supposed now that leaving off the part about drugs other than alcohol wouldn't bother her too much if it proved necessary.

The discussion went throughout the room as various members talked about changes in their lives and how they'd reacted to them. As always, Amy felt much better by the time the meeting closed.

"Now the fact that you're moving doesn't mean that you have to become a stranger," Megan said as they walked out after the meeting. "Fifty miles isn't all that far, after all. It doesn't cost much to call in the evenings, and you can come visit me and my brood anytime — you know you're always welcome in our home."

Amy felt at a loss for words after receiving good wishes from everyone in the group, and now this from her sponsor — a woman so different on the outside from Amy and yet so similar in feelings and with such understanding. Megan never seemed at a loss for empathy with Amy, despite Amy being younger and single and a career woman. They hugged, and Amy promised to call Megan as soon as she was settled into her new place.

The next morning, the movers showed up at Amy's apartment promptly at 8:00 A.M. She'd gotten everything ready, and she watched the men carry her possessions out to the moving van, congratulating herself on having an employer generous enough to pick up the tab for the professional move.

Amy took a final look around her three-room apartment after the men had carried out the last carton. She'd taken this apartment just after she'd gotten sober, and although that hadn't been a terribly long time ago, there were still memories connected with this place. She quickly closed the front door and headed out to start her car, leading off with the moving van following.

The drive was pleasant. The first half of the trip was on an interstate, but the second twenty-odd miles was on a two-lane highway that wasn't overly busy in mid-morning. The day was sunny, and Amy was glad — having to move on a dark, damp day would've been more than she felt she could bear.

The further they traveled from the city and the four-lane highway, the more rural the surroundings became. The highway passed farms, some large, most small, and went through stretches of forested land. Flocks of crows policed the fields and perched in trees alongside the road. A groundhog stood like a small brown furry post on the shoulder of the highway.

The town that was to be Amy's new home was probably bustling on this bright morning, but compared to the city it seemed sleepy.

Main Street was lined with handsome old oaks and maples. Most of the downtown buildings were of red brick, three or four stories tall, built in the years between the two World Wars.

The town had one movie theater, two supermarkets, one fast-food restaurant, a hardware store, a feed-and-seed supply, several service stations, and a collection of other small businesses that served the needs of small town life.

Amy's new place was half a duplex, considerably larger than her old apartment. After the movers had unloaded her furniture and placed all of it, the space still seemed rather bare. Well, with the raise coming with her transfer and promotion, she could realistically consider buying more furnishings.

She unpacked her clothes and dishes and began setting up housekeeping. Once she'd put things away so that she at least had an even chance of finding them, she went out and shopped for groceries. She'd deliberately used up her supply of food to avoid moving it.

By the time evening arrived, she'd fixed herself a meal in her new place, taken a shower and washed her hair, and done most of the things that make a place home. She'd gotten the address of the meeting place of the Step-by-Step group, and at seven-thirty she'd found the AA meeting room, off an alley that ran behind the buildings on the west side of Main Street.

A dozen or so people were already in the meeting room when Amy entered. A pretty, middle-aged woman came forward to greet her.

"Hi, I'm Anna," she said.

"I'm Amy."

"New here?"

"Yes, this is my very first day in town, in fact. I've been a member of AA for about a year."

"You did well, coming to a meeting your first night in town," Anna said. She had a soft Southern accent; she'd pronounced "you" as "yuah" and "here" as "heah."

"I thought I'd better get established in AA right away," Amy said. She told Anna about her job with the bank and her transfer here and promotion to assistant manager. They went over to the long table at the side of the room and got coffee. Unlike her other meeting, here there was no tea or hot chocolate, although there was a smaller pot of plain hot water and a jar of decaffeinated coffee. At least two dozen ashtrays were stacked on the table, and the smoke was already noticeable, even though the meeting hadn't started. Obviously, this was no nonsmoking meeting.

"Is this your home group?" Amy asked Anna as a couple of men approached them.

"Yes," Anna said, "I have to help the rest of the gals keep these guys civilized." She deliberately raised her voice for the men to hear.

"Aw, Anna," the bigger of the two men said. "We're fairly decent. Don't give this young lady the wrong impression." He stuck out a big hand to Amy. "I'm Chet."

Chet was in his fifties, a large man with silver hair swept back over his ears like Hollywood's idea of a rural politician. He wore a sports shirt in a violent shade of blue, the tails outside his trousers in what was probably an effort to disguise his rather large stomach.

"Arnie," said the other man in a soft voice. Arnie didn't look Amy in the eye as he shook her hand, a sign she took to mean he was very shy rather than slippery. Arnie, a few years younger than Chet, was a thin man wearing matching shirt and pants that were the uniform of some trade. His name was stitched on a patch over the shirt's left pocket. Arnie's sideburns were a decade out of fashion; he wore a thin mustache of the sort Amy had seen in pictures of early pilots.

Amy met more people before the meeting started. She was relieved to see that there were a fair number of women in the Step-by-Step group; she'd worried about being the only female in some forsaken AA group out in the boonies.

Herb, a man of Chet's general age with a military-style haircut, chaired the meeting. He asked an elderly man named Grover to read "How It Works" and Arnie to read the Traditions. Both men were poor readers, and Amy felt embarrassed for them, but no one else seemed to notice how slowly they plodded through the readings.

When they were done, Herb asked if anyone had a problem concerning staying sober or living sober to discuss. Amy was having a problem with her move and new surroundings, but something kept her quiet.

"Well," Herb said after a moment, showing no surprise that no one had brought up a problem or suggested a topic, "we'll do well to stick to AA basics." He leaned back in the chair behind the chairperson's desk.

"When I took Step One," Herb said, "I admitted I was powerless over alcohol.

"Alcoholics Anonymous tells me that if I'm an alcoholic, I can't ever safely drink again. A lot of people say that alcoholism is a disease and that it's incurable. They say that alcoholics are always at risk of drinking again. So, let's talk about the First Step and alcoholism and what being powerless over alcohol means to each of us. Frank?"

Frank was a short, thickset man with bushy black eyebrows and a head so smoothly bald that it glistened as if waxed.

"I don't think I'll ever be 'cured,' " Frank said. "I think I'll always be an alcoholic. I think that once I became an alcoholic, I lost my ability to drink reasonably or safely.

"But I'm not so sure about this disease business. I think that calling alcoholism a 'disease' could be a cop-out. If I was still drinking, for instance, and somebody told me that alcoholism is a disease, it would be easy for me to just say, 'Oh, it's not *my* fault; you see, I have this *disease.*' I think personally that a lot of people are doing that now, making excuses for alcoholics. Since we've had all the doctors and psychologists researching and analyzing alcoholism and lawyers using it as a defense for their clients in court.

"'I drank — nobody made me do it, nobody held me and forced it down my throat. It's up to me to take responsibility for my own alcoholism and for my own sobriety."

Amy tried to follow Frank's line of thought. The part about taking responsibility for one's own actions made sense, of course.

But she couldn't see how Frank considered alcoholism as anything other than a disease or an involuntary disorder. She knew she certainly hadn't chosen to become an alcoholic herself.

Herb next called on a man named Wylie.

"I go along with Frank about the cop-out of saying that being an alcoholic means I have a 'disease,' " Wylie said. A little man, his hair had once been red but was now a sort of grey-orange. His voice was surprisingly loud for his small size, and he spoke with careful enunciation of each word, as if he might have dentures that interfered with clear speech if he spoke too quickly.

"I've heard this talk about how alcoholism might be hereditary," Wylie went on. "I'm sure not going to blame my daddy for my alcoholism. He didn't even drink — he hated liquor, on account of his father's drinking."

It seemed to Amy that Wylie had just contradicted himself about alcoholism's hereditary factor; he'd said he didn't accept it, and then he'd implied that his grandfather's drinking had been a problem for his father. Amy had learned that although alcoholism tends to run in families, it can skip generations. The fact that Wylie's father didn't drink was no proof against the hereditary factor in alcoholism.

Herb called on big, silver-haired Chet next.

"I agree completely about not blaming others for my alcoholism," Chet said. "I hear about these people who call themselves 'adult children of alcoholics' — they blame everything wrong with them on their alcoholic parents. That makes me feel like throwing up! Giving an alcoholic that kind of excuse is the worst thing you could possibly do for him!"

Amy felt her anger flaring. She belonged — or had belonged, back in the city — to an ACoA group. Chet's view of the Adult Children of Alcoholics recovery program was obviously based on gross ignorance. Although some adult children of alcoholics came into ACoA blaming their parents for their troubles, they soon learned that a vital part of recovery is letting go of the blaming. And refusing to see the effects of growing up in an alcoholic home was simply hiding your head in the sand.

"I don't particularly care if people call alcoholism a disease or not," said the next speaker called on, a man named Grady. Grady wore a somber dark suit, white shirt, and black tie. With his slicked-down hair and solemn face, he could have been an old-fashioned minister or perhaps an undertaker.

"I don't think it's so important what we call alcoholism or how we define it," Grady said, "as long as we ourselves know we can't safely drink alcohol. I think that Bill W. and Doctor Bob knew that very well when they founded Alcoholics Anonymous back in the thirties. I think God gave this AA program to Bill and Doctor Bob. I think that AA is divinely inspired, that it takes God to help an alcoholic get sober and stay sober. . . ."

Something about Grady's fervor made Amy uncomfortable. He had the sound of a fanatical evangelist. Amy had found her own understanding of a Higher Power early in recovery, but it was not like this fervent belief that Grady seemed to have.

"There're all kinds of folks coming into AA these days," said the next speaker, a smallish, white-haired man named Brad. "Some of them want to talk about being overeaters, or children of alcoholics, like Chet was saying, or drug addicts. I don't think any of that has any place in Alcoholics Anonymous. We're here to stay sober and help other alcoholics get sober. That's what AA is all about. . . ."

Brad had finished his tirade and another speaker started talking when Amy realized Brad hadn't even mentioned his own addiction to alcohol or how he came to accept the First Step.

Herb had called on only males until nearly the halfway point of the meeting. Amy supposed this could be simply a coincidence. It might at least be a relatively innocent kind of unconscious male chauvinism on Herb's part, calling on so many men before asking the women present to say something, but a part of Amy wasn't at all convinced of this.

The second half of the meeting saw a gradual return to the topic that Herb had suggested — that of the First Step and what being powerless over alcohol meant to the individual. A dark-haired woman named Annette, a huge, bearded man named Joe, a well-dressed man named Phil — all talked about their first experiences with powerlessness and unmanageability. The bashing of the disease concept and ACoA's and other problems ceased in the second half of the meeting, but no one seemed inclined to refute anything Frank or Chet or Brad or the others had said.

Amy wasn't called on. After the meeting, she talked a little more with Anna. She was tempted to ask Anna about some of the rather hostile comments she'd heard concerning problems other than alcoholism, but she didn't feel she knew Anna well enough yet.

Before she left, Anna gave Amy her phone number, saying, "It doesn't hurt to have some contacts when you're new in town."

Amy was grateful for Anna's friendliness. But she couldn't help wondering how much she'd be able to communicate with a woman of Anna's age. Especially since Anna seemed to simply accept the kinds of attitudes Amy had heard expressed by some of the male members of the Step-by-Step group tonight.

Driving back to her new home, Amy was experiencing feelings she'd not had before upon leaving an AA meeting, feelings of frustration, anger, and resentment. Some of the attitudes she'd heard expressed tonight were completely at odds with her understanding of what it meant to be alcoholic.

Most AA members Amy had met were quick to say that alcoholism wasn't a moral issue. She'd often heard it said that, "We're not bad people trying to get good; we're sick people trying to get well."

And yet several of the men tonight had used the word blame in connection with alcoholism, especially when the hereditary issue was raised. If alcoholism was in fact a disease, and not a moral issue, it was no more "blaming" to say that someone inherited his or her alcoholism than to say a person's diabetes was hereditary. And one man at tonight's meeting didn't even want to call alcoholism a disease!

But in spite of her negative feelings, she certainly didn't feel tempted to drink. She'd done the right thing by going to an

AA meeting her first night in town; it wasn't *her* fault that she'd run into these people with their strange ways of looking at things. She was physically tired, and she'd learned by experience that fatigue could cause her to overreact emotionally. She managed to more or less put the events at the meeting out of her mind and got a fairly good night's sleep.

The next few days on her new job as assistant manager of the branch bank kept Amy's attention focused on work. She found herself going in early and staying after regular working hours, snatching meals when and where she could. By Wednesday night she was more than ready for a meeting.

Wednesdays meant speaker meetings, and the speaker on this night was a big, bearded man from another town. Named Webb, he was in his late forties or early fifties. Webb's story up until the point of his getting into AA was similar to those of several other men his age that Amy had heard. It was when he reached the point of talking about his life in Alcoholics Anonymous in the present that Amy began to feel a strong dislike for him.

"I believe in AA the way the founders meant it to be," he stated bluntly. He had a gruff, raspy voice that grated on Amy's ears.

"I don't care much for all these treatment centers that are springing up all over the place like weeds after a rain," Webb went on. "The old-time AA's used to detox drunks themselves. It wasn't unusual for an AA group to keep a bottle of paraldehyde, or a bottle of whiskey, with a member they trusted to stay sober, and they'd use that if a drunk started to go into delirium tremens or convulsions or seizures from alcohol withdrawal.

"These treatment centers —" Webb gave a snort of scorn. "They're just out to make a quick buck, off the insurance companies and the new DWI laws and all the lawyers who're trying to get their drunk clients off the hook by having them go through programs at the drunk farms.

"And I don't care too much for the twenty-eight-day wonders that these treatment places turn out, either. They've had their heads stuffed full of psychological garbage and fancy theories about what causes alcoholism. They think they know it all. Give me an old drunk off the street any day!"

Amy was stunned. She looked around incredulously to see how others in the audience might be reacting to Webb's opinionated and, to her, rude comments.

A few faces looked irritated; most were neutral; a few, those of Chet and Wylie and Frank among them, were smiling and giving little nods of agreement with Webb.

Amy felt anger and disgust and some defensiveness. She was one of those "twenty-eight-day wonders" herself. Webb's remarks were insulting and degrading to anyone who'd gone through treatment; she only hoped there were no newly sober treatment center graduates in the audience.

That night she was thoroughly angry when she left the meeting. She was angry not just at the speaker, Webb, but at the whole Step-by-Step group of Alcoholics Anonymous. Perhaps not everyone in the group was like Chet and Wylie and Frank and — God forbid — like Webb, but this group obviously condoned the kind of attitudes she'd heard tonight.

Underneath her anger, Amy was beginning to feel fear; she had never dreamed she'd feel this way about Alcoholics Anonymous. She'd been told that "AA won't ever steer you wrong." But now the messages she seemed to be getting from this AA group were in direct conflict with some important things Amy had come to believe. In the back of her mind was a disturbing question of whether or not she might be the one in the wrong — perhaps there was an idea or message that she was missing.

She stewed over it for the next couple of days, but her previous AA experience and the concept of "take what you like and leave the rest" began to calm her fears. She decided that she could disagree with people like Webb, Chet, Frank, and Wylie without getting down on AA. After all, no one person spoke for AA as a whole. . . .

Amy made the sudden decision that next Saturday afternoon to drive back to the city and visit her old AA group. The fifty-mile drive didn't cool her enthusiasm for her impulse, and when she arrived back at the meeting room across from the hospital, the warm reception from people so dear to her made the trip more than worthwhile.

Amy and Megan began catching up on events before the meeting and took up again when it was over.

"So how're things out there in Small Town U.S.A.?" Megan asked.

Amy told Megan about the Step-by-Step group and about some of the doubts and misgivings she was beginning to have about AA in her new town.

"Sounds like you've run into a very traditional group," Megan said when Amy finally realized she'd been almost ranting and stopped talking.

"Try Stone Age," Amy said.

"I think I know what you're feeling right now," Megan said. "I sort of fell into a supertraditional AA group not too long after I got sober. This was a group so traditional that everybody had a seat — all the regular members, that is. You didn't sit in someone else's seat more than once; you were told, more or less politely, that that seat belonged to so-and-so.

"It took me a while to sort out my feelings about those people. It seemed at first that they'd have liked to do away with every advance in the knowledge and treatment of alcoholism and practice some kind of AA 'voodoo' instead."

"That's the impression I get of this group," Amy said. "The business about not considering alcoholism a disease, and the speaker's criticism of treatment centers and the people who go through them. . . ."

"Have you ever thought about how some of the AA members who came in 'off the street' might feel about those who've gone through treatment?" Megan asked. "The reason behind their attitudes, I mean?"

"No," Amy admitted. "But it's hard for me to imagine *why* they're so negative about people who've gone through treatment."

"I didn't go through treatment myself," Megan said. "I was more or less detoxed by my family doctor. Then I went to my first AA meeting with a friend of the doctor who was a recovering alcoholic. I used to think that people who'd gone through treatment had somehow had it easier than me."

"Treatment's no vacation at a resort," Amy said. "Or at least it wasn't for me."

"I found that out," Megan said. "I did some volunteer work at a treatment center; I came in and heard patients' Fifth Steps while they were still in treatment. After meeting a lot of those women who were patients at that center, I began to realize that treatment center AA's didn't have it all that easy. Spending a month or more away from home, with all the problems they'd gotten into while drinking facing them when they got out. And being in a place where they heard little else but talk about chemical dependency almost twenty-four hours a day. I changed my mind about treatment center AA's being somehow 'softer' than me."

"Tell that to those people in the Step-by-Step group," Amy said. "That speaker was more than just condescending toward people who've been through treatment; he acted as if he almost hated them!"

"Maybe there's something to that," Megan said. Amy looked at her in surprise. "I don't mean hatred, in a personal sense — I doubt that many traditional AA's hold real hatred for people who've gotten modern treatment for alcoholism — but resentment. That might be the key to some of the attitudes you've been seeing.

"A lot of the older AA's, and even some not-so-old members, hit pretty low bottoms before they got sober. Some of them lost just about everything — jobs, families, reputations, credit — the works. I think that they sometimes see people who go through treatment as being more privileged than themselves."

"But that's not necessarily so," Amy objected.

"I know that and you know that, but it's still a perception among a lot of AA members that going through a treatment center is something that the well-off drunks are able to do. Sure, there are people who lose jobs, who lose spouses, who face jail time when they're discharged from the treatment center, who have all kinds of unpleasant things happen despite going through a treatment program. But the perceptions people get can be awfully hard to change, and, unfortunately, a lot of AA members see treatment as some kind of country-club vacation."

"But that isn't fair!" Amy said.

Megan raised one eyebrow slightly — what Amy had come to know as her sponsor look. "Say," Megan said with mock surprise, "that must mean that some AA members aren't perfect! We can't have that, can we? I mean, they need to shape up and do things the right way."

"All right," Amy said, "maybe I am a little obsessed with this business, but..."

"'Live and Let Live,' that's one of our slogans, right? You don't have to agree with the treatment-center bashers in that group, do you?"

"No," Amy admitted.

"So there you are," Megan said. "Look, it's too late for you to drive back tonight; stay at our house."

And with that it was settled, at least for the moment. Amy spent the night in Megan's guest room, ate a leisurely breakfast Sunday morning with Megan and her husband and two boys, then drove home.

It was a beautiful late-summer morning, and Amy was amused at herself for having been so frustrated over the incidents in her new AA group. Talking with Megan had helped put it in much different perspective; she could take what she liked, leave the rest, and get some practice in toleration in the bargain.

This workweek began less hectically than her first week on her new job. When she went to the Wednesday night speaker meeting, the speaker turned out to be a woman, Fran, a member of the Step-by-Step group with whose story Amy felt considerable empathy.

By the time the Saturday night general discussion meeting rolled around, Amy was feeling remarkably more serene and confident than she had the previous week.

"Hi, Amy," said big, silver-haired Chet when she walked into the meeting room on Saturday evening. "How're you doing, sweetheart?"

Amy felt a flash of irritation at the "sweetheart," but she was glad enough to have her name remembered to let it slide off. She reminded herself that Chet was, after all, old enough to be her father and from a generation of males who found it hard to understand the modern woman's resentment of patronizing nicknames.

Arnie came over and greeted her in his shy way, as did Wylie and Herb and several other members. They seemed to be genuinely glad to see her, and something of the old warmth she'd felt toward AA began to come back.

Chet chaired the meeting this evening, and after he'd suggested the Higher Power and its importance in recovery as a topic, he totally surprised Amy by calling on her first.

"I'm Amy and I'm an alcoholic," she said, remembering not to add "and addict." Her mind raced — it was always difficult to be the first speaker in a discussion meeting.

"I now choose to call my Higher Power God and, before I joined AA, I didn't know that God had a place in my everyday life."

She wondered if she'd committed an error in judgment by the remark about choosing to use the word *God*. She'd picked this up from other AA's in her early recovery, but she didn't know how well it would go down with this group. Still, there was nothing to do but plow ahead.

"To me," she went on, "God was somebody the priest prayed to and talked about at mass. God was all tied up with confession and absolution and penance and duties and doctrine. God wasn't somebody I could just talk to, as a friend. God was someone to fear and to step very carefully around.

"AA taught me that I could have my own understanding of God," Amy continued. "I didn't have to accept what somebody else told me God was like. I could see Him — or Her — in any way that made sense to *me.*''

Had she made another possible boo-boo in the little witticism about God possibly being a Her? The middle-aged men in the room might see her as some kind of militant feminist. She quickly finished what she had to say with the feeling that she might have alienated some of her new AA acquaintances.

When Amy finished, Chet called on Grady, the man who'd reminded her of an evangelistic preacher. She mentally held her breath to see how Grady might respond to the things she'd had to say.

"I liked what Amy had to say about God maybe being a Her," Grady said with a dry chuckle. "I think she made a good point about how each of us can have our own personal understanding of God."

Amy felt a wave of relief and gratitude. Grady had actually complimented her! Grady went on to say that he, too, had had a religious background that seemed to stress the harshness of God. And that it had taken him a long time to accept the AA idea of finding his own personal Higher Power.

The meeting went well — great, in fact, from Amy's point of view — particularly since she'd been having such negative feelings about the Step-by-Step group. She now felt a little foolish over her near panic at what she'd seen as this group's ultraconservative nature. *Tolerance, that's all I needed*, she told herself.

Things went very well for a couple of weeks. The problems in her new job were challenging but not overwhelming. She bought herself a new sofa, a dining table, and some chairs for her larger living quarters. She went to three meetings a week in her new AA group and visited her old group on Saturdays. Things seemed to be going very well indeed. Then came the Friday night meeting when the woman named Loretta showed up.

Loretta, a chunky woman whose dark hair was already turning grey, was perhaps ten years older than Amy. Loretta's face carried the unmistakable signs of alcoholism for anyone who could read them. Amy felt a deep gratitude for having gotten sober relatively early in her adult life; the physical toll on women seemed more noticeable, severe — perhaps because of the great emphasis on physical beauty for women.

The men all seemed to know Loretta. She introduced herself to Amy, but it was obvious that she was more at ease kidding around with the men than talking with the women in the group.

When the meeting started and Wylie, the chairperson, asked if anyone had a problem, Loretta's hand went up.

"I haven't been to many meetings lately," Loretta said after she'd identified herself. "In fact, I haven't been to *any* meetings for some time. I've been away too long, but I'm glad I came here tonight."

Amy could see now that the kidding around she'd seen Loretta doing earlier had been an alcoholic's front; Loretta was in a lot of emotional pain.

"I've been living with a guy who's a practicing alcoholic," Loretta said. "I knew that wasn't a good idea, but..." Her voice trailed off as she swiped at her eyes.

"Last night he left," she said after she'd composed herself. "He just packed his things and went. I told myself it was better this way; being around somebody who's drinking isn't good for me, but..." She stopped again as her voice cracked.

"I felt really lousy after he left," Loretta said after she'd once more drawn herself together. "My sponsor's out of town. I tried to call some people in AA, but it seemed that every number I tried either didn't answer or was busy. So, I came to this meeting tonight."

Wylie was toying with a pencil on the chairperson's desk, looking uncomfortable. When Loretta finished speaking, there was a long, profound moment of silence. Then Chet, who was sitting just behind Loretta, spoke up.

"It sounds to me like that's a problem you should talk with a sponsor about, honey," he said to Loretta. "Alcoholics Anonymous is about staying sober; it's not about dealing with your romantic problems."

Amy was shocked and embarrassed at Chet's blunt rejection of Loretta's problem. To Amy, this was an issue of staying sober. For a woman to have a man leave her, even if he was a practicing alcoholic and no good for her, was the kind of emotionally painful situation that could easily lead her to drinking.

Up at the chairperson's desk, Wylie cleared his throat.

"I, uh, I can't help but agree with Chet," he said, not meeting Loretta's eyes. "We do have to stick to the basics of Alcoholics Anonymous. Maybe you could talk one-on-one with someone after the meeting?..."

Loretta didn't respond immediately. She sat quietly for a moment, looking down at her hands in her lap, then got up and, without a word, walked out of the room.

Again there was a pin-dropping silence. Then one of the female members of the group, Doris, rose and followed Loretta out. Wylie cleared his throat again and said, "Well, does anyone else have a problem?"

"I don't have a problem, Wylie," said Frank, "but I think maybe I have a topic, considering what's just happened. How about 'singleness of purpose'? We say that AA can't be all things to all people. Maybe we should talk about what we mean by that...."

Amy was aware that the men in the room had shot each other glances while Chet and Wylie were in the process of rejecting Loretta and she was leaving. But none of them had met the eyes of any of the females present.

"I feel sorry for the person who just left," Frank was saying. "But I don't think that problems of that sort should be discussed at an AA meeting, any more than problems like drug addiction or eating too much or gambling or anything else not connected to staying sober should be discussed."

"I agree with Frank," Grady said, raising his hand. "AA is very specific about what its primary purpose is — to stay sober and help other alcoholics to achieve sobriety. AA can't be Dear Abby or Ann Landers."

Amy waited for someone to challenge Chet, Wylie, Frank, and Grady, to say that helping an alcoholic deal with an emotional crisis was helping that person stay sober, no matter what the crisis was. But no one spoke up.

The discussion, such as it was, went around the room. Most people said more or less what the first few speakers had. To Amy, it sounded like a group rationalization for having cut Loretta off.

Amy was called on near the end of the meeting, but she simply said, curtly, "I pass." She left immediately after the closing.

Amy was furious over what she'd seen tonight. *There had been, the flavor of moral disapproval in the air,* she thought. *Perhaps this conservative, traditional group disapproved of Loretta living with a man to whom she wasn't married.* Amy thought that, had Loretta been a male, the attitude might've been considerably different.

She thought of calling Megan when she got home, but she remembered that Megan and her family were out of town for a week. Then she thought of calling someone else in her old group. The problem was that they wouldn't know the people and situation involved in tonight's fiasco.

It was then that she remembered having Anna's phone number and invitation to call. Although Anna hadn't been at the meeting tonight, she'd know the people involved. Amy wasn't sure how Anna might see the incident, but she needed to talk with someone about it.

"No, it isn't too late for you to call," Anna said when Amy apologized for calling at the fairly late hour. "And I'm not sick or anything; I'd just decided to give myself an evening at home. How're you doing?"

"Not great," Amy said with the honesty she'd learned to practice. "I've run into a problem I've never had before."

"Really? Sounds intriguing. Tell me."

"This AA group," Amy began, and then stopped. She really didn't know how to begin. How was she to know, after all, if Anna wasn't as conservative and traditional-minded as any of the people at the meeting tonight?

"You mean the Old Guard?" Anna asked with a chuckle.

"I, uh, well, I guess so," Amy stammered. "I hadn't thought to call them that...."

"I probably shouldn't call members of my own group sarcastic little names like that," Anna said. "But I do love them, despite their quirks. Tell me what's bothering you specifically."

Amy told Anna about the incident with Loretta, not using anyone's name. She told Anna how angry she'd felt and how she was now feeling fearful that her source of recovery was now somehow threatened by her experiences with this group.

"The first and most important thing," Anna said, "is to not let this put you off AA in general or let it put you off the Step-by-Step group itself; there's a lot of good AA in this group, no matter how narrow-minded or shortsighted a few of its members may be occasionally. The fact that individual members of an AA group hold certain opinions doesn't mean that they speak for the whole group."

"I know," Amy said. "But nobody in my old group seemed to be like this. The way that woman was just cut off tonight wasn't right."

"I understand how you feel," Anna said. "I'm inclined to agree with you that her problem shouldn't have been just dismissed out of hand. But I can also see how a middle-aged man chairing a meeting might feel inadequate in trying to deal with a situation like Loretta's."

"I didn't mention her name, did I?" Amy asked.

"No, you kept everyone's anonymity very well, Amy, but I guessed who the person with that particular problem was. She's been taking a risk, a big risk, one she's been advised more than once against taking, by living with that guy. Loretta's done the all-too-typical thing, I'm afraid, of asking for advice and then not taking it. And it wasn't a case of her already being with the guy when she got sober; she went into that relationship *after* she got sober."

"Well...," Amy said. This put a slightly different complexion on the whole thing; she hadn't, of course, known about Loretta's failure to heed some basic advice concerning relationships in early sobriety. And she hadn't considered the possibility that Wylie might have felt out of his depth in dealing with Loretta's issue.

"But still," she said to Anna, "the whole group seemed to spend the rest of the meeting in justifying the way Chet and Wylie cut Loretta off."

"You know how good alcoholics are at rationalizing their own behavior after the fact," Anna said dryly. "The fact that they're sober doesn't make them immune against rationalization; they can rationalize for others as well as for themselves when the situation seems to demand it."

"Well, that's true," Amy admitted. The logical part of her was agreeing with Anna, but her emotions were still finding it difficult to accept Anna's calm assessment of the situation.

"Tell you what," Anna said, "why don't we meet tomorrow evening before the meeting and talk some more about this?"

Amy looked at her watch and said, "Oh, goodness, I'm sorry to keep you so long at this hour. I'd like very much to talk about this some more...."

And so they agreed to meet early on Saturday evening.

At seven-fifteen, Anna was already in the meeting room. Amy got a cup of decaffeinated coffee, and they moved over to a corner where they wouldn't be disturbed by later arrivals.

"You sounded, as my teenaged granddaughter says, pretty 'bummed out' last evening," Anna said.

"I was," Amy admitted. "I still am, although I guess I feel better than I did last night. I got used to an AA group with a lot of younger people in it...."

Amy stopped and her face turned as red as her hair as she realized what she'd just said to a woman who'd mentioned having a teenaged grandchild.

"That's all right," Anna said, laughing. "I know that there're a lot of older folks like me in this group. There're even a few old fogeys — I don't consider myself one of them, so I'm not offended by your feelings."

"Well," Amy said, trying to compose herself, "a lot of the people in the AA group I belonged to in the city also belonged to other support groups. We'd discuss anything that happened to be bothering us when we were in AA; we felt that anything that had an effect on our emotions and our serenity therefore had a bearing on our sobriety. I just can't seem to adjust to people who want to talk only about not drinking."

"I think I understand how you feel, Amy. Tell me, was the group that you belonged to in the city a fairly new one?"

"Yes, I guess it was. I mean, it was older than my sobriety, but then, *anything over thirty days was* when I first joined that group. But I guess the group was maybe a couple of years old at the time I joined."

"Let me tell you about the Step-by-Step group's history, Amy," Anna said.

"It was started over forty years ago, back in the days when a large number of people in this country hadn't even heard of Alcoholics Anonymous, let alone knew anything about it.

"The man who started the Step-by-Step group had reached the level of town drunk and skid-row bum before he got sober. He and the first few members of the Step-by-Step group, all of them men, were in almost the same situation as Bill W. and Doctor Bob at the time they founded AA in 1935.

"Those first few members were scared to death that their new AA group might fall by the wayside. No one knew then for sure that AA would even survive, let alone grow and spread all over the country and the world.

"Anyway, there wasn't another AA group in this area then. The members had heard stories of AA groups breaking up over all sorts of things. That's why those early members of the Step-by-Step group concentrated on keeping things basic and simple, and that tradition has come down over the years."

"I can understand that," Amy said. "But times have changed. From what I've learned, AA has changed too. It seems to me that some people here are living in a sort of never-never land of yesterday."

"In the case of a few members, there's maybe some truth in that," Anna said. "There are AA members who still think that treatment centers are just a flash in the pan, although it's pretty obvious that they're here to stay.

"There're AA's who are afraid that treatment centers are threatening AA — somehow taking over AA's job. But the truth is that AA has grown by leaps and bounds because of people being introduced to it while in treatment.

"The first AA members, all men, were worried about letting women alcoholics in; they were afraid there'd be sexual hanky-panky and AA would be driven out of existence by angry spouses. Of course that didn't happen."

"But what about the people who don't seem to want to change with the times?" Amy said. "I know it's not that they're stupid — surely they can see that times change!"

"People fear change," Anna said. "How did you feel about moving here from the city, for instance?"

"I see your point, but —"

"Take a simple thing like vocabulary," Anna interrupted. "I expect that a good many people in the AA group you were a member of in the city had been through treatment. They'd read the kind of self-help books that are now coming out for children of alcoholics and for people with other kinds of

problems — some related to alcoholism directly, and others in-
directly — right?"

"Well — yes," Amy said.

"Acquiring that kind of knowledge means acquiring a vocabulary to go with it, a vocabulary that a lot of older AA members never had a chance to learn. Few of us like to admit we
don't know what a word or term means. When people who've
been through treatment say things like 'cross-addiction' and
'psychological addiction' and speak of being the 'family hero'
in a 'chemically dependent family,' some of the older AA members can well feel left out by virtue of not knowing, what's to
them, a new language."

"I hadn't thought of it just that way," Amy admitted. "But
their reaction seems so drastic. I mean, putting people down
who've been through treatment and all...."

"Amy, some of them are never going to change. Some of them
are living in a kind of nostalgia for the 'good old days' of AA.
It's the same thing as those people who talk about how great
life was before modern technology messed everything up. The
same people are glad to have the modern advances when it
comes to things like air conditioning in the summer and central heating in the winter and modern medical care if they get
sick or hurt."

"Have you ever gotten frustrated at people in AA who act
that way?" Amy asked.

Anna smiled. "Many times. Take the thing about the early
AA's keeping a bottle of whiskey to detox drunks. It's hard to
imagine a responsible AA member today who wouldn't consider taking a person to a detoxification facility much better
than playing do-it-yourself doctor.

"But I've had to learn to accept that there are going to be
the Old Guard guys around, guys who want to keep everything the way they imagine it was 'way back when.' I have to
Live and Let Live — keep my own opinions and let others
have theirs."

"But I don't know honestly if I can get what I need from a group like this one," Amy said. "I mean, if I have to go to meetings and sit there and bite my tongue and practice tolerance, how can I get the full benefit of AA?"

"Have all the meetings of the Step-by-Step group you've attended been like that?"

"Well — no."

"Wasn't there ever a time in your former group when you had to practice some tolerance?"

Amy thought of the time when the man with the massive case of denial had come to meetings because a judge ordered him to and how he'd gone on and on about how *he* wasn't an alcoholic. And about the time the seductive young woman just out of the treatment center had messed up the minds of half the males in the group. And about the time a few of the members had wanted to hold all closed meetings. . . .

"Well, there were times like that," Amy said. "But it seemed different then, somehow. I felt a part of that group; now I feel like an outsider."

"Give it a little time," Anna said. "And it wouldn't hurt to let some people in the group know how you feel about some things, in a tactful way. Like Chet calling you 'sweetheart,' for instance."

"Oh, no, he didn't do that to you, did he?"

"He did until I asked him not to," Anna said. "I told him very politely and sweetly but firmly that I didn't care to be called anything other than my name."

"How did he take it?"

"He pouted a little at first, but he got over it."

"I guess I'll not give up, yet anyway," Amy said. "Thanks for the talk."

"The Step-by-Step group needs you, Amy, as well as you needing it."

"Needs me?"

"Sure. New members with new ideas are what causes an AA group to grow. If there were just the same old faces all the time, the group would grow stale. Whether you've thought about it or not, you're as important to Alcoholics Anonymous as it is to you."

When Amy walked into the Step-by-Step meeting room the following Saturday, she was greeted by Chet with a "Hi, Amy, how're you doing, sweetheart?"

There were only a couple of other people there so far — Wylie and a young man Amy didn't recognize, a newcomer from the look of him. They were talking together off to the side; it was as good a time as any to talk with Chet.

"Chet," she said, putting her hand on his arm in a friendly gesture, "I really don't feel comfortable with people casually calling me 'sweetheart' and other things like that. It makes me feel that they're not taking me seriously, simply because I'm a female."

Chet's eyes narrowed a little. "I didn't mean any harm," he said stiffly.

"I know you didn't," Amy said, "and I —"

Just then Frank and Grady walked in, and Frank called out to Chet and the moment was lost. Amy wondered if she'd created an enemy in Chet, or at least lost a potential friend. Well, what was done was done; she resigned herself to accepting however it might turn out.

The meeting that night was chaired by Phil, who suggested as a topic how the AA members in the room had reacted to their very first exposure to Alcoholics Anonymous. Amy had the feeling that the newcomer's presence might've had something to do with Phil's choice of topic. The young man's hands were none too steady as he carefully held his coffee cup; his eyes were dark-circled and a bit red, though he didn't appear to be under the influence.

About halfway through the meeting, Phil called on Amy. She identified herself and began telling briefly how she got to AA and about her first meeting.

"I'd identified myself as a drug addict before I realized that I was an alcoholic," Amy said. "I'd had the notion that alcoholics were people — mostly men — who'd done a lot of really rough drinking and carousing.

"I was young, and a female, and I'd done drugs other than alcohol, prescription drugs, and I thought that 'real' alcoholics would probably look down on me as a sort of sissified drug addict. Besides, the drugs I'd done seemed sort of *clinical* to me; boozing wasn't as refined as I'd considered myself.

"The counselor at the treatment center I finally checked myself into told me about the relationship of alcohol with other drugs, not only in their immediate physical effect but also in the addictive process. I began to see that even though I hadn't done the kind of drinking that I had thought 'real' alcoholics did, when I began drinking, the trouble started.

"I'd drink too much at night, and then I'd need a stimulant drug to get me going in the morning. By noon I'd be coming out of my skin with withdrawal from the alcohol and the effects of the uppers. I couldn't drink while I was working, but I could sure take some downers to get me through those long afternoons. By evening the process would start all over again.

"I went to my first AA meeting while I was in treatment. By that time, I'd already learned a good deal about alcoholism and addiction from the staff at the center. But it wasn't until I heard people in AA talking about their own experiences in living and dealing with alcoholism that I began to accept my own alcoholism and need for recovery in my heart. The people at the treatment center were the 'experts'; they had the theoretical knowledge. But the people in AA had been personally involved with what I was going through."

Amy realized she'd had quite a bit to say. She finished by saying, "I'm grateful I found Alcoholics Anonymous. I've learned that it doesn't matter how you get here, how much you drank, what other drugs you may have used. It just matters that you admit your powerlessness over alcohol and that you have a desire to stop drinking."

After she'd finished and Phil had called on someone else, Amy looked around. Wylie grinned at her. The new young man was looking at her with some amazement. He obviously hadn't expected to see an attractive, well-dressed young woman at his first AA meeting, let alone hear her say the things Amy had said.

When the meeting was closed with the Lord's Prayer and Amy was moving across the room in the general direction of the door, she found her way blocked by Chet.

"Don't pay me too much mind, Amy," Chet said with a grin. "I'm getting to be an old geezer, a little behind the times. I didn't mean to act as if I didn't take you seriously. I hope you don't have any resentment?. . ." He held out a big paw to shake her hand.

She bypassed the hand and gave Chet a hug. His big smile, after a second's surprised look, showed his pleasure.

Amy stopped and talked with this person and that as she unhurriedly worked her way toward the door. She had a considerably different feeling about this group, and perhaps, she thought, about AA in general.

She'd had what some called the AA "honeymoon" in her original group. She'd looked at that group through rose-colored glasses, and almost everything and everyone had seemed perfect.

She had now experienced some of the inevitable imperfections, in both individual AA members and in an AA group. Oddly, that no longer seemed to bother her. She knew this wasn't the last time she'd have feelings of frustration and exasperation with some of the quirks of some of the members of her new AA group. And she would still need to go back to the city and visit her old AA group and friends there.

But she no longer felt the sense of dismay and near panic she'd felt earlier about the Step-by-Step group. She paused now near the door and looked at the people staying around after the meeting — Nick and Buddy and Phil, Herb and Chet, Richard and Annette and Anna, huge Joe in his leather jacket, Brad with his pipe, old Tom with his chew of tobacco, tiny big-voiced Wylie, Bonnie and Laura and Janey, all the people whose names she was learning and who were becoming acquaintances and potential friends.

The Step-by-Step group wasn't like her first home AA group, but it was becoming more familiar to Amy and therefore more comfortable. Traditional some of its members might be; opinionated certainly some of them were — but Amy now felt that she had found a new home group.

Appendix One

THE TWELVE STEPS OF ALCOHOLICS ANONYMOUS*

1. We admitted we were powerless over alcohol — that our lives had become unmanageable.

2. Came to believe that a Power greater than ourselves could restore us to sanity.

3. Made a decision to turn our will and our lives over to the care of God *as we understood Him.*

4. Made a searching and fearless moral inventory of ourselves.

5. Admitted to God, to ourselves, and to another human being the exact nature of our wrongs.

6. Were entirely ready to have God remove all these defects of character.

7. Humbly asked Him to remove our shortcomings.

8. Made a list of all persons we had harmed, and became willing to make amends to them all.

9. Made direct amends to such people wherever possible, except when to do so would injure them or others.

10. Continued to take personal inventory and when we were wrong promptly admitted it.

11. Sought through prayer and meditation to improve our conscious contact with God *as we understood Him,* praying only for knowledge of His will for us and the power to carry that out.

12. Having had a spiritual awakening as the result of these steps, we tried to carry this message to alcoholics, and to practice these principles in all our affairs.

---

*The Twelve Steps of AA are taken from *Alcoholics Anonymous* (3rd ed.), published by AA World Services, Inc., New York, N.Y., 59-60. Reprinted with permission of AA World Services, Inc.

Appendix Two

THE TWELVE TRADITIONS
OF ALCOHOLICS ANONYMOUS*

1. Our common welfare should come first; personal recovery depends upon A.A. unity.

2. For our group purpose there is but one ultimate authority — a loving God as He may express Himself in our group conscience. Our leaders are but trusted servants; they do not govern.

3. The only requirement for A.A. membership is a desire to stop drinking.

4. Each group should be autonomous except in matters affecting other groups or A.A. as a whole.

5. Each group has but one primary purpose — to carry its message to the alcoholic who still suffers.

6. An A.A. group ought never endorse, finance, or lend the A.A. name to any related facility or outside enterprise, lest problems of money, property, and prestige divert us from our primary purpose.

7. Every A.A. group ought to be fully self-supporting, declining outside contributions.

8. Alcoholics Anonymous should remain forever non-professional, but our service centers may employ special workers.

9. A.A., as such, ought never to be organized; but we may create service boards or committees directly responsible to those they serve.

10. Alcoholics Anonymous has no opinion on outside issues; hence the A.A. name ought never be drawn into public controversy.

11. Our public relations policy is based on attraction rather than promotion; we need always maintain personal anonymity at the level of press, radio, and films.

12. Anonymity is the spiritual foundation of all our traditions, ever reminding us to place principles before personalities.

---

*The Twelve Traditions of AA are taken from *Twelve Steps and Twelve Traditions,* published by AA World Services, Inc., New York, N.Y., 129-87. Reprinted with permission of AA World Services, Inc.

Other titles that will interest you . . .

Things My Sponsors Taught Me
by Paul H.

A no-nonsense lifeline for sobriety shared by one man and his sponsors. Its practical wisdom answers some of the the tough questions that face newcomers to A.A. and will bring a smile to anyone living the Twelve Step way of life. 76 pp. Order No. 5155

Take What Works
How I Made the Most of My Recovery Program
by Anne W.

Insight into some popular fellowship wisdom that is often accepted without question, and perhaps should not be. Anne W. shares how thinking through these sayings and axioms helped her to expand and enrich her recovery program. 75 pp. Order No. 5412

The Slogans
Basic Tools for Successful Recovery
by Mel B.

A simple, insightful look at seven slogans traditionally acknowledged by people in A.A. and other Twelve Step programs. It's all here, from "Easy Does It" to "Live and Let Live." 32 pp.
Order No. 5233

What Is A.A.?	**What Is N.A.?**	**What Is C.A.?**
Leaflet	Leaflet	Leaflet
Order No. 1445	Order No. 1396	Order No. 5584

For price and order information, please call one of our Telephone Representatives. Ask for a free catalog describing more than 1,500 items available through Hazelden Educational Materials.

HAZELDEN EDUCATIONAL MATERIALS

1-800-328-9000	**1-800-257-0070**	**1-612-257-4010**
(Toll Free. U.S. Only)	(Toll Free. MN Only)	(AK and Outside U.S.)

Pleasant Valley Road • P.O. Box 176 • Center City, MN 55012-0176